THE MINNESOTA KINGSTONS | BOOK TWO

CONRAD

THE MINNESOTA KINGSTONS | BOOK TWO

CONRAD

SUSAN MAY WARREN

SOLI DEO GLORIA
· PUBLISHING ·

Conrad
The Minnesota Kingstons, Book 2
Copyright © 2025 by Susan May Warren
Published by SDG Publishing

Ebook ISBN: 978-1-962036-31-3
Print ISBN: 978-1-962036-30-6

Scripture quotations are also taken from the Holy Bible, New International Version®, NIV®. Copyright© 1973, 1978, 1984, 2011 by Biblica, Inc®. Used by permission of Zondervan. All rights reserved worldwide.

For more information about Susan May Warren, please access the author's website at the following address: www.susanmaywarren.com.

Published in the United States of America.

Cover design by Emilie Haney, eahcreative.com

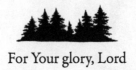

For Your glory, Lord

ONE

I F THEY'D BEEN ON THE ICE, CONRAD KINGSTON, center for the Blue Ox hockey team, would have done time in the penalty box.

And pretty-boy television-talk-show host Ian Fletcher would have a broken nose, maybe a few gaps where teeth used to be.

Instead, the smug man sat across from Conrad on the set of *The Morning Brew*, the "In the Locker Room with Fletch" segment, sporting a perfectly groomed fade-style haircut, blue eyes, and a too-wide smile, prying into Conrad's life.

This was not a locker room Conrad had ever seen, with the chesterfield sofas, a backdrop of fake lockers, and most importantly, bright lights that burned into his eyes, so that the cameras could capture every expression in slow motion as he went over the glass coffee table and neatly put a fist into Ian's prying piehole.

Or at least wished it.

But Conrad was working on his impulse control, on and off the ice, and using his words instead, and so far, so good.

See, he could play nicely.

"So, do you have a date for tonight's event?" Ian asked, waggling his eyebrows. "Seems to me that you might have a lineup after your centerfold."

"It's not the centerfold," Conrad growled.

"Sorry. Mr. *June.*"

He should have expected the too-personal, off-script questions, what with his half-naked picture on the screen behind him. He couldn't look at the photo.

One more of his many, *many* bad yeses.

Instead, of course, he smiled. "Maybe we talk about the charity event tonight."

"Of course." Fletch leaned back, crossed his legs, his grin a sort of victory pump.

Please. Just thirty seconds without the cameras—

No, no. No. The last thing he needed was a splash on social media about King Con being unhinged. Not with the trade season still alive. Conrad flicked his wrist and managed a glance at his Rolex Daytona. Four more minutes and then he could flee—

"I've heard tonight's auction already has bids in the triple digits. Everyone wants a piece of Mr.—"

"It's really about raising money for the kids who've been affected by crime."

Something of a challenge flashed in Ian's eyes, but Conrad didn't flinch.

"EmPowerPlay. Play strong, heal stronger, right?"

"Exactly." Conrad kept his smile, tried to recall what Felicity had told him to say. "EmPowerPlay is dedicated to empowering young victims of crime by facilitating their involvement in sports. We fund local sports teams, helping children build confidence and resilience, fostering emotional healing and personal growth, and offering kids a constructive outlet to channel their energies and reclaim their strength after facing adversity."

Bam. Just like he'd rehearsed.

"And it was founded by the Pepper family, who are shareholders of the Blue Ox hockey team, right?"

"Apparently." He refused to let Penelope Pepper flash into his brain, although the memory of her in his arms a month ago, after the craziness at his sister Boo's wedding, had done a little number on him. Occupied his brain for far too long.

She'd texted him once, asking to meet for dinner. He'd promptly gone on the road for nearly two weeks with the Ox, and when he'd returned, she hadn't answered his reply text.

So, whatever.

Still.

Nope. Not going back there.

"And you've *met* the Peppers, or at least Penelope." Ian grinned and glanced at the screen behind him, and Conrad tightened his jaw at a bootleg paparazzi picture of exactly his memory—him carrying Penelope up the stairs into the wedding reception after she'd been attacked in the parking lot.

Great. He kept his gaze even, smiled. "She needed a lift."

Ian laughed. "Ah, that's a good one, King Con." He turned to the cameras, somewhere out in the darkness, and finger quoted the word. "Just like the 'lift' you gave to Jasmine Hartwell."

Aw, shoot. That's what he got for trying to be clever.

His mouth tightened. "That was different."

"Right. That was Tyler Anderson's girlfriend. Bit of a messy dustup there, if I remember right." He winked at Conrad.

Conrad only needed ten seconds. *Less.*

He lifted a shoulder. "Just a misunderstanding. Torch and I figured it out."

"Didn't you take a restraining order out on Jasmine?"

He said nothing.

"And then there was that fight on the ice—"

"That's in the past."

"Maybe not"—Ian leaned forward—"given last night's game.

You deliberately kept the puck three times when Torch was open, and took failed shots on goal." His smile dimmed. "Are you at all worried about the fact that your contract expires after this season?"

"Listen, it's a fast game, and Torch wasn't as open as you think." Conrad's smile had also vanished. "And no, I'm not worried."

Really. He and Torch had ironed out the misunderstanding long before social media had made it a deal. Bros over—well, ice bunnies.

Ian held up his hands as if surrendering. "Just wondering, given the fact that rookie Justin Blake scored for the win."

"Blade is a solid young player, great potential." Oh, Felicity would be so proud of him.

"And a center, ready to take your spot."

Maybe those were veneers. Conrad had a couple of his own veneers, for different reasons.

"It's Coach Jacobsen's call. I'm just there to play hockey." He looked at the camera, gave them a photoshoot smile. "The calendars are available at the Minnesota Blue Ox website—"

"Right," Ian said, following Conrad's lead. "Visit the website to donate or volunteer." He turned back to Conrad. "Thanks for being here today." He stretched out his hand.

Conrad took it. Gave him a firm hold. Added a squeeze.

Ian's eyes flashed and Conrad let go, then waved to the camera.

"And we're out," said a voice in the shadows, and Conrad stood up, ripped off the mic, turned to Ian.

Ian stood also, his smile gone.

And oh, the urge—

No. Impulses always turned to regrets.

Conrad shook his head, moved toward the set.

"All press is good press," Ian shouted after him.

A PA met him. "Mic?"

He dropped the mess into her hands and stormed out into the hallway. Ian stayed on set, probably saving his life.

"I thought that went great." Felicity Grant stood in the hallway, holding two cups of coffee, wearing an earbud, her blonde hair cut short, an athletic build. She'd played women's hockey at the U of M and of course knew the sport well enough to talk shop with the players. Now, she shoved a coffee into his hand. "Just breathe."

Conrad headed down the hallway toward the greenroom. "None of those questions were in the preinterview chat."

"He does that." She followed him inside and stood at the open door as he grabbed a couple wet wipes and ran them over his face. Makeup coated the cloths, and he scrubbed under his chin, hating how it'd stained his dress shirt.

"I'm never doing this again." He threw down the wipes and grabbed his coat, headed for the door.

Felicity put out her hand and even stepped in front of him. "Yes, you will." She arched a brow. "Attendance is down, and a little goodwill from our starting center doesn't hurt. You were handsome and fabulous, and who cares what Ian says?—you got our message out. Live above it."

"I hate the press. Torch wasn't even dating Jasmine—"

"Drama sells." She lifted a shoulder.

His gut tightened. "Wait—you didn't . . . I mean . . ." He met her eyes. "You weren't the one who called the cops that night, right?"

Her mouth opened. "And possibly get you pulled over for DUI?"

"I don't drink."

She smiled.

He frowned, narrowed his eyes. "That photo with her made me shut down my Instagram account."

"I know. I set up the new one, remember?"

He did know. "Just—no drama tonight, okay? I don't even want to be there."

"You have to be there. It's required in your contract."

"I just . . . are they really auctioning off *dates*? C'mon—the 1990s called, and they want their charity gimmicks back."

She laughed. "It's not a date. It's a seat at the table. Calm down."

"It's hard to stay calm about being property." He stepped past her, headed down the hall.

"You're a professional athlete," she called after him. "Of course you're property!"

He took a sip of the coffee, made a face, and dumped it into the garbage on his way out of the building. The Charger sat in the lot under a dour, gray mid-February sky, the air brisk, the snow piles grimy. Winter refused to surrender, a forecast of snow and ice over the next week, which made it überfun to live in Minnesota.

He got in, turned the car on, and let the motor rumble a moment, the heat turning him from ice-cold to warm.

Maybe he should visit his sister Austen down in the Keys during his next bye week.

The sun hung low, casting late-afternoon shadows over the river as he drove out of the city, into uptown, and to his remodeled mid-century-modern home on W 24th, near Triangle Park in South Minneapolis.

Black exterior, angled roofline, too many floor-to-ceiling windows, and inside, despite the hardwood flooring and beamed ceiling, the place felt too austere, too modern.

Another yes he should have thought through.

He pulled into the underground garage, got out, and took the elevator up to the main floor. Amber sunlight streaked the white wooden floor, the bouclé sofa, the concrete countertops. He picked up a remote and shut the shades to the street, then voice activated his audio system.

He had his shirt unbuttoned and off, sprayed on stain remover as Tommy Emmanuel came on, plucking out a rendition of "How Deep Is Your Love?" on his acoustic guitar.

Breathe.

The sunlight had found Conrad's master bedroom through the transom windows, but the picture window (covered in a one-way film that his brother Doyle had helped him install) overlooked the back of his property and Cedar Lake, still snow-covered.

Any day the cold would break, and the thaw could turn the ice on a lake deceptively lethal, cracking and snapping as the currents beneath awoke. But for now it was a glistening, brittle beauty under the twilight hues.

He threw the shirt in a hamper, jumped in the shower, and felt recovered by the time he emerged, donned a towel, and leaned over the sink for a beard trim. His cell buzzed from the bedroom, and he recognized Jack's assigned ringtone—"Go Your Own Way," Fleetwood Mac.

Although, recently Jack had decided to put down roots at the family homestead some sixty miles west, at least until he sorted out his relationship with reporter Harper Malone. So maybe Conrad needed to change up songs.

Maybe "Home," by Daughtry.

Video call. He thumbed it open. "'Sup, bro?" He turned his video off, left the call on speaker.

Jack sat in the kitchen of the Norbert, one of the heritage homes their parents rented out on the King's Inn property. Jack's dark hair lived below his ears and had its own mind, just like Jack. He wore a flannel shirt and a dark grizzle of beard, the perfect look for a handyman, despite his real job as a finder of all things lost.

His most recent finds had been himself, forgiveness, and a second chance with the girl next door he'd never forgotten. And a job, taking over for little bro Doyle, who took care of the grounds and lived in the Norbert. For now.

Apparently, Doyle had decided it was time to escape his grief and the broken dreams of the past and start new. He hadn't yet left for the Caribbean, but their mother was planning a sendoff party next weekend.

About time, really.

"So, just a heads-up," Jack said in greeting. "Penelope is going to be at tonight's gig."

Conrad had been filing through his suits—not the Armani, of course, but maybe the charcoal cashmere-wool Canali Kei. He pulled out the jacket. Slim fit.

He'd put on some muscle since he'd purchased this a couple years ago.

"I figured, since it's her family's gig." He put the suit back, pulled out the HUGO BOSS. "The Pepper Foundation started EmPowerPlay, and they're sponsoring the event."

"You two ever connect?"

Again wool, slim fit. And boring. He put the suit coat back. "No. I texted her after I got back from Nashville. She never answered."

"Probably because she's still working on her murder podcast."

He pulled out the TOM FORD windowpane. He'd worn it for the Blue Ox Man of the Year awards ceremony last year. Understated. Elegant.

"Her only lead in the Sarah Livingston case—Kyle Brunley—was killed the night he posted bail," Jack said.

Conrad stilled, his hand on the midnight-blue velvet-and-silk Brioni smoking jacket. "Wait. Kyle Brunley is dead? The guy who tried to kidnap her and Harper?"

Penelope had vanished from his sister's wedding event last month in a move many pegged as a PR gimmick for her show. *Nope.* Conrad might never forget her worn but tough-edged expression when she'd been found . . . having escaped on her own and hidden out.

"Yep. He was arraigned, posted bail, and the next day, vanished. They found him in his car about a week ago in a ditch off Marsh Lake Road. Harper told me about it last night at dinner."

Conrad carried the smoking jacket out to the bedroom. "That's the third person murdered in the Sarah Livingston case."

"If you don't include Sarah."

"Right."

"Harper's worried about Penelope. Penelope hasn't answered her texts either, so . . . track her down, and find out how she's doing."

Conrad found a light-blue shirt, matching trousers. "My bet is that she's just fine. She's smart, resourceful, and tough. After all, she did survive three days in a freezing icehouse—"

"For *ratings*."

Well, not quite, but Conrad could see why Jack, who'd found her, might think that.

"Which makes a guy wonder just what else she'd do for her story," Jack continued.

Conrad put on a T-shirt, then the dress shirt. "I'm not sure what I can do. She's got her own mind."

"Just . . . I don't know. Harper asked me to call you. She seems to think that Penelope likes you."

He pulled on the trousers. Still a good fit. Then he returned to his wardrobe and opened his tie drawer. Grabbed out a black satin bow tie and flipped up his collar. "Fine. Sure. But let's not overthink this. I have a full roster of games, and I need to be on point if I hope to be in a position to renegotiate this summer. And frankly, Penelope is . . . she's all over social media. I'm not going there again, bro." He flipped down his collar. Smoothed it out. "Besides, I doubt she has any bandwidth in her life for anyone extra."

"Even Mr. June?"

He stilled, walked out to the bed and picked up the phone. Jack was grinning.

Conrad turned on his own video.

Jack raised an eyebrow as Conrad's mug showed up. "Wow. Seriously?"

"I swear to you, if I see one calendar at the King's Inn—"

"Dude. I caught your 'In the Locker Room with Fletch.' You're going to sell truckloads. Did you wax before you—"

Conrad hung up. Threw the phone on the bed. Clenched his fists for a second, staring into the mirror.

The sweat broke out along his spine, his heart slamming against his chest.

And just for a second, the world narrowed.

Breathe. He sank down on the bed. Put his hands on the cool comforter. *In. Out.*

Visualize. His eyes opened, his gaze finding the picture of the sailboat, the one pitched at an angle, the splash of the deep-blue lake catching the sun. He sat holding the tiller, hair wild, no beard, barefoot.

He could smell it. Lake water. Wind. Spray.

His heartbeat softened. More breaths.

Getting up, he went to the bathroom, downed a glass of water. It sat in his gut without returning. *So far, so good.*

He just might live through this night without being the center of paparazzi attention. *Please.*

His Rolex said he had thirty minutes before the event—so great, he'd be late. Maybe he could slip in the back.

Except, as he drove up to the event—at the historic Frederick mansion in Minneapolis—the coned entry directed him to the valet entrance.

He surrendered his keys to some youngster in a suit. "Don't dent anything."

The kid—okay, probably a college student—nodded, and Conrad got in line to enter the building. He recognized a few of the other Blue Ox players—rookie Justin, of course, grinning for the press, and Wyatt Marshall, their goalie, with his pretty, petite wife, and player Kalen Boomer, and even Coach Jace with his wife Eden.

A heater blasted the portico, so he wasn't cold as he stood at the bottom of the grand staircase.

A plaque near the walk said the place had been built in the late 1800s. It bore an Italian Renaissance aura, with pillars flanking the doorway of the covered entrance.

Massive floral arrangements in the blue and white of the Blue Ox stood in urns on either side of the door. And from the terrace over the entrance hung a banner with the EmPowerPlay logo.

Music spilled out—Pharrell Williams's "Happy."

This might not be a disaster. He'd get inside, glad-hand a few donors, eat some shrimp cocktail, give Coach Jace a thumbs-up, endure dinner small talk, and then skedaddle.

No harm, no foul, and he'd escape the media chaos.

Except, as he neared the door—*no. Oh no.*

Inside the foyer, larger-than-life posters of the calendar models flanked the stairway leading up to the ballroom, and even from here . . .

He looked like he might belong in a *Magic Mike* movie. Shirtless, his body photoshopped into a tan. What hockey player sported a tan in April (when they'd taken the shots)? His beard was tangled, the red hues accented, his hair mussed, and *good grief,* they'd added blue to his eyes.

Forget *Magic Mike*—he could be on some sordid magazine cover, or worse, a romance novel.

No, he couldn't do this—

He turned, and nearly plowed over—

"Conrad!"

Penelope Pepper. She held her hands up, catching his wrists, balancing herself a little.

If he thought he'd lost his breath before . . . He just stared at her, not sure if his thundering heartbeat was panic or . . . awe.

He'd forgotten—or maybe simply tried to forget—the effect she had on him. The high cheekbones that framed the curve of her face, those golden-brown eyes, dark on the outside, radiating to a glimmer of light around the irises, her full, shaped lips, now smiling.

She wore her dark hair swept back and up, trickling in chocolate waves around her slender neck. A white faux-fur shawl wrapped over a white V-necked silk top with puffy sleeves, and a belted long teal skirt. And she smelled—well, not quite exotic, but exciting and fresh and tempting.

And right then, something he'd dismissed awoke inside him.

"Penelope," he managed, aware of her hands on his wrists. He turned them and grabbed hers back. "I'm sorry—I didn't mean to plow you over."

"I missed you too, Con." She laughed, pushed out of his grasp and smoothed her hands on his chest. "And I should know better than to stand too close to a Blue Ox." Then she winked, and *yes, Jack,* Penelope seemed *Just. Fine.* "A gal can get knocked over way too easily."

He had no words for that.

She peered past him toward the foyer, and her eyes widened, her mouth opening to a perfect O. "I see the problem."

"A poster-sized problem."

Then, just like that, she turned him around, stepped up beside him, and slipped her hand around his arm. "Steady on, soldier. This is for the kids." Then she looked up and winked. "Don't worry, I got you."

Cameras flashed as she walked him into the event.

And he didn't know whether to hold on, or run.

———•———————•———

It didn't have to be fake. Penelope liked Conrad—really.

Who wouldn't love a guy who stood over six feet, with tousled dark-blond hair, a rakish beard, devastating blue eyes, and owned the room with his smile?

If a gal went for athletes, that was.

He cleaned up well too, in that velvet-and-silk jacket, the cute bow tie, all the red highlights standing out in his trimmed beard. He even smelled good. Woodsy, with a little cinnamon spice thrown in. *Yum*. And his grip on her as he'd nearly knocked her over—well, a girl might hold on to that.

If she needed help.

Which she didn't.

But he made good cover, and tonight was all about subterfuge. For the *kids*.

She didn't have to show an invitation at the door, of course, and neither did Conrad. She simply pointed to his overlarge and—*wow*—blown-up picture, and security waved them inside the Frederick mansion.

"I'm sorry I didn't text you back," she said as he walked her into the foyer jammed with guests making their way to the second-floor anterooms and the third-floor ballroom. A grand chandelier splashed light on the blue carpet that led up the mahogany staircase with the scrolled banisters. The place felt even more regal than her own home, and that history stretched back to the 1880s.

In each of the second-floor rooms, a representative from one of the many EmPowerPlay sports teams offered more information about their respective team—soccer, baseball, volleyball, and of course, hockey.

Probably, Tia would be upstairs, mingling, glad-handing, and stoking the charitable fires.

"I'm sorry I didn't text back earlier," he said as they moved forward, toward the stairs, and she couldn't resist a glance at the magnificent poster. Not just of Conrad, of course, but the whole first line, the goalie, their leading wings and defensemen, and the other center, a rookie.

The caption on the top said *Sons of the North*.

"I feel like you should be wearing a little halo."

He glanced at her. "Please stop."

"What? I heard this year's calendar sales are through the roof. Tia is over the moon."

"Tia?" They started up the stairs. She held up her dress with one hand, wishing she'd worn her Converse.

Of course, then her mother would have had a stroke, so there was that.

"My sister. She heads up the event every year and runs the foundation. So she's a big fan. You can sign her arm or something."

He rolled his eyes.

She'd glanced back, into the crowd below. *Shoot,* no sign of Anton Beckett, although she'd only seen a picture of him. Still, narrow face, dark hair, sort of a pinched personality—she should be able to spot a conniving lawyer amidst all the athletes in the crowd.

She nearly tripped and Conrad caught her, glanced over. "You good?"

And just like that, the memory of him sweeping her into his arms to carry her up the stairs at the Kingston wedding whooshed in. He'd smelled of the woods then too, along with the breath of the crisp winter air, strong and capable, and considering she'd just nearly broken her nose, her lip fattened, and felt like she'd spent the night in a dumpster, yes, his embrace had made an impression.

Hence her crazy text later that night, inviting him to dinner. To which he hadn't responded, so *full breath and calm down*. He wasn't into her, despite his help on the stairs. Again.

They navigated up to the third floor and stood at the entrance to the ballroom. Chandeliers hung from an arched ceiling, puddling light on the round tables that surrounded a dance floor. Blue lights, angled from the floor, turned the walls a Blue Ox blue, and the gold chairs around the tables, along with the white and blue faux votives, added a celebratory hue to the room. A DJ worked at a mixer, now playing a Maroon 5 song.

At the front, pictures of the twelve guests of honor were perched on easels with numbers and auction baskets under them. People lined up to offer bids and drop them into the baskets.

Penelope spotted her father, Oscar, wearing a black Armani suit, looking like a gray-haired Sly Stallone, talking with a group of his fellow investors, some of their faces familiar. He didn't see her, so all things normal. However, her mother Sophia, standing in her own conversation circle, glanced her way. Elegant, with her dark hair back, wearing a shimmery blue floor-length dress, she had never seemed to wonder what her role in the Pepper family might be.

Grand matron, all-around socialite, and the woman who kept Penelope's father grounded.

Glancing around, Penelope also spotted Tia working the crowd. Tia wore an elegant black dress, poised and perfect and everything Penelope was not.

Although, Tia had her own facade, so Penelope had no desire to switch places.

She noticed a few from the family security detail pocketed around the room too. Geoffrey, her father's personal bodyguard, and her own shadow, Franco. But with an outside firm guarding the event as well, the private Pepper team had notched down to DEFCON 4.

Her gaze fell on a man near the front. *Target acquired.* Anton Beckett stood watching the bidding and holding a glass of red wine. Gray suit, white shirt, one hand in his pants pocket, the man who had the answers she needed. But wasn't getting. *Yet.*

Conrad's mouth twitched. He looked at Penelope. "Can I get you something?"

"A glass of Cab. And be sure to pick up one of those scallop avocado toast appetizers. My sister's concoction, but they're amazing."

She released his arm and threaded her way through the crowd, working over to Beckett.

He glanced at her, took a drink, then looked at her again, and his eyes widened.

That's right, buddy. I'm coming for you.

She kept a smile and glided up to him.

He stiffened. "I'm not sure what game you're playing at, Miss Pepper—"

So he *did* know her. *Fine.* "I just need to recover what Kyle already gave me."

"It's out of my hands—"

"I know you share a cloud at the office. I just want the files he put on the jump drive." The *corrupted* jump drive, the one he'd given her before he'd clearly changed his mind and tried to . . . well, who knew what he'd planned on doing when he'd shown up at the wedding and tried to drag her away.

"I just want this over." His voice, still in her ears, right before he'd hit her. The bruises had finally faded. But *yeah, buddy,* her too.

Nothing, especially not some uptight lawyer, would stand between her and the truth of who had killed Sarah Livingston.

And beyond that, who had killed Edward Hudson.

But she'd get to that.

"Those are protected files, Miss Pepper."

Her voice softened. "The files never belonged to Kyle or the firm. They were from Sarah Livingston's laptop. She gave them to Kyle for safekeeping. And he gave them to me."

"And you lost them." He took a sip of wine.

"No. When I opened the drive, it had a formatting error. He must have saved over information and corrupted the drive. I just need access to his cloud. Or his computer—"

He shook his head, cut his voice down. "Not here."

She stared at him, and maybe it was the last month of hunting for Kyle—and then discovering his dead body, so that had been awesome—or even the nightmares, waking her in the dead of night, replaying running for her life across a frozen lake—but she was just over it. Tired of lies and missing leads and injustice, and the simmer in her gut just lit up.

He lifted his drink, and a woman walked by, and Penelope used the moment to trip into him.

Red wine splashed across his chin, down his shirt.

Oops.

"What the—" He backed away from her, shaking the wine from his hand, grabbing up a napkin to blot his shirt. "What is wrong with you?"

"Everything okay here?" Conrad walked up carrying a glass of wine and a plate of appetizers.

He could carry the room the way he sauntered up, almost like a dare. Anton glared at her, then spun and strode away.

Conrad glanced after him, frowned.

"He's getting away," she said, not really meaning that, but, well, meaning *exactly* that because he just might head home, and she'd lose any hope of talking him into—

"Getting away?" Conrad raised an eyebrow. "Who is that?"

"Anton Beckett, from B & B Law Firm."

He wore a blank look.

"Kyle Brunley's firm. Beckett and he were partners."

Conrad's expression sharpened with recognition. "Kyle Brunley, the guy who tried to kidnap you at my sister's wedding."

"Yes. Maybe. I dunno."

"I was there. I'm going to say that's a hard yes." His mouth tightened. Looked a little fierce and lit a strange tiny spark in her.

She lifted a shoulder. "He's dead, so really, we'll never know."

"Jack told me."

"The problem is that the jump drive he gave me before . . . well, before everything went down is corrupted. So I never got the information he intended to give me. But I know"—she put a hand to her chest for emphasis—"that he stored it on his computer. Which of course is backed up to his cloud. I've already searched his house, and his computer isn't there, so—"

"You *searched* his house?"

"I was worried, okay? And if it weren't for me, maybe no one would have found his body."

His eyes widened.

"Listen—I know the working theory is that Kyle Brunley killed Sarah Livingston in an act of passion, but he *did* care about her. They were lifelong friends. I believe the information he gave me was real, that he was trying to help me find her real killer—who I think is a man named Swindle. More, that information also implicated Swindle in a slew of other crimes—"

"Like the death of your sister's fiancé."

How he knew that, she didn't know, but a lot had gone down at the Kingston wedding fiasco, so who knew what she'd said? "Yes." She sighed. "I need that information. And Beckett is the gatekeeper."

He glanced at the door where Beckett had disappeared. "Okay." Then he turned and headed across the room.

What? She followed him. "Where are you—"

Conrad pushed out into the hallway. There, at the end, sat the bathrooms.

The hallway was empty. He handed her the glass of wine, scooped up the last appetizer, popped it into his mouth, then entered the men's room.

She stood in the hall, not sure what to do.

A second later, the door opened. Conrad popped his head out. "All clear."

All . . . clear?

He held the door open. "Now or never."

Right. She stepped inside the room.

Beckett stood at the sink, his shirt saturated as he tried to wash it. He glanced up at her. "You've got to be kidding me."

"I don't think murder is something to be kidding about. And if you're hiding information that implicates your client, that makes you an accessory."

"No, it doesn't." He turned off the water, his shirt pink.

"Yes, it does. If you hold information that suggests more crimes will be committed, you're legally bound to turn it over."

Beckett had reached for towels, was vainly trying to dry the shirt.

Penelope grabbed a couple more, held them out to him. "Since I've been investigating this case, I've been kidnapped and seen two men shot and people murdered. So it's a fair guess that whatever Swindle is up to, it's not over."

He stilled at her words. Frowned. Swiped the towels from her. "Kyle wasn't murdered."

"Tell that to his car, the one upside down in the ditch with side-swipe dents on it. But it wasn't the crash that killed him." She handed the wineglass back to Conrad. "I'd blame the 9mm JHP bullet in his chest. But whatever."

He swallowed.

"Sarah's apartment was looted, her first computer stolen three months before her death. That's when she gave Kyle the jump drive. And then she was killed. Whatever was on that jump drive is incriminating enough to kill for." She cocked her head. "Still want to hold on to it?"

His mouth tightened. Opened.

And right then, a patron walked into the room, past Conrad. He stopped, glanced at Penelope, then the two men, and froze.

Beckett pushed past him, fleeing. She turned to go after him, dodging the man and—

Bam! Right into Conrad, standing in the doorway.

Oh, she was clumsy tonight. The wine splashed down the front of Conrad's shirt, soaking his torso.

He held out the wineglass, looked at her.

"Sorry."

The patron had also fled.

Red wine dripped down Conrad's front onto his expensive dress pants.

She grabbed a couple paper towels, ran them under water. "I'm so sorry—" Her eyes burned. What had she been thinking, trying to—

"Hey." He'd put the glass down on the marble countertop. Met her eyes through the mirror. "This isn't over. You gave him a lot to think about."

"Yeah, which he'll use to look up some case law and hunker down on top of it like a junkyard dog on a pile of old hubcaps."

She got a smile.

He took off his jacket and hung it on an open stall door. And then he took off his soiled shirt.

And the undershirt.

Which left only his stained skin. He cleaned it off while she ran his shirt under cold water, soaping it up and scrubbing. It worked out much of the stain, leaving a cloud of gray, but maybe with some bleach. . . .

He threw the undershirt into the trash. Then he took the wet shirt from her, ran the dryer and held the garment under it.

Penelope leaned against the tile wall, her arms folded. Tried not to admire the view, but yes, so much better than a stupid calendar. Washboard stomach, burly shoulders, muscled arms.

The man was beautiful.

Too bad she didn't date. Athletes or otherwise.

He finished with the shirt and tugged it back on. It was still wet, and it stuck to his skin in places, but he grabbed his jacket and pulled it on too. Shoved his bowtie into his pocket.

"I have an auction to attend," he said.

"And I'm in the mood to spend money."

He held out an elbow. She looped her arm through it, and he opened the door.

He stepped out first, and by the time she followed him, the press had already grabbed their shots. They blocked the hallway, shouting.

"Miss Pepper, why were you in the bathroom with Conrad Kingston?"

"Conrad, is Penelope Pepper your good luck charm?"

"Penelope, is he your plus one?"

Maybe.

Conrad held up his arm and ushered her out into the hall.

She spotted Franco near the door, his arms folded, a look of annoyance on his face. *Oops.* Thankfully he hadn't made a scene. Calm down. Conrad was harmless.

Even, maybe, safe.

Now, Conrad ushered her into the event area, shutting the door on the paparazzi.

She looked at him. "Thank you."

He smiled down at her. "Anytime." He winked.

And she couldn't help but lift herself up and kiss him. Sweetly, on the cheek. Like a friend.

Then she lowered herself back down and patted his chest. "Now. Let's see if I can win me Mr. June."

TWO

NEXT TIME SHE TEXTED, HE WOULDN'T WAIT two weeks to answer.

Conrad sat next to Penelope at his assigned table, watching her tell the other eight guests about her previous murder-podcast investigation—one involving country-music star Oaken Fox, now his brother-in-law, and the attempt on reality-show star Mike Grizz.

She was animated and brilliant, and he still couldn't believe she'd taken him up on his invitation to invade the men's room.

Gutsy.

A server leaned over him and took away the plate of quail, new potatoes, and asparagus. Penelope had barely touched hers, but she'd been laughing at his stories. Like they might be teammates, hosting the table.

Of course she'd won the auction for him—outbidding the nearest offer by miles. The gesture stirred the heat inside him that had grown to a simmer over the evening.

Maybe he'd text her first next time.

A speaker got up, and he remembered Penelope calling her Tia, her sister. Pretty, with shoulder-length black hair and a solid, determined look about her, she thanked everyone for coming and then explained their organization as well as key accomplishments for the last year.

"We believe sports are life, and when children are able to be physically fit and participate in a team, they build confidence and life skills that help them heal." She then showed a short video of three kids who'd survived violence in their community and then thrived—one on an inner-city baseball team, another with a community hockey team, a third on her local volleyball team, all sponsored by EmPowerPlay.

"Our biggest need is for coaches to volunteer," she said as the lights came back up. "And, of course, funding. You're changing lives. Be generous." She then invited guests to visit the various rooms on the second floor, where team members waited to meet them.

"And then be sure to stick around for the dancing." She grinned, winked. And Conrad saw the family charm in her smile.

"How did EmPower start?" he asked Penelope as servers set down chocolate cake at their places.

"My dad's idea. We had a friend whose family survived a hostage situation, and he wanted to help them heal. Children heal better when they feel strong and safe." She picked up her fork, considered the cake, then put it back down. Glanced at him. "Should we go visit the rooms?"

He, too, pushed away the cake, excused himself from the table, and followed her through the crowd, down the stairs to the second floor. Already, guests mingled in the rooms. Three rooms—volleyball, baseball, and hockey. Inside each, mounted posters on easels depicted teams, and action shots hung on the walls. Representatives fielded questions and handed out team brochures.

"Each team is funded both individually and through the main foundation," Penelope said. "We usually have a younger-teen and an older-teen group. The difference is that our coaches aren't there to make champions but to invest in lives. The teams do compete with small private schools or other community teams, but really it's about drawing kids out of themselves and helping them trust and try." They had walked into the baseball room, and she greeted the representative, took a brochure. "Did you ever play baseball?"

He nodded. "One year. And I hated it. All that waiting around for the ball to come to you? No, give me the fast action of hockey all day." But he pocketed the brochure, perused the signs. "Is this just a Minneapolis/St. Paul organization?"

"Oh no. We're in small towns too—in fact, we've discovered that many small towns don't have the money for local teams, so we have a number of sponsored teams around Minneapolis. And we're growing—thanks, Stef." Penelope lifted a hand to the representative and led him out of the room. "We have a team in Duluth, and one in Grand Rapids, and even over in Moorhead." She walked into the volleyball room. "The only criteria is that the players aren't already in a school sport."

"It costs money to be in an extracurricular sport," he said, reading the boards. Again, teams and action shots and even a couple medals from local tournaments. A teenager, maybe sixteen, with long blonde hair, wore an EmPowerPlay T-shirt and dress pants, and he shook her hand.

"I'm Emily," she said, turning a little red.

"Conrad."

She nodded. "I know."

"You from here?"

"Out west. Waconia area. I play on the Northwest Smash." She pointed to an action shot of herself three feet off the ground, mid-spike.

"Nice moves."

She grinned.

He greeted the coach, a woman in her mid-thirties who held a volleyball casually under her arm.

"Lydia is a coach for a local high school. Donates her time."

"Are most of the coaches professional?" He followed Penelope out of the room. She headed for the hockey display.

"Not all of them. Some. Most of the time they're former players, or just people with experience." They entered the hockey room.

This one contained a couple trophies along with team posters and more action shots. A man, late twenties, stood talking with a couple near a window. He seemed familiar but Conrad couldn't place him. *Or wait—*

"Simon McHale?"

The man turned, and a smile spread over his face. Sandy-brown hair, still lean, although he'd filled out, he wore a pair of dress pants and a hockey jersey. "King Conrad."

Heat rose at the high-school nickname that had followed him into the league, but Conrad didn't refute it as he shook Simon's hand. "McHalestorm."

Simon laughed, pulled him in, and clamped him on the back. Then he turned to Penelope. "Oh, I see how it is. I should have guessed you might be involved with EmPowerPlay." He held out his hand. "Miss Pepper."

She took his hand, glanced at Conrad.

"Simon and I played together in high school," he said. "He's a couple years younger than me, but an excellent left winger."

"I just tried to keep up with His Excellence."

Penelope raised an eyebrow, a smile playing at her lips, and he didn't make a play at shutting Simon down. Not with that spark in her eye.

"So, you're coaching the . . ." Conrad glanced at the jersey. "Ice Hawks?"

"Yep. Hey, Jeremy, c'mere. I'd like to introduce you to—"

"The King." The voice, just a little gasp behind him, made Conrad turn. A kid, maybe fifteen, tall, skinny, walked up. "Wow." The kid held out his hand. "My dad is a huge fan."

"Really." Conrad shook his hand. Good grip.

"Yeah. Wait until I tell him that I met you!"

"Your dad already knows the King, kid," said Simon, putting his hand on Jeremy's shoulder. He looked at Conrad. "You remember Joe Johnson. Security Guard at the North Star Arena back when we played? That was before his accident."

Conrad didn't move, managed to keep his smile, but everything inside him seized.

Yes. *Of course* he remembered Joe. *Oh.*

Breathe.

He managed a nod, his body on autopilot, and then, "How is Joe?"

"Aw, Dad's good. Getting around better since he had his leg amputated. Sometimes helps at the games."

But Conrad's brain stopped on *amputated.*

He might be ill.

Penelope was watching him, a small hitch in her brow.

"You should come to a game," Simon said. "We play at the new arena—the Arctic Edge—or at least we practice there. We play all over Minnesota. But we have a great team—mostly kids from Chester, although we get a few from Duck Lake. A lot of them are recovering from the trauma of the tornado a few years ago, of course. But others just need a way to burn off energy. And then there are kids like Jeremy here, who's a natural. They just need a little support getting onto a team."

A.k.a. funding. Because Jeremy's dad probably lived off disability.

His knees might buckle. "I'd love to come to a game," he said, his smile still fixed. "Good to meet you, Jeremy."

Conrad pointed at Simon and then met him in a hand grab. He hoped his palm didn't feel as sweaty as his body.

Then he practically fled the room, walking with his hands in his pockets. *Don't run.* But he desperately needed air.

Penelope instead led him back to the ballroom. Ed Sheeran's "Photograph" played and a few people danced. Penelope looped her arm through his. "Dance?"

No. "Sure."

Just breathe.

He took her hand, led her to the middle, where other guests were slow dancing, and pulled her into his arms.

Certainly she couldn't feel his thundering heart—

"You okay?" She'd circled her arms around his neck, searching his face.

"Me?" He cleared his throat.

"No. I'm talking to Justin Blake, the rookie—yes, you. You went pale down there, like you'd seen your life flash before your eyes."

He swallowed. "Oh. Um. Just . . . you know. High-school memories—hey, is that Stein?" What was his older brother doing here? Stein wore a plain black suit, stood near the wall with his hands clasped, watching, *wait*—"He's with Declan Stone."

The billionaire had hosted Oaken Fox's bachelor party at his lake estate near Duck Lake a month ago.

She glanced over. "Yeah. Declan and my dad are friends. He gives a lot to EmPowerPlay. I didn't know your brother knew him."

Or worked for him? *Huh.* But it suddenly made sense why, after their sister's wedding, Conrad's former-SEAL brother hadn't returned to his life in the Caribbean teaching tourists how to scuba dive. And why he'd been a little tight-lipped about the deets.

He'd gotten a security gig. *Interesting.*

The song changed, again Ed Sheeran, and Penelope started to hum.

"I found a love . . ."

He stared down at her. She could take his breath away, really. Cause him to lose himself in the golden layers of her eyes, sink his gaze onto her full lips tinted with a hint of pink. Desire crested over him.

"I never knew you were the someone waitin' for me . . ."

Maybe he would survive, because he'd stopped shaking. *So see,* he was fine. Just fine.

And just like that, the image of Jeremy—not fifteen, but one year old—toddling onto the ice with his dad at the arena flashed into his mind and—*aw*—

The room started to turn fuzzy around the edges.

He stepped away from Penelope, the sweat rushing over him, and headed through the crowd for the hallway. Pushing through the doors, he leaned against the wall, then bent over and grabbed his knees.

Hot, the room spinning—he needed air.

Door, at the end of the hall. He practically sprinted for it, barreled through, down the back stairs to the second, then first floor, his gut still roiling—

Then out into the brisk winter air with the stars sparkling overhead, watching as he paced the parking lot filled with limos and SUVs and even his Dodge Charger. He looked up, heavenward, not asking any questions, because frankly, well, maybe he had enough answers for tonight.

It didn't matter how much Conrad lied to himself, clearly God hadn't forgotten.

He finally braced himself against the back of his car, taking in cool breaths, his body still shaking.

Focus.

He closed his eyes, trying to conjure up the boat, the waves, the wind—

"Bro?"

He stiffened, opened his eyes. Turned.

Steinbeck stood in the lot, pale blue eyes on him, worried.

"Hey," Conrad managed, standing up. And right then, of course, his gut decided it had waited long enough. He pushed past Stein and beelined to a nearby dumpster.

Don't lose it, don't—

He held on to the edge, gulping in breaths, fighting.

"You eat something bad?" Stein again. "Don't tell me you had something to drink."

Conrad held up a hand. Swallowed. *Maybe . . .* He turned to Stein. "No." But suddenly, his stained shirt, the dampness against his body, made him shiver. "Just . . . yeah, something didn't sit right."

Like running smack into his dark night of the soul.

He ran a hand across his mouth. "You working for Stone?"

Stein lifted a shoulder. "Short-term gig. How'd you know?"

"You have a look."

"I'll work on that."

"Good luck. You were born with it. How'd you get that gig?"

"Long story. I'll tell you about it next weekend at Doyle's party. But this isn't about me. What happened in there?"

What was he going to say? The last, *very* last thing he wanted his family, especially Stein, to know was that the panic had returned. In force.

See, this was why he shouldn't do calendar shoots and public events and . . . generally leave the safety of the ice—

The door opened, and of course Penelope came out into the darkness. *Aw . . .*

He walked over to her, still wobbly. "Sorry to leave you—"

"Are you okay?" She put her hands on his arms, concern in her beautiful eyes.

"Probably the quail," Stein said, arms folded.

"Really? Are you allergic?"

He didn't want to lie, but . . . *oh . . .* "Maybe. I don't know."

"I'll get your keys," Stein said and headed around the building to the valets at the front.

Conrad blew out a long breath. "You're cold. Go back inside. I need to go home."

She blinked, swallowed, then nodded, stepping back. "Okay, I, uh . . ." She wrapped her arms around herself. "Right." She took another step away, and he fisted his hands at his side to keep from doing something crazy, impulsive, even pedestrian like reaching for her.

Telling her that he sort of, a little, might like her.

After one date that wasn't a date but a rescue, really?

No. Still, "Can I text you?"

She shook her head. "I don't think that's a good idea . . . "

And as his heart stilled, a rock in his chest, she added, "This was fun, Conrad. You're . . . Anyway, thanks for what you did in the bathroom. Take care."

Then she turned and quick walked back into the mansion, leaving him standing in the dark parking lot.

Again trying not to throw up.

By the time Stein returned with his keys, Conrad was leaning on the back of his car, arms folded, sufficiently chilled, breathing easier. Still, as Stein handed the keys over, he wore a question in his eyes.

"It's nothing," Conrad said. "Like you said, bad quail."

"So we're going with that?"

"Absolutely." He took the keys. Because not even he could voice the truth.

But he couldn't help but glance one last time at the bright lights of the mansion as he pulled out of the lot and into the cold night.

———•————————•———

She hadn't hated the charity event.

For once. For the first time, really, in longer than she could remember.

Penelope sat at the massive granite counter of her parents' expansive kitchen overlooking the frozen lake, a spoon in her granola and yogurt, stirring. Stirring. Stirring.

"Okay, give, Pep. Who was that hottie you were dancing with?"

She looked over to the door where her sister Tia walked into the room. She blinked and gathered herself away from the moment in the shadowed parking lot. Away from Conrad's beautiful blue eyes clouded with hurt—*maybe* hurt, although she could be dreaming that part up—after her words *"I don't think that's a good idea."*

Tia raised an eyebrow and set down her coffee mug to pour more from the French press on the counter. Clearly big sis had already been up for hours despite their late-night return from the party. Penelope had opted to overnight at her parents' lakeshore home in Wayzata instead of driving home to her uptown bungalow.

Of course, Tia looked perfectly put together. Aside from her dark hair, pulled back in a sleek bun, Tia wore an ivory velour leisure suit, gold earrings, and a pair of fluffy UGG slippers. No wonder Edward had fallen for her.

Tia glanced at Penelope's pajama bottoms and oversized maroon University of Minnesota T-shirt and raised an eyebrow.

Hey, she wasn't the event planner, the foundation head, the beauty and brains of the Pepper family philanthropy, thank you.

Just a murder podcaster trying to find justice. One men's bathroom at a time.

Her mouth tweaked at the memory of Conrad holding the door open. *"Now or never."*

Shoot, it might have been *never* if it weren't for him.

"Pep. The guy. Give." Tia had poured the coffee and now slid onto a chair at the black-and-white granite island. Reached for one of the fresh blueberry muffins that Greta had made before leaving for the grocery store.

"You've never met Conrad Kingston?" Penelope kept her voice casual. "Plays center for the Blue Ox. They call him King Con."

Tia broke apart the muffin onto a napkin. "Oh, I know what they call him." She winked. "Just wanted to make sure you did. But what I want to know is *how* you know Mr. June."

Right. Poor man—he'd looked like he'd wanted to bolt when Tia had introduced him. He might have relaxed a little, however, when Tia read off Penelope's winning bid.

"He was in the wedding I was in last month."

" Boo Hoo Kingston's wedding."

"I think they're just calling her Boo," Penelope said.

Tia took a bite of the muffin. "Sorry. Habit. And I forget that you two are friends. I saw the pictures in *People*. Beautiful wedding."

Penelope nodded. No need for Tia to know about the three days that Penelope had spent hiding from a killer, right? She'd just alert security, and suddenly Franco would be following her home to sit in her driveway, and "Pep" would be right back to her high-school days when everyone knew she came with security checks and babysitters.

"So you met Conrad at the wedding?"

"Briefly. We're just friends."

"Mm-hmm." Tia took a sip of coffee, set it down. "Not the way you two were slow dancing."

"Oh, good grief, it was a slow dance. Nothing more."

Tia took another bite of muffin. "You might want to rethink that. He's a doll. All that scruffy, long blond hair, the hockey beard, and those eyes—" She put her wrist to her forehead. "Swoon."

Penelope laughed, and Tia grinned. "Yeah, I don't think so."

Tia pushed the other half of her muffin toward Penelope. "Please. The no-athletes rule?"

"One was enough for me."

"Ted was hardly the example of a good boyfriend. So what he had other motives—"

"That's the thing, T. You lucked out with Edward, right? You knew him from childhood, knew he wasn't trying to get anything from you—"

"I think you're safe with Conrad Kingston. He has his own money."

"Pay attention. His contract expires this year. Dad is a part owner of the team. Don't you think his contract will come up in conversation? He dates me and suddenly there are stakes. Broken heart equals broken future."

"Only because Dad is desperate for you to find 'the One.'" She finger quoted the words.

"I don't need 'the One.'" Penelope mimicked the gesture. "I have a job I love, and not everybody gets what Mom and Dad have."

Oops.

Because Tia's mouth tightened and she looked away, drew in a breath.

"Sorry."

"No. It's fine." She turned back to Penelope. "Listen, Pep. I'll always miss Edward, but . . . I need to let go. Keep moving forward."

"Isn't that what you're doing with the Pepper Foundation and EmPowerPlay?"

Tia went quiet. Sighed. "Maybe. Or maybe I need a change. Something different. Away." She glanced at Penelope again. "A fresh start."

Penelope took a sip of coffee, set it down. "Listening."

"I talked with Declan Stone last night. He has an orphanage down in the Caribbean in need of a manager."

"You're going to move to the Caribbean to take care of *kids*?" *Oh.* She didn't mean it how it sounded, but—"What about the foundation? I mean—"

"Maybe you could step up."

The voice came from behind her, from the hallway that led to her parents' wing, with her father's private home office, her mother's library, the master-bedroom suites and off-rooms.

She turned as her father walked into the room. Clean-shaven, still built even in his early sixties, he wore a pair of dress pants, a black pullover V-necked sweater, and carried a coffee mug. He came over, set it on the counter, and met her gaze. "I think it's time, Pep."

"Dad—"

He held up a hand, his gray eyes on hers. "Listen. It's time to stop horsing around with this podcast gig and invest in the things that matter." He glanced at her sister. "Tia's done her service. And frankly, it's your turn to do your part."

She stared at him. "Dad. I'm not a philanthropist. I don't want to change the world."

"Of course you are. Why do you think you've been on this crusade to find a killer responsible for Edward's death for the past three years?"

She stilled, glanced at Tia, back at her father. "Because no one else has?"

Tia's mouth opened, closed, and she gave her father a hard look.

He sighed. "Pep. You need to stop the fantasy. Edward's death was an accident. A terrible, cruel accident that we all grieved." He put a hand on hers, warm, solid. "And I know you grieved just as much as Tia. He was, after all, your friend first."

Her throat thickened even after her father let her hand go. "He was murdered," she said softly, barely. "I know it."

Silence. Tia looked at her coffee. Her father didn't move his gaze from her.

"The forensic report came back inconclusive," Tia said finally. "And you carrying on with this belief only makes it harder for us all to heal." She looked up, her eyes glistening. "You need to let me have a future."

Oh.

"Can you just do this for me?" Tia wiped her cheek almost violently.

"I'm not a financial wizard like you," Penelope said, then looked at her dad. "You know that."

He sighed. "I'll hire a foundation manager. But we need you to be the face. Show up at events, give interviews. Be a spokesperson. That's all I ask." He lifted a shoulder. "You can still do your podcast if you want."

Like it was a hobby. "Dad. I make money with the podcast. We're nationally syndicated. It's a big deal." Or could be, if her ratings hadn't tanked after she'd failed to fulfill her promise to uncover Sarah Livingston's killer on her podcast a month ago. She'd even received more than was fair thumbs-down and hate posts calling her a fraud.

So that hurt.

And now her father arched a brow and delivered a zinger. "A three-point-four-million-dollar-charitable-fund big deal?"

"Wow."

"Just saying. You want to change the world, maybe look closer to home."

"Strong-arm much?" She finished her coffee, then got up and put her mug in the sink. Turned to face her oppressors.

Her father wore a frown. Tia looked away, outside, probably to the future that Penelope was keeping her from pursuing.

"Don't you guys want peace? To be able to sleep through the night knowing you did everything to find justice for Edward?"

A beat, and then, "You don't have to have justice to find peace," Tia said.

Whatever. "Fine. Okay. I'll . . . show up and smile. Just tell me when and where."

"Great," her father said. He cast a gaze at Tia.

Tia sighed, her smile tight. "Thanks, Pep. We have a small photo event with a local team later this week. The news wants to do a feature on us and what we're doing. I'll text you the deets."

She slid off the chair, then came over and pulled Penelope into a hug. "It's okay to let go of the past. It doesn't mean you didn't love him."

Maybe Tia's words were for herself. Still, Penelope nodded.

Tia let her go, grabbed her half-full mug, and headed out of the room.

Her father stood there watching her go, compassion in his eyes for his oldest daughter. Of course.

Funny, but she'd never seen him look at her that way. Then again, she'd never quite measured up to Tia, who took after him in nearly every tangible way, from her no-nonsense business head to her athletic spirit to her ability to lead.

Still, it wasn't a terrible gig. Show up, support the kids. She could do this.

"I saw you talking with Conrad Kingston last night."

Oh. She had picked up her phone and now glanced at her father. "Yeah. He's a friend."

"Be careful with that one, Pep. We don't need any drama. Investors are on social media too."

She frowned. "Are you talking about the scandal with Torch and his girlfriend?"

He held up a hand. "No. I don't believe a word of social media. But scandal affects ticket sales. And it's not just his rep. I get Blue Ox team reports. King Con's stats are dropping, and the truth is, investors are worried. He might get traded, and I don't want him to break your heart." He walked over, delivered a kiss to her cheek, then squeezed her forearm and headed out of the room.

Aw, shoot, that was information she didn't need to know. So maybe it was a good thing she'd turned Conrad down.

She picked up her phone, opened her email, and spotted a message from Clarice, her new manager, thanks to Harper's rec-

SUSAN MAY WARREN

ommendation. And she could hardly ignore the "Open Me Immediately!!" subject line.

No greeting, text above a picture—

Clarice
_____

Did you do this on purpose?

And then a photo of . . . *oh boy.* Her and Conrad on the dance
floor, his big hands on the small of her back, her arms wrapped
around his neck, and *shoot* but he was sweet and handsome and
looked down at her with a hint of a smile.

She couldn't take her eyes off the smile. Because it seemed . . .
oh no . . . it seemed like he actually liked her. At least, from the
warmth in his gaze.

Hitting Reply—

Penelope
_____

It was just a dance.

She sent it. Set down her phone.

And it didn't take much for her to remember his chest against
hers as they'd danced, the strength of his arms cocooning her, the
woodsy scent of him—

Her phone rang and she swiped open the call, put it on speaker.
"I promise, it's not a thing."

"Looks like a thing." Clarice, probably in her cute Franklin,
Tennessee home office, already three cups of coffee into her day.

"It was a charity event for EmPowerPlay. He plays hockey—"

"I know who King Con is, Penelope. And who he should be
to you."

What?

Clarice's chair squeaked, as if she might be leaning forward.
"You should date him."

"No. What? No, absolutely not."

"I don't mean for real. I get it. Conrad Kingston is a player. He
stole a teammate's girlfriend from right under his nose. He has at

43

least one restraining order out on a previous girlfriend. And at least a half dozen shadow Instagram accounts who post sightings. Who knows if he's behind them, but let's say his combined reach is nearly double yours."

It is?

"You post a few pictures of you two out, tag him, and your podcast will explode."

"Wait. You want me to join the ranks as one of Conrad's ice bunnies?"

"No. Okay, maybe yes. But frankly, you'd help him too—he needs a bit of a reputation cleanup. I already have a call in to Felicity—"

"Who?"

"The publicist for the Blue Ox. Listen. It doesn't have to be forever. Just a few events, you two smiling, and boom, it's Travis Kelce dating Taylor Swift. Although you'd be Kelce in this situation."

"The football player?"

"Who had a podcast. That exploded when he started dating Swift."

"I think he was popular before he started dating her—"

"Didn't hurt his reach though, did it?"

A beat. "You want me to use Conrad for his social-media audience? That's . . . um . . ."

"Done all the time, sweetie. And like I said—it's a win for Conrad too. To be dating a Pepper? Think of what it might do for your little charity. What's it called—Power Play?"

"EmPowerPlay, and it's hardly little—whatever. It feels slimy."

"Not if you really like him. Then it's a meet-cute, with wins all around."

"What are you, a screenwriter?"

"That's not a bad idea. Maybe I'll put out a Request for Proposal—"

"Stop." She picked up the phone, took it off speaker, and walked to the window. Outside, the sun shone down on the frosty lake, gilding it, the sky a glorious blue.

"He might get traded." Her father's words pinged back to her, along with the squeeze of her heart.

She'd met his family. The last thing Conrad would want is to have to move. Probably.

Except Tia was suddenly in her head. *"Dad is desperate for you to find 'the One.'"*

If he thought Conrad and his daughter were dating, maybe her father wouldn't be so eager to trade him, right?

It still felt slimy. "How long do I have to do this?"

"A month, tops. By then, it's old news. Show up to a few of his games wearing his jersey, give him a hug, maybe go out for dinner—someplace public. Snap some shots of you two doing something fun—whatever. One month of content, one million new followers, and suddenly you're back in the black, solving crimes, finding justice."

Doing something that mattered, on her own.

"Okay. You talk to Felicity. If Conrad agrees, then . . . one month. Then I'm out."

"If you don't fall in love first."

She laughed. "Don't hold your breath." Because if he said yes, then he was using her too.

And she'd been there, done that, thank you.

She didn't care how beautiful his eyes, his smile, the aura of protection, or even his Mr. June physique. She wasn't going to fall for a liar.

THREE

MAYBE HE SHOULD JUST HANG UP HIS SKATES. Conrad stormed into the locker room and sent his helmet crashing against his locker. It bounced, hit the floor, and spun out, just like his gameplay today.

Behind him, his team came in, a few slapping Justin's—Blade's—shoulder pads for his game-tying goal.

Blade shot Conrad a glance, a hint of challenge in his eyes, before he sank onto the bench and unlaced his skates.

Conrad already had his off, his socks sweaty, his body one giant ache thanks to the beating he'd gotten from the Colorado Sting.

He'd given out a few too, spent at least a minute in the box for boarding, but it had rattled the Sting and given Torch, his left winger, a chance to score.

And then, somehow, after the second period, he'd lost his mojo, his verve, and he was bouncing shots off the pipes, ringing the iron on all his attempts, if not outright sending the puck into the cheap seats.

He'd looked like the rookie out there.

Wyatt Marshall—their goalie—came in and sat down next to

him. Pulled off his jersey, then picked up Conrad's helmet from the floor, set it on the bench. "Could be worse."

"How?" He put his skates in the sharpening bin above his locker. "We could have lost."

"We tied. I lost a half dozen face-offs, turned over the puck at the blue line three times, we had more broken plays than wins, I missed too many back-checks, and by the end of the game, I was just slapping at anything that moved. No wonder coach took me out."

"Everybody has a bad day."

"Try a bad month. Sheesh, if I were coach, I . . . well, I don't want to jinx the ice, but . . ." Dropping his breezers, he stepped out of them, pulled off his jersey and pads, then headed for the showers, grabbing a towel on the way.

Ten minutes later, he emerged, towel at his hips, his clothes in their mesh bag, which he dropped into the hamper, still steamed at the game.

Although, the chilly shower had cut his anger into mere frustration.

Until he spotted Blade, the rookie, talking with a female reporter.

In their locker room.

He walked over, not caring that he might be in the shot. "You're supposed to stay in the designated interview area."

Justin looked at him, back at the reporter, flashed her a grin. "The old man is worried about you seeing all his saggy parts—"

And that was it. Conrad put a hand over the camera, shoved it down and away, and looked at the woman. Couldn't remember her name, although he'd seen her before. *Wait.* "Ava. You know better. Team rules—media stays in the media area—" He pointed to a space on the far side of the room, behind the showers.

She held up the mic. "Wanna respond to Blade's stellar performance out there tonight? Or maybe your time in the penalty box?"

He turned his back to her, put a hand on Justin's chest. "You know better too."

Justin slapped his hand away. "Don't touch me, old man."

Old. man?

He dropped his hand, took a step into Justin's face, lowered his voice. "Listen, pup. Respect your team."

Justin's jaw tightened, and he shot a glance behind him, then took a breath and backed away.

Conrad rounded back to the reporter. But the movement, of course, jostled his towel, and he got a hand on it just before it unlatched.

Ava's mouth twitched.

"Did you not hear me?"

She narrowed her eyes but gestured with her head for her cameraman to follow her.

Conrad stood, a hand on his towel, watching until they retreated.

He got a couple high fives as he returned to the locker area. Wyatt had also returned, his hair wet, wearing a pair of jeans, barefoot, bare chested.

"Thanks, man. That's not the first time she's pushed the edge. Apparently, she thinks rules don't apply to her."

Conrad pulled on pants, then reached for a T-shirt, his chest a little less tight.

Wyatt closed his locker, holding his jacket in one hand. "See you at Sammy's?"

"Dunno. Maybe." Although, maybe he needed to spend some time in the darkness of his home theater, rewatching the game.

Rewiring his reactions.

He sat, pulled on his boots, tied up his laces, and looked up to see a few of the guys now meeting with media in the designated area. His contract stated that he needed to stop in, offer himself up like a tasty morsel after every game. Even Wyatt stopped by, now cornered by a different female sportscaster, probably pinning him down on the two goals he'd let slip by, completely ignoring his twenty-plus shots-on-goal saves.

That's how it was though. The reporters only wanted to talk about the worst. Or—and he spotted Justin, talking again with Ava—the best.

No, not the best. Justin had gotten lucky, taken advantage of his moment in the spotlight while Conrad had sat out with his line for a breather.

Whatever. He had his moment in the sun.

"Old man." Hardly. He had at least three, maybe five good years left.

Okay, two. One more contract, however. And please let it be with the Blue Ox. He just had to make it past the trade deadline in three weeks, and he'd finish the season with the Ox.

He always played better in the last forty days before the end of the regular season.

Grabbing his gear bag, he got up and headed for the door.

Coach Jace Jacobsen emerged from his locker-room office, just by the door, and leaned his big shoulder on the frame. Gestured with his head for Conrad to join him.

Perfect. Conrad sighed and followed the coach into the office.

Jace shut the door behind him.

Posters of former teams from the last twenty years hung on the walls around the room, with a few blowups of their stars over the years. Jace, a former winger and enforcer for the team, had his own mug blown up, looking fierce as he stared into the camera. Now he wore the same dark expression as he folded his arms.

"Sit, Conrad."

Oh, this would be fun. Conrad sank into one of the folding chairs, dropped his bag on the floor. "'Sup, Coach?"

Jace took a breath. "The Department of Player Safety is reviewing that hit you did on Kowalcyzk."

"What? They were hitting just as hard. Besides, I already sat in the box for it."

Jace held up a hand. "Listen. I know how it gets. Believe me—I had my share of hits, both given and taken. But hockey's changed since I played. Player safety is a priority. They're reviewing the hit for a charging infraction to the neck and head."

"C'mon—he was shorter than me—"

Jace again held up a hand. "More than that—you played like a third grader tonight. What's going on?"

Right. Conrad leaned back, looked away, out at the media room. Maybe he should be grateful Coach had pulled him in here. But the last—very last—thing he could admit was that he hadn't been sleeping.

That he *was* like a third grader, waking in the middle of the night for the past three days, sweating, bursting out of a sound sleep. Maybe even doing a small pillow hug.

Memories, not nightmares, and in every one of them, he was the one who lost a leg.

Although, sometimes the nightmares shifted and he found himself in frigid water, the earth having given out beneath him.

And in between the nightmares, when he woke and stared at his coffered ceiling, Penelope Pepper walked into his head. And it wasn't just her "I don't think that's a good idea" to his offer to text, but the other words, spoken to the skinny lawyer in the bathroom earlier that night. *"Since I've been investigating this case, I've been kidnapped and seen two men shot and people murdered."*

So, hurt and worry were a stupendous combination for getting back to sleep.

He might have worked out a little harder than he'd needed to, so he'd blame tired muscles, too.

He looked back at Coach. "Just not sleeping great, maybe."

"Fix it," Jace said. "And in the meantime, you're suspended from this weekend's road games."

He blinked at him. "What?" He found himself on his feet. "Coach—*c'mon*. I'll get it together—I always do—"

"Sit down, Conrad." Voice low, steady, a hint of the old enforcer in his tone.

Conrad's mouth tightened. but he lowered himself back into his chair.

"I know that's not what you want to hear—especially with the draft deadline coming up, but frankly, maybe you need a head swap. Get your brain out of the game for five minutes, or ten, and do something that activates your muscle memory. You can play hockey—no one is doubting that you're a legend in the league. But you've got the yips."

"Don't say that. It's like referencing Macbeth at a theater. Now you've jinxed me."

Jace held his gaze. "It's that kind of thinking that leads to the yips."

"Please, for crying out loud—"

Jace smiled. "Fine. I get it—I used to not wash my socks the entire Stanley tournament." He blew out a breath. "Still. You're close to burning yourself out." He walked around his desk. Picked up a bulky, oversized package and tossed it to Conrad.

"What's this?"

"Congratulations. You're the new assistant coach for the Northwest Ice Hawks."

"The who? I'm what?" He opened the package. A jersey, a whistle, and a schedule. He pulled the gear out.

"EmPowerPlay has a team that's going to the regional playoffs in a couple weeks. They need a coach. Someone who can help them win."

"What? I'm not a coach." He looked up. "Jace. Please—"

Jace stood, arms folded, unmoving.

Aw . . . "Listen, you need me. The team needs me—even if I'm on the bench—"

"We're playing the Boise Blizzard. Trust me, we got this." Jace leaned on the desk. "I'm going to be honest. I like you. A lot. You're a Minnesota guy, a homegrown favorite, and I don't want to see you go. But there's talk about trading you."

Shoot—he knew it. But still, the words landed like a blade in his heart.

"However, this game isn't all about stats. Not when it comes to hometown love and ticket sales. Truth is, the crowd, *our* crowd, loves you. And if you can make them love you even more, the powers that be will think twice about trading you. At least mid-season." He stood up. "Like you said, you always seem to land the last forty days until playoffs. And there's no doubt you've carried us through the last few years." He folded his arms again. "I don't want to lose you. So . . . work with me."

And what was he going to say to that?

He sighed. "How many games am I out?"

"Just this weekend. And you just have to coach up to the tournament. Then call it good." Jace gave him a smile. "It wouldn't hurt if you won, either."

"Right." Conrad stood up. "I'll do my best."

"That's never in doubt." Jace reached out to shake his hand.

Conrad met the grip, not sure why, despite his temporary banishment, the terrible fist had loosened in his chest.

"I think you're safe." Jace lifted his head, indicating the media room.

Conrad turned and saw that most of the reporters had left.

"Just pray you don't end up on social media, clutching your towel. But way to take one for the team." Coach grinned.

Conrad rolled his eyes. "If they haven't seen enough of me. Next year, count me off the calendar."

Jace laughed. "As the former, ahem, *clothed* centerfold for *Hockey Today,* I get ya. Hang in there. Think of the lives you're saving."

Conrad groaned and headed out the door and into the tunnel

to the exit. The breath of the ice lingered, almost a challenge, but he ignored it, setting his bag over his shoulder.

But not before he heard laughter, words.

He turned, headed back down the tunnel to the ice.

One of the two swinging doors was still propped open, and as he stood at the entrance, he spotted Justin.

On the ice, his arms around Ava, teaching her how to shoot a puck.

She must have a good five years on him, but Justin didn't seem to mind, his twenty-two-year-old brain clearly on sparks between them as she leaned into him.

Yeah, that was trouble waiting to happen.

He turned and headed out to the parking lot. Dropped his duffel in the trunk, then got in the Charger and dropped the package on the passenger seat. Picked up his phone, where he'd left it charging during the game, no distractions.

Thumbed open his text messages, just in case. Of course, nothing. Not that he expected anything, but . . .

Aw, shoot. He'd hoped, maybe. A little.

Clearly, Penelope Pepper had meant what she'd said.

Jace was right. He needed a brain transplant. One that didn't include Penelope Pepper and her murder mystery.

It might help if said brain could erase the past, too, thank you. He'd give his Ducati Panigale V4 for a decent night's sleep.

While he waited for his car to warm up, he glanced at the package on the passenger seat. Picked it up and pulled out the jersey.

Icy blue and silver with a hawk on the chest, wings wide, talons out.

He groaned. *No, no*—how had he not put together Jace's words with Simon's team?

Conrad sighed, leaned his head back.

So much for escaping his nightmares.

•————————————————•

Her opening music—a seductive saxophone melody—faded out, and Penelope leaned into her Shure SM7B microphone, her voice smooth, even, and perfect for her late-night audience. Or whenever her listeners wanted to download her podcast.

"Hello, puzzlers! You're tuned in to *Penny for Your Thoughts,* the podcast where no clue is too small and no theory too wild. I'm your host, Penelope Pepper, diving deep into the twists and turns of the Case of Sarah Livingston."

She sat in her basement office, remodeled after she'd bought the 1927 home on Wood Lane in Minneapolis, a tiny dead-end street that backed up to Minnehaha Creek. A Tudor with sweeping rooflines and a slant-ceiling second-floor attic, she'd gutted the place and redone it to give it the vintage-modern vibe that felt like home.

Unlike the Pepper palace on the lake.

The basement office was her haven. Wood flooring with a plush lamb's-wool rug, an antique oak desk that sat in the middle of the room, whitewash over the original brick walls, and Tiffany lighting. Behind her, a shelf stocked with vintage Agatha Christie mysteries, and a teal-painted wooden cabinet that held her research. Above that, on the wall, an old map of Minneapolis–St. Paul held pushpins that indicated places in her investigation.

For inspiration, on the other walls hung movie posters—*Rear Window* and *North by Northwest.* But her favorite spot was her grandmother's blue velvet Queen Anne chair, worn yet decadently comfortable, seated in the corner with books piled on the floor nearby.

On her desk, two monitors captured her notes for today's monologue.

"Sarah, a vibrant real estate agent, was murdered in her own home under circumstances that grow stranger by the day. No forced entry, and witnesses saw a masked man running from her townhome late at night. Her ex-boyfriend, Holden Walsh, alibied out, which left the police with no motive, no leads, and a cold trail. And the *Penny for Your Thoughts* listeners on the hunt. Since our last episode, the plot has thickened, and today I've got some critical updates and theories that might just blow the roof off this case."

A glance at the starburst clock on the wall suggested she needed to get moving. The publicist for EmPowerPlay expected her out at the rink in two hours. She pitched her voice low, adding a bit of play to it.

"First off, remember Kyle Brunley? Sarah's best friend, suspected of the murder by some because of his rumored jealousy over Sarah's ex-boyfriend Walsh? Tragically, Kyle was found dead, his car crashed in a ditch." She leaned into the mic, changed her voice again. "Accident . . . or silenced forever?"

She pushed a button, and a sound effect of a gasp emitted into the recording.

"And then there's Tommy, Sarah's neighbor, recently out of surgery after being shot in what was described as a 'freak accident.' But, folks, how many freak accidents can one case have, hmm?"

Glancing at her notes, she continued. "Adding more mystery, we learned that before her death, Sarah's home was burglarized. Her computer was stolen—why? What was on that computer? Was it connected to the fire at the Stone Arch Condos, leading to the death of one man?"

She hadn't yet announced who that man was—and maybe, given the conversation with Tia . . .

No. Edward's death *had* to have been a murder. She felt it in her gut.

"These weren't just any condos, folks—they were owned by none other than Walsh and his elusive partner, Derek Swindle. Did Walsh share something dangerous with Sarah before their breakup? And where in the world is Walsh now? He's missing, and as each day passes, the questions pile up like clues in a detective's docket."

She pushed another button, and a telephone rang. "Let's see what you have to say. I want to hear your theories, no matter how out there they might seem. Let's go—a penny for your thoughts."

The calls came in, recorded on her site earlier in the week, and she posted the most juicy. The first call came on the line. Eager. "Hi, Penny, longtime listener here! I've got a theory—what if Walsh and Swindle are in witness protection because they stumbled onto a real estate laundering ring? Maybe Sarah found out and . . . well, you know."

"Fascinating take!" Penelope said. "Witness protection is a twist I hadn't considered. Thanks for your thoughts!"

Another telephone ring.

"Caller two, hit me with your theory."

This one could be a podcaster, with her conspiratorial tone. "Hey, Penelope, here's what I think: aliens. Yes, aliens are using real estate to infiltrate our society. Maybe Sarah caught on to their plans!"

"Okay, caller two. Our armchair PIs never disappoint with their creativity. Thanks for adding some extraterrestrial intrigue to the mix."

She'd cued up two more calls.

"Hi, Penny, love the show. Here's my theory: what if this whole thing is a cover-up for a bigger scandal? Maybe Sarah discovered fraudulent activities tied to the real estate market, involving not just Walsh and Swindle but higher-ups in the industry. Her computer might have had evidence that could bring down a lot of powerful people!"

This one she liked, a lot. Had already jotted that angle down for more investigation. "Oh, a classic corruption angle—nothing like financial scandal to stir the pot. Thanks for weighing in with that sharp insight! And our final caller for tonight . . ."

"Hey, Penny, I've been thinking—what if it's all about personal vendettas? Maybe someone from the apartment-complex fire saw something—even Sarah at the scene—and thought she had something to do with it through her connection to Walsh. Perhaps they sought revenge not just on her but on everyone close to her, like Kyle and Tommy. Remember, 'If the fact will not fit the theory— let the theory go.'"

An Agatha Christie quote—she'd heard it before from this caller. But this theory stilled her. She hadn't considered that Sarah might have been complicit in a crime that had led to her murder. "Revenge—a motive as old as time itself. That's a chilling but entirely possible scenario. Thank you for your thoughtful contribution."

Two interesting theories, at least.

She didn't have time for the last one, but it also sat in her brain. *"Hi there, Penny! Here's a wild card: what if Sarah was part of an undercover investigation? Maybe she was working with the police or a private detective to expose illegal activities in the real estate business and her cover was blown."*

Penelope needed to recover the information from Kyle's jump drive, or sussing out the theories would be like herding cats.

She cued her transition music. "Keep these theories coming, folks. Every angle provides a new piece of the puzzle in unraveling the secrets of Sarah Livingston. Call and leave a message, and let's unravel this mystery together on *Penny for Your Thoughts*. In a world full of puzzles, your thoughts might just be the missing piece. See you next time—toodles!"

She hit her outro, a mix of jazz music, and then stopped recording. Saving it to the cloud, she sent her producer a message, then picked up her phone.

A text. And no, she didn't expect Conrad to text her—after all, she'd been the one to shut him down. But she couldn't deny the craziest, unmerited disappointment that Lucas Reid, newly promoted PR director for the Pepper Foundation, had sent her a digital reminder to BE AT THE NORTH STAR ARENA BY FOUR P.M., all caps.

Sheesh, calm down. She closed her computer, then slid the barn door open and headed through her finished basement to the upstairs, through the open great room/kitchen, to her second-floor bedroom, the entire top level, with a master bathroom that overlooked the river. After changing into yoga pants and an oversized EmPowerPlay sweatshirt, she pulled back her long hair, added a white furry headband, then headed downstairs, donned her UGGs, grabbed her keys, and was out the door.

See. She could be on time.

She headed west on Highway 7, out past Waconia, listening to a murder mystery on tape—a book about an art thief in Boston.

She finally pulled up to the North Star Arena, a massive steel building just east of Duck Lake, with a star on the apex of the building and trucks and SUVs filling the lot.

Hopefully Lucas would be here with his iPhone, or whatever he planned on taking pictures with, and she could buzz in, buzz out, get on with her day.

Not that she had any plans beyond a bubble bath and the rest of her audiobook.

The icy air met her as she walked inside, shouts echoing along with the crisp shots of pucks and the swish of skates. She glanced at her watch. Twenty minutes late. Practically fashionable.

A smattering of parents sat in the bleachers, watching, a few shouting encouragement and bleacher advice to the coach.

She spotted Lucas sitting on a bench a couple rows up from the entrance. He waved to her—nice-looking guy, late twenties, clean-shaven, wearing glasses, his dark hair behind his ears, a little of a renegade aura despite his suit pants and puffer jacket.

"Sorry I'm late."

"They started early," he said. "Apparently the new coach changed the time." He gestured to a couple of guys across the ice. One of them Simon, whom she recognized when he skated nearer to the edge, blowing his whistle.

The kids—a motley crew dressed in worn jerseys, a few in jeans—*what?*—passed pucks to each other in pairs as they raced down the ice.

The other coach worked with a group of players, crouching down as he talked with them, his back to her.

"They're not bad. They were pretty unorganized when I got here, but that coach stepped in and they did a three-puck relay."

She glanced at him. "Did you play hockey?"

"I'm a Minnesotan. Of course I played hockey." He smiled up at her, winked.

Wait—was he flirting with her?

"Did you get any shots?"

He handed over his Canon DSLR.

She flipped through the shots of the players in huddles and then moving up the ice, then the coaches skating up to assist, and then a close-up of one of the coaches instructing a kid, maybe thirteen, about correct hand placement on the stick—

Her breath hitched. *Wait—what?*

She looked up at Lucas. "Is that Conrad Kingston?"

He took the camera, looked at the screen. "I think so."

Aw.

"I told them we'd get some shots of you and the team when they break." He frowned. "Where are your skates?"

"My, um . . . skates?"

"Aw, shoot. I texted you. Or—" He pulled out his phone. "Yeah, here it is, unsent." He dropped the phone back into his pocket. "Okay, so I'll see if I can find some. You do know how to skate, right?"

"In *hockey* skates?"

He shrugged. "Aren't all skates the same?"

She sighed. "No. But I am Minnesotan. I suppose I can figure out how to stand up."

Or not. Because twenty minutes later, oversized used skates on her feet, she ventured out onto the ice like a toddler.

It didn't help that she'd spent the previous twenty minutes watching Conrad, her insides knotting up with a heat that she didn't want to interpret. He looked good. Better than good—solid, a hockey superhero out there as he worked with the kids and then showed off a little as he taught them how to flick in shots from the crease, Simon suited up as goalkeeper.

He wore a serious, grim look—a close-up she nabbed via Lucas's viewfinder—and she discovered he'd trimmed his beard even shorter than at the gala, had a sort of whiskered north-woods look about him, especially with the thermal shirt that poked out of his jersey. Not a Blue Ox jersey either, but Ice Hawks, so clearly he was buying street cred with the team.

While she looked like an idiot. Oh, this was a bad idea—

"You need a hand there?"

She looked up, and of course Conrad skated right up to her like he might have been born on skates.

Of course he had.

He smiled at her, but it seemed a little tight, even as he held out his hand.

She grabbed it, wobbled, and he grabbed her other arm.

"Ho-kay. First time on skates?"

"Not even a little. I grew up on Lake Minnetonka, thank you." She didn't mean to snap, but—*seriously*. He needed to stop being so . . . fantastic.

Like holding her up as they skated to the center, where the team posed with their sticks. And then even kneeling in front of her so she could steady herself as she gave a thumbs-up for the camera and smiled.

More shots, and he was *right. there*. Even caught her again when her feet defected.

"Gotcha," he said.

Oh, no, no—because he smiled at her and winked and . . .

Lucas snapped a shot.

And then she got it. Clarice. She'd called Felicity, and the game was on. The entire thing was an act—all the charm, all the music, the bone-weakening smiles.

Well, two could play that game—actually two *should* play that game.

She winked back.

His eyebrows arched.

She gripped his arms, pulled herself close, then encircled his waist. Grinned up at him. "Don't let go. I might end up a splotch on the ice."

He seemed have gone a little pale but nodded.

She looked at Lucas and smiled.

Flash.

They finished the shoot, and Conrad helped her back to the side. Let her go. "Okay, that was . . . unexpected."

She sat on a bench, unlacing her skates, looked up at him. "Yeah, for sure. I didn't think . . ." She sighed. "Anyway, thanks for the photos."

"Yeah, well, it's part of the deal, right? Show up, smile, do some good for the team."

"Land a new contract."

He blinked at her. Then his smile faded and he nodded. "Hopefully."

And if she'd had any lingering ideas or even hopes that this might be real . . . well, really, she got it. And didn't blame him at all.

Hockey was his life. He couldn't lose it.

She fought with the skates, and he knelt and helped her, pulling the blade. She leaned back, held on as he wrenched it off, nearly stumbled back.

She held up her other foot, spotted Lucas again with the camera, waved, and then grinned as Conrad pulled off the other skate.

He held them in his grip as she reached for her UGGS. He started to say something, but seemed to hesitate.

Lucas had skated—of course—over to the other bench.

Then, "The team is going over to Lakeside Pizza Company. You want to come along?"

Oh. "Is Lucas going?"

He glanced over. "The photographer?"

"Yes. He's with EmPowerPlay."

His mouth opened, closed. Turned into a grim line. "Dunno. I mean, we can invite him."

Clarice would be thrilled. More personal shots. And maybe Penelope could do an end run around Conrad until Clarice ran out of posting material. "Okay."

"Okay," he said, and sighed. "See you there."

Then he stepped out onto the ice and skated his magnificent deceptive self away from her.

FOUR

How had he gone from a superstar to the tagalong?

One minute, Conrad had been congratulating himself for not melting down in front of a group of hero-worshipping teenagers . . . the next, She Who Would Not Text Him had replaced him.

At least, that's what it felt like as he watched Penelope and Lucas walk out of the building, chatting like a couple.

What. ever.

Wow, had he pegged that wrong. And worse, he'd made a royal fool out of himself, acting like he might be her hero.

He wanted to floor it back to Minneapolis instead of following Simon and the other team members to Lakeside Pizza Company, on the shores of Duck Lake.

"Just go," said the voice on the other end of the phone, a.k.a. his sister Austen, the One Who Knew. Because she'd been there that night when his panic attacks had started.

Seagulls cried in the air on her end, so she probably sat at dock in her trawler-slash-live-aboard boat.

He slowed, driving through Duck Lake to the west end, where Lakeside Pizza Company sat on the edge of the namesake lake.

Light puddled on the streets, cleared of snow and rubble that had been dumped into the municipal parking lot for now. A few shops remained open—Duck Lake Market, Sip and Paint, and the Lumberjack's Table, a couple neon signs glowing in the bar-side extension.

He should really swing by and see his parents out at the King's Inn, but then there would be questions and maybe some dodging of the truth, and he hated secrets. Hated lying.

Hated his stupid mistakes.

"The more you show up, the easier it will get," Austen said through the speaker in his car.

And of course, she was referring to practice and the fact that he'd made it through without the world closing in on him. Without even having to find a small quiet place and breathe.

As if his nightmares hadn't begun on this very ice so many years ago. Fifteen, to be exact.

"It's just through next weekend; then I'm out."

"But you had fun, right?"

Fun. Maybe. "I don't know. Simon's doing a good job. I showed up and helped him with some drills, taught them some shooting techniques."

"You represent everything they can be. Everything they dream about. It doesn't hurt to give them a piece of yourself. You have a lot to give."

Funny, it felt like the kids had given to *him*, at least for that brief hour of practice. He'd found pieces of himself he'd forgotten as he'd taken shots on goal against Simon.

"Well, at the very least, I didn't throw up on them."

She laughed. "That's always a win. Maybe it was all those visualization exercises you did over the past four days."

He heard rain pinging on the other end of the line. "Where are you?"

"On the *Fancy Free*. There's a little squall moving in."

"Please tell me you're at a dock."

"Yes. Calm down. But tomorrow's my day off. I'm heading out to a dive—serious treasure debris about sixty feet down. We'll see."

A clunk—maybe she was filling tanks.

He turned onto the drive toward Lakeside Pizza ahead.

"So, was he there?"

A beat.

"Jeremy."

He sighed. "Yeah, I know. No, he didn't show up for practice."

"Maybe that was God on your side. Baby steps."

He didn't attribute any of that to God's involvement. But he didn't want to argue with her theology. Leave well enough alone and maybe everything would be fine.

"By the way, their Hawaiian pizza is amazing. Stein and I went out before I headed back to the Keys. How is he? It's been a minute since I've heard from him."

"I saw him last weekend, at the EmPowerPlay charity event. He's working with Declan Stone. Stone offered him a job after Stein returned his phone." Their brother had weirdly found Declan Stone's phone in his suit pocket after Boo's wedding reception.

"He was still thinking about the offer when I left. Did he ever figure out how Stone's phone ended up in his pocket?"

"I don't know. Maybe the man mistook Stein's jacket for his own."

"Well, I'm glad he took it. He needed something besides teaching kids how to snorkel." Another thump. "Listen. Eat some pizza, relax. This could be fun—just don't overthink it."

"Have you met me?" He pulled into a space.

"Right. What Conrad wants, Conrad gets."

"Ha. I'd like to live in your fantasy."

"Love you, bro. Stay groovy." She hung up.

Geez, his sister, the surfer girl, marine biologist, deep-sea treasure hunter.

Maybe he *was* overthinking the entire thing. The past. His career. Penelope.

"What Conrad wants, Conrad gets."

Hardly, but . . . what *did* he want?

His gaze landed on Penelope the moment he entered the former Pizza Hut with red vinyl booths and black tables. The place smelled of garlic and Italian sausage and tomato sauce, and he lifted a hand to a couple locals as he came in, including Deputy Jenna Hayes, who sat at a booth with a man he didn't recognize.

A glance around the room said that Lucas hadn't joined them. But Penelope had, and now she sat at a booth across from a table of raucous boys, reading her phone.

She looked up as he walked over. "Hey."

"This seat taken by anyone under the age of thirty-two?"

She arched a brow, but offered a slim smile. "Don't break a hip sliding in."

He sat down, waved to Simon, sitting with a couple kids, and turned to her. "What are you doing?"

"Looking up hockey suppliers." She met his eyes. "These guys need gear. New helmets, new skates, new pads, new everything. I had a talk with Simon—they got a bus to transport kids last year, and that ate up their entire budget."

Oh. "I didn't know."

A waitress came over and he ordered a Coke.

"Pepperoni?" he asked.

"Whatever you want. But I heard the Hawaiian is good."

From who? "Sure," he said, and the waitress left.

He glanced at the other table, where a serious arm-wrestling match was going down.

She turned to him. "Okay, I can admit I didn't expect to see you at practice. I mean—I guess I figured we'd connect, you know, but you seemed a little . . . weird, I guess, after seeing Simon at the gala."

Oh, right. "Yeah. Um, actually, Coach Jace asked me to help. I'm sitting out a couple road games—"

"*Sitting out a couple road games?* Holy cats, Conrad. *Why?*"

He didn't want to smile, but her concern felt . . . genuine. So maybe they were friends. He could do friends. "I was a little . . . grumpy, let's call it, during the last game."

"Oh, you mean the brawl with the Colorado left winger? The penalty call?"

And now, *really*? "You saw the game?"

"It was on while I was making dinner."

"Late dinner."

"Sometimes. Research. I get sort of wrapped up in it, and it drags me down, holds me captive. I can even forget to eat."

"Yeah. Me too. Only, my addiction is sailing shows on YouTube."

She gave him a look.

"Right? Crazy. But once upon a time, my grandfather had a little daysailer on the lake, and he taught me how to sail. Someday." He lifted a shoulder.

"I didn't see you as a sailor."

"It's very quiet. Sometimes . . . I like quiet."

Why had he said that? But maybe friends were honest with each other, right?

He found himself tracing her smile, then trying to figure out the exact color of her eyes.

She nodded. "I like quiet too," she said. "But what I'd really like is peace."

"Don't you have peace?"

"I have questions," she said.

He blinked at her, the candor undoing him a little. But before he could chase down her comment, the pizza arrived.

And that's when trouble showed up in the form of Tyler Bouchard, the center he'd been helping with strategy today. "Dare you to a pizza contest, Coach."

Conrad's stupid mouth, and maybe a little ego, said yes.

Forty minutes later, he stared at a pile of crusts, his stomach hurting as he went toe to toe with Tardis-for-a-Stomach Tyler.

The kid had him by four slices, easy.

For her part, Penelope stood at the end of the table, watching, her arms folded.

"You tapping out, Coach C?"

Coach C. He could live with that.

He held up his hands, and behind him, people clapped. He hadn't realized they'd gathered an audience.

Tyler's father, Steve, came up and shook his hand. "Didn't think you could get beat by a kid, right, King Con?"

The guy was a little paunchy, wore beer on his breath. Conrad smiled, kept it easy. "He's a champ, for sure."

Steve grinned, threw an arm around his wife, plump, wearing an Ice Hawks jersey. Conrad had noticed a few other parents in the bleachers. Some had followed him to the pizza joint.

The team took a few photos with him, and even Penelope hopped in, moving in right next to him, her arm around his waist.

Huh. He settled his arm over her shoulders. Like they belonged together.

Then he and Simon huddled up to go over details for the next practice.

When he walked back to Penelope, she was reading her phone. Something in her expression seemed unnerved. "You okay?"

She looked up, flashed him her phone screen. "Beckett texted me. Said he has information for me. Maybe he got Kyle's computer."

Beckett—it took a second but, "The guy from the men's restroom."

"Please say that a little louder." She glanced around her.

He shook his head. "So—he wants to meet up?"

"Yeah. Gave me his address." She dropped her phone into her bag and grabbed her jacket. "Good to see you, Conrad."

And—*wait*. "Where are you going?"

"To Beckett's house?" She wore a little confusion.

"Over my dead body."

Silence.

Maybe he'd said *that* too loud.

"What did you say?"

"I said . . ." He schooled his voice. "This guy gives me, to quote my father, the *willies*. You're not going alone."

"I can handle myself." She pulled on her jacket.

"I don't care if you're a Navy SEAL, you're not going alone." He also nabbed his jacket. "And you're not a Navy SEAL, in case you're wondering."

Her mouth opened, just slightly. Then, "I am aware that I am not a Navy SEAL."

"Good. I'll follow you." He lifted a hand to Simon and went to the door. Held it open for her.

"You don't have to—"

"Where does he live?"

She glanced at her phone. "In the Golf Terrace Heights area in Edina."

"Perfect. I know exactly where that is. Let's go."

She raised an eyebrow, but headed out to her Nissan Rogue.

He got in the Charger and glued to her tail as she motored out of the lot, his chest tighter than it should be. What was it about this woman that he couldn't help but be worried about her?

He turned on the radio, found some jazz, and settled in for the ride, the night crisp, the stars bright in the dark sky, her taillights in view. They finally reached the city, but as they got on 100, heading to Golf Terrace Heights, the stars vanished, the lights of the city blurring the panorama.

And up ahead, a glow pressed against the darkness.

She got off 100, onto Vernon Ave., and as he looked across the snow-blanketed golf course, he spotted the source of the light.

House fire. One of the stately homes that edged the golf course.

They headed down Wooddale, and the knot in his gut tightened. He'd been in one house fire—or rather, garage fire—as a child. Terrifying.

Red lights flashed against frozen pavement and snowy banks as they turned onto Golf Terrace Road. Smoke billowed from the back of the house, flames crashing through the main-story windows of a once-gorgeous Tudor with tall angled rooftops and a brick facade. Three fire trucks sprayed the home, turning the air soggy. Snow melted around the house.

Penelope stopped a short distance from where police cars cordoned off the area.

A few onlookers dressed in jackets and hats stood watching the peril.

Conrad pulled up too. Shut off his car. Got out. Penelope had gotten out and ventured closer, wrapping her arms around herself as she watched the firefighters.

"What happened?" Conrad addressed his question to a bystander, a middle-aged man in a parka and slippers, hands shoved into his pockets.

"I don't know—the house just exploded about twenty minutes ago. Must have been the heater. It's an old house."

Right.

He walked up to Penelope, stood behind her. "That's Beckett's house, right?"

"Yeah," she said quietly.

And then, just to confuse him even more, she turned, put her arms around his waist, and hung on.

Let go.

Let the poor man go.

The thought pulsed inside Penelope, in her head, even her chest, but it just couldn't make it out to her arms.

Which were viced around Conrad like he might again be an anchor.

A buoy in the sudden tsunami of despair.

Okay, that felt overly dramatic, but not a bad line—she might use that in an upcoming podcast. Still—

His big hands held her arms and finally went around her, probably as he was thinking through the fact that this was not in his *contract.*

Whatever.

But as if to confirm her thought, he loosened his hold, then took her arms and moved her away from him.

Right. His gaze was on the house, so she turned and spotted firefighters emerging from the blazing structure.

Between them, they carried a bagged body, heavy, and to her guess, one Anton Beckett.

"Oh no. Beckett was home," said the man near her, wearing a parka and slippers. He'd come up next to them near the police barricade. "Poor man—I saw lights on just before the house blew up."

The cold night slid into her soul.

And then, probably because he was still a nice guy, Conrad put a hand on her shoulder, squeezed. Heat poured through her at the gesture, but she didn't move.

The firefighters put the body into an ambulance, which pulled away into the night.

Her last lead had just been cindered. Another man killed. To her knowledge, Beckett didn't have a wife or kids, but he *did* have a life.

Or had.

Her throat thickened.

"Let's go," Conrad said softly. "I think maybe you need a cookie."

She glanced up at him, turned, frowned. "A *cookie*?"

"Trust me." He gestured with his head to their cars, and she followed him, stood at her open car door.

"Where are we going?"

"Follow and learn." He got into his sleek Charger and backed into a driveway, pulled out. Like a woman hypnotized, she obeyed.

And yet, her heart banged in her chest, her breaths hard, her thoughts tangled as she pinned her gaze to his taillights, red and glowing like a beacon in the night.

She followed him through the maze of streets leading to St. Louis Park, and weirdly, just south of her own neighborhood, then over to Lake of the Isles and, tucked back a couple blocks off Hennepin, into the lot of a vintage-train depot. Yellow awnings over the windows, decorated with twinkle lights that lit up the space. He was waiting by the door, holding it open as she walked up. "What is this?"

"Ironclad Desserts." He wore a grin, and she frowned but headed inside.

The aroma of chocolate baked goods filled the eclectic space. Small wooden tables with votive centerpieces, a long, high wall shelf crammed with used books, and hanging industrial lights gave the place an easy vibe. Leather chairs circled around wooden coffee tables, creating conversation nooks by the windows.

He stopped at the order station. "Hey, Marcie. I'm going to need a chocolate toffee-chip, stat."

The woman—pretty, in her twenties—grinned, a few stars in her eyes as she took his card, swiped it, and handed it back. "Right away, Mr. Kingston. And your regular coffee order?"

Huh.

"Times two, but make them unleaded," he said. Then Conrad gestured to a leather chair grouping.

She sat, leaned back, closing her eyes. "It's late. I should go home."

"Me too. I have practice in the morning."

"You're going to practice even though you're suspended for two games?"

Marcie came over with a couple decaf coffees. "You forgot these." She winked at him.

"Thanks, Marce." He picked up the coffee. "I come here after games sometimes. Habit. My mom used to make me chocolate chip cookies after every game . . . Sort of a lucky charm." He took a sip of coffee. "Best late-night brew in Minneapolis. And I'm not suspended. Just . . ." He made a face. "Let's call it a mental time-out."

She took a sip of the coffee. "This is good."

"They call it the late-night latte. Decaf, milk, a hint of vanilla." He set the cup down. "Now what?"

"Now what?"

"If that body was Beckett, then clearly whatever he wanted to tell you is dead with him, so . . . what's next?"

Oh. She had the weirdest sense that this might be a continuation of that hug he'd given her. Only without any contact. Because hello, no cameras. But she'd met him—this was Men's-Bathroom Guy, and maybe Carry-Her-Up-the-Stairs Guy. Not I-Am-into-You Guy, so *calm down.*

Marcie walked over again, this time carrying a sizzling skillet that she set down, along with two plates and forks, on the table between them. A giant chocolate chip cookie with whipped cream melting over the top. She cut the cookie into pie angles, then lifted one onto a plate, gave it to Penelope. The other onto a plate for Conrad. "Enjoy."

Penelope picked up her fork. "How do you stay in such good shape with this kind of late-night sugar?"

"Sometimes I don't eat the entire thing." He took a bite. "At once." His eyes closed, and he made a deep, rumbly sound in his chest.

Dangerous man, with the cookie, and the hug, and now a lion grumble.

Good thing this was all just pretend. And maybe, right now, therapy.

She took a bite. "How do you not eat the entire thing? Holy cats."

"Right?"

She set her fork down. Picked up her coffee. "I needed that information."

He also set down his fork, picked up his coffee. "Why?"

"Because I think Sarah Livingston knew that my sister's fiancé, Edward, was murdered."

He didn't flinch, just looked at her, steady on. "I'm listening."

She set her coffee down. "Okay, so, Sarah was a real estate agent, and she did a lot of work with Walsh and Swindle's management group. They owned a high-end condo along the river, downtown, and Edward lived in one of them. One night, it burned to the ground, with him in it."

He cocked his head. "Like Beckett."

"Just like Beckett. An explosion out of nowhere. But I got the official report. They said it was a gas leak ignited by a cigarette—or even a lit joint. Which is a complete lie because Edward didn't smoke, didn't do drugs. The man was a fitness junkie. He barely even used his stove. Smoothies galore."

Conrad was nodding.

"They ruled it an accident, and S & W got the insurance money, and the case was closed."

"What did Sarah have to do with it?"

"Edward had given his notice, had a house pending for him and Tia once they walked down the aisle. Sarah was handling the transaction. She'd also gotten him into the condo, so they were longtime friends." She drew in a breath, met his eyes. A beat, then, *why not—*

"What no one knows, even my audience, is that I met with Sarah before she was murdered. About a month before, in fact. I told her what I thought, and she said she'd do some digging, see if S & W had any information about the fire or how it might have happened. And at the time she was dating Holden Walsh, so . . ."

Her eyes started to burn, and she looked away.

"That's why you picked up Sarah's case. You went from a closed-case podcast to a cold case."

She looked at Conrad. "You listen to my podcast?"

"While I cook."

She smiled, his reference to her watching his game hitting home. "On Friday nights?"

"I live a boring life."

"Sure you do. I've seen your Instagram."

His mouth tightened and he looked down at his coffee. *Oh, shoot*—and now it all felt very awkward. She'd sort of forgotten, at least for a second, just what had brought them back together.

At least, on his end.

For her part . . . *shoot.* She looked down at her share. "I can't eat all this."

"It didn't go down like it played out on social media," he said then, softly. She looked up, frowned.

"I don't need to know—"

"I need to tell you." He drew in a breath. "Torch had been seeing this girl—Jasmine. Mostly hookups. She was what we call an ice bunny—"

"Girls who hang around the players."

"Yes. He brought her to an after-game event at Sammy's, a restaurant in St. Paul, and she got a little drunk—as did he. He got a cab home and left her there, so I offered to drive her. I was in the Charger, and muscle cars don't do well on the ice. It was slick out, and I hit a patch of ice . . . Anyway, I got pulled over. It was weird—like the cop was following me. Maybe. Anyway, they pulled me out of the car, and she got out of the car too, and the cops made me do a sobriety test, and she was there, making a scene—it all got caught on video, got posted, and went viral. Torch was really hot when he saw it—but when she started showing up at games and then at my house, he realized she'd moved on. I had to take a restraining order out on her . . . But people accused me of . . . well—"

"I can imagine." She hated the way his eyes had darkened, the story quieting his voice, as if he carried shame. "It wasn't your fault."

"I should have called her a cab." He shook his head. "It was an impulsive decision. I'm working on that." He offered a wry smile.

Wait—had this been an impulsive decision? "I'm not going to stalk you, Conrad."

His eyes widened. "I didn't—"

She held up her hand. "And just to be clear, I'm not going to fall for you. So don't worry."

He frowned.

"You probably shouldn't fall for me either." She looked at him, winked, desperate to deflate the sudden tension between them.

"Right," he said. "Gotcha." He set his coffee down and motioned to Marcie. "So, why not leave Sarah's case to the police?"

Oh. The abrupt change of subject made her blink, scramble to catch up. *Right. Sarah's cold case.* "Because it feels like they're not looking very deep. They don't see the connection, I guess."

Marcie came over with a couple Styrofoam take-out boxes.

"I do." He lifted his cookie slice into his box.

She did the same. "S & W, right? They had everything to gain from the fire. But why kill Edward? That's the connection I'm missing."

He leaned back, frowning. "Seriously? You don't see it? Edward and Sarah and Kyle and now Beckett, not to mention the attempts made on Ty and Tommy back in Duck Lake a month ago?"

She closed her box, licked off some whipped cream that had gotten on her finger. "Sure—the Sarah Livingston case."

He leaned forward. "No, Penny. Not the Sarah Livingston case." He paused, his blue eyes on hers, something fierce and solemn and unmoving in them, the sense of it rooting her to the spot, seeping over her. "You, Penelope Pepper, are the connection."

A chill washed through her.

"Everyone you knew—even Edward—dead. Someone is watching you . . . and taking out people around you and your investigation." He picked up his box. "Now, never mind me while I follow you home and make sure you get inside okay. Do you have an alarm system?"

She nodded, her words trapped.

"Good. And then tomorrow I want you to call your rich father and tell him you need personal security, or you can expect me to show up on your doorstep, hockey stick in hand." He didn't seem to be kidding as he got up and held out his hand to her.

Oh. my.

"Listen. You don't have to do that. I have security—it's just that I don't . . . well, I don't like them following me around, so I sort of fired them."

"Well, unfire them." He held the door open for her.

"Night, King Con," said Marcie as they left. He smiled and waved and followed Penelope out into the night.

And followed her all the way home.

The last Penelope saw of him was his headlights as he backed out of her driveway.

No, the last she saw was her memory of him, the smile on his handsome face, his gaze on hers.

Offering her a cookie.

He was back in his skin.

Steinbeck stood away from his boss, of course, letting Declan have his space, move around the rooftop terrace of the Majestic Hotel in Barcelona, glad-handing colleagues here for the conference. And sure, jet lag sent a buzz through him, turned him hot and punchy. But it only stirred up memories of a day when he'd been someone, done things that had sent a fire through him.

He didn't miss the beach for one lousy millisecond.

And this view topped any beachside cabana. The rooftop bar stood eight stories up, offered a panoramic view of the city. The air was still a little crisp, hovering in the mid-sixties today, so the hotel had fired up the outdoor heaters and served the food inside the adjoining restaurant. The picture windows looked out on a view of the soaring multitowered cathedral, Sagrada Família, and the wide Passeig de Gràcia boulevard, with Gaudí's famous casas and works by other modern architects.

Stein knew Antoni Gaudí might be deemed a little unconventional, but a strange part of Stein liked the unconventional nature-themed architecture that defied reason and felt a little like a theme-park attraction. Declan had planned an outing to the cathedral during the conference this week, so Stein hoped to get a closer look.

He could get used to traveling with Stone. Working for Stone. The guy had a level head, wasn't an eccentric billionaire, and had even asked Stein to spar with him on a couple occasions.

Maybe to see if the former SEAL really could hold his own. Stein had tried not to hurt his boss when he'd taken him down. Again. And again.

Then again, he'd had to tell Declan the truth about his scars and why he'd left the teams, and while he'd left the story sketchy, he'd told him enough about the Krakow disaster for Declan to realize the decision to leave the Navy had been agonizing.

And out of patriotism.

He just couldn't slow his team down, not with his knees.

But he could slow down someone trying to take out his boss, or even rob him, which Declan thought had happened when Stein had returned his phone after finding it in his coat pocket the night of Boo's wedding.

Weird.

Now, he watched as Declan, dressed in a velvet navy sports coat and tweed pants, his dark hair freshly cut, stood with a couple men from Germany.

Speaking German, of course.

Stein caught a few words, but he wasn't really listening.

He was watching. Watching the delegation of men from Hungary, scientist types, talking with a researcher from Prague, a woman with dark hair. There were only three women at the conference, which felt strange since AI technology didn't discriminate. But add that to the defense applications—hence the AI-Genesis Conference, a summit of technology-progressive thinkers.

And Declan Stone owned one of the largest AI research programs in the world—Spectra. Stein had done some not-so-light reading on the plane on his way over about Axiom, the AI program that had a number of—in his opinion—frightening defense applications. But only in the wrong hands.

It gave Stein the reason why Declan might be unnerved about someone stealing his phone, and more specifically, his passwords and any other gateways to his program.

Like personal coercion.

His gaze fell on a blonde grabbing a drink at the bar. Vermouth with an orange slice.

"Your tan is fading."

He glanced over at the voice and grinned. "What are you doing here, cuz?"

Colt Kingston held out his hand. Colt stood the same height as Stein, his dark hair clipped short, in a blue suit that stretched over his shoulders, a white oxford, dress shoes. "Same thing you are. Shadow work."

"Really." He released Colt's hand. "I thought you were on a boat in Florida."

"And I thought you were teaching bikinis how to scuba dive."

Stein laughed and Colt grinned. "So, who are you with?"

Stein lifted a chin. "Declan Stone."

"The tech guy. Yeah, we know him. His AI program is leading edge. The DOD has used it with some of their cyber soldiers—"

"I really don't want to hear the end of that sentence."

"Can you say *Terminator*?"

"'Come with me if you want to live'?"

Colt nodded. "It could be prophetic."

"And I'm working for the creator of the Terminator—Skynet." He glanced at Declan. "He doesn't seem like a power-hungry dictator. I ate a plate of patatas bravas last night with him in the Gothic Quarter."

"No. He's been vetted. Actually served in the Marines, so a patriot. But Logan Thorne has us just . . . watching."

"You're here with Logan Thorne?"

"You know him?"

"Of him," Stein said. "He's from Chester, a small town near ours. Went missing after he joined the SEALs. I didn't realize he'd been found."

"Oh, that's a story, but yeah. He works directly with President White, for a group called the Caleb Group."

"Like Caleb from the Bible?"

Colt nodded. "Not bad."

"I'm a Kingston. You and I have the same blood for fathers. Bible at the dinner table."

Colt nodded toward a tall man, brown hair, dressed in a suit, now talking with Declan. "That's Logan."

Another man stood with him, lighter brown hair, but definitely a military bearing. "Who's that?"

"Another guy on the team."

Maybe he'd said his name, but Stein's gaze had returned to the blonde he'd seen earlier. She stood near a window, staring out, but even he could see her gaze fall on Declan.

She was studying him.

Maybe it was just female appreciation—he supposed his boss looked a little like a movie star with his dark hair, pale gray eyes. And he had money.

But this felt different. As if she might be sizing him up, considering him—

Her gaze shifted to Stein. Just like that, she caught his eyes, held them.

He couldn't move, his heart slamming into his ribcage. He *knew* her. Not a name, not even a face, but those eyes—

No. That smile. Those lips, full, formed ... with a *smirk*?

For a second—a long, beautiful, intoxicating second—he was back at his sister's wedding, dancing with a stranger, the kind of dance that had him forgetting his name, moving in sync with a woman who seemed to fit him, who knew how to follow and yet possessed her own power, enough to make him want to keep up, to match her.

She'd left without a name, without a look back, the aura of mystery in her wake.

His throat dried.

She'd had blonde hair too, blue eyes, and—no, it couldn't be her. Couldn't be the same, captivating smile. Couldn't be—

And then another image hit him. Something ... further back.

Same smile. Different aura. Fierce. Angry. Desperate. So no . . . it couldn't be Phoenix.

Especially since she was dead.

The woman looked away, sighed, took a sip of her drink.

He looked at Colt. "What?"

"I didn't say anything." Colt held a glass of water, sipped it, his eyebrows up, a side-eye at Stein. "But I think that blonde over there just shouted across the room."

"You're hilarious," Stein said, but couldn't help turning back for another glimpse.

She was gone.

He glanced around the room, frowned.

"Interesting," Colt said, then lifted his glass and walked away to where his boss had left Declan.

It couldn't be her.

Really.

Focus, Stein. The last thing he needed was for his boss to get hurt—or worse—during Steinbeck's first gig back in the game.

FIVE

"SO SHE *HUGGED* YOU?"

Jack's question made Conrad look up from where he had unscrewed the base of yet another bus seat in Jack's newly purchased 1973 GMC forty-five-foot passenger transit bus, which sat tucked away from the elements in a rented heated garage in Duck Lake.

"Don't get excited. It doesn't mean anything." Conrad tossed the nut and bolt into a bucket as Jack loosened a seat on the other side of the aisle.

The bus was a classic, vintage find, and Conrad fought a small twinge of envy, despite the mountain of work ahead of his brother. The mint-green vintage bus, with its metal racing stripe down the side, flat windshield, fishbowl headlights, and angled safari-style windows looked like something out of an old 1970s photograph. It would make cool digs for Jack when he hit the road again, traipsing America in search of the lost.

Maybe when Jack hit the road again, Harper Malone would join him as his wife, given the fact that Conrad had walked in on them kissing this morning.

For her part, Harper seemed already invested in the project, painting ceiling boards and trim laid out on sawhorses, the piquant smell of fresh paint sharpening the brisk air. She listened to music, wearing paint clothes, and a bandanna over her short blonde hair.

Cute.

And just then, the sight of Penny sitting across from him at the Ironclad, her eyes wide at his words, sat down in his brain and didn't budge.

"You, Penelope Pepper, are the connection."

He'd never been so ice cold as in that moment he'd realized that. Until then, he hadn't been able to get his brain off . . . the hug.

"What do you mean 'It doesn't mean anything'?" Jack worked the seat free from its mounts.

"She's not into me—or maybe not now. I did a stupid thing and told her the story of Jasmine."

"Why?"

"I don't know, okay? I just . . . I didn't want her to think I was that guy." He got up and helped Jack wrench his seat free, then took one end as they hauled it out of the bus. "Let's focus on what really matters."

"What's that? Donuts?" Jack angled the seat down the steps.

"For the love. What do you know about the mystery of Sarah Livingston?" He let go as Jack carried the seat to the corner to join the other forty-five seats on their way to an eBay posting.

Jack set it down, smacked off his hands. "Pretty much every-thing since Harper is helping produce the podcast. She's writing copy and managing the forum." He glanced at his girlfriend, who was humming a song Conrad couldn't make out.

Jack wore a silly grin now as she took the paintbrush and sang into it like a microphone. "Don't stop believin'—"

Oy.

"She's not great at karaoke," he said, laughing.

Nice to see his brother happy. Jack had spent so many years as the prodigal. His return home seemed to have set their family to rights.

And had freed Doyle, maybe to finally find his future.

Conrad slapped dirt from his hands too. "First, like I said, let's not get crazy about the hug. It was an impulse. Just—a reaction to seeing Beckett's house on fire. And good thing, because about ten minutes later, the firefighters carried his charred corpse from the house. At least, we thought it was Becker. They identified his body in today's paper."

"Charred corpse? That's a little harsh, Conrad." This from Harper, who clearly could hear them over her music.

He glanced back at her. "Sorry. Good copy, though—you should use that for the podcast."

"You just play hockey. Let me do the writing." She dipped her brush into the paint, tried to catch the drips, and finished the end of the board. Her clothes resembled a Jackson Pollock painting.

Conrad followed Jack into the bus.

"So, what's the point we've been missing?" Jack bent over another bench.

Conrad worked his seat free. "*Penelope* is the connective tissue here. Did you know that she talked with Sarah Livingston *before* Sarah was murdered?"

Jack glanced up at him with a frown. Tossed a freed bolt into the bucket. "What about?"

"Long story, but she thinks Sarah had information about the murder of Edward Hudson, her sister's dead fiancé."

"That's why she thinks the crimes are connected."

"Yes. But what if they're connected because of *Penelope*?" He carried the seat out of the bus and set it on the garage floor, then climbed back inside.

Jack's power drill buzzed. He dropped in another bolt. "How?"

"I don't know." Conrad picked up the drill. "I think we need to figure out if Edward was really murdered. So I'm thinking we probably need the forensic report. And then—"

"Wait—what's this *we*?" Jack stood up. "You're going to investigate this with her?"

Oh. "Uh . . ."

"And what, join her on the podcast?"

He unscrewed a bolt. "What—no. Of course not. It's just . . ." Conrad finished unscrewing the others, then stood up. "She gets in over her head."

"You think?" Jack worked his seat free. "This is the girl who hid for three days in an icehouse, waiting for her podcast to drop, after thinking someone was trying to kill her."

"Someone *was* trying to kill her," Conrad said, his voice quiet.

Jack's mouth pinched. "We'll never know, will we?"

"I think the evidence is pretty clear. Whoever took her drove her out to Loon Lake to shoot her and leave her with the fishes."

"Thank you, Michael Corleone, for that reminder. I was there." He picked up the seat, and Conrad grabbed the end. "I'm just saying, she could have gone to the police. But she didn't."

"My point exactly. She's a little impulsive—"

They'd brought the seat outside—not heavy, but awkward—and set it next to the other. Jack looked up at him. "That's the pot. Sheesh."

Sometimes his big brother seemed so different from him. Sure, he'd played hockey and had been raised by the same parents, but Jack had a sort of individual spirit about him, the ability to separate his emotions from his job of finding the lost, to see the big picture.

Conrad had always let himself get too wrapped up in the frenzy of the game, the emotions. Struggled to step out of the brawl. "Hey. I'm working on that."

Jack stood up. "The fact is, you care—it's just part of who you are. You care, you get involved, and suddenly you're in over your head too. I just don't want to see you get hurt." Jack picked up his seat, heading for the pile. "Although, I'm not sure it's not too late, given your recent social media."

Conrad had followed him. "What?"

Jack set down the seat, turned to him. "Harper showed me. Pictures of you and Penelope at Lakeside Pizza Company? Looked like you were having a good time. Something about a pizza-eating contest?"

What? "Yeah, pictures were taken, but—who posted them?"

"Penelope. It's on her account, but she tagged you, I think. They came up on Harper's feed. Lots of likes, buddy. So, are you two dating?"

"No." Conrad probably set down the seat harder than he needed to. "She specifically told me that she wasn't falling for me."

Jack raised an eyebrow.

"Listen. I don't know what to think. One minute she's flirting with me, the next she ghosts me. I dunno. She's a mystery. I can't figure her out."

"So maybe don't try. Stop overthinking it."

He frowned, following Jack over to his workbench, where Jack opened a vintage thermos and poured a cup of coffee. Handed it to Conrad. Poured one for himself. "Bro. It's got to be exhausting being in your head."

"What are you talking about?"

"You make everything way too complicated. You're constantly reviewing your life, looking at your mistakes"—he held up a hand as Conrad's mouth opened—"and if you're not doing that, you're trying to figure out how to navigate your next play. In life, on the ice, dating . . . You gotta relax. Stop worrying."

"Please. It's not like you didn't let your mistakes drive you away from . . . well, everything." Conrad glanced at Harper, who had set down her brush and now climbed into the bus.

"Agreed. So this is newly minted advice. Maybe you stop trying to figure everything out and just trust that God has a good path."

He narrowed his eyes as Jack walked over to the bus to join Harper.

Yeah, well, he made his own path. Had to.

Conrad climbed inside the bus to a discussion about designs.

"If you want a king-sized bed, Jack, you need to put the bed across the back." Harper was motioning out her design with a cup of coffee from Echoes Vinyl Café.

"But what if I want just a queen bed? I can put it along one side and then there's a walkway."

Harper cocked her head at him, raised an eyebrow.

Jack grinned, a twinkle in his expression.

And that only made Conrad's mind go to Penelope sitting across from him, tasting an Ironclad cookie, ribbing him about his late-night sugar habits.

"You probably shouldn't fall for me."

"Conrad," Harper said, "I heard you're coaching an EmPowerPlay team." She climbed up to sit on a seat while Jack loosened one of the last ones.

"Yeah. The Ice Hawks. How—"

"Penelope, of course. She called me this morning, said something about eating a cookie with you?"

"Sounds like a date to me," Jack said, glancing up at him.

It did, didn't it?

Maybe they *were* dating. Which meant, what? . . . He should text her?

Stop overthinking it.

He picked up his phone and pulled up her text from ages ago. Stared at the note, not sure what to say . . .

Conrad

Hey. Wondering if you're free—

Nope. Delete.

Conrad

Hey. Just checking in—

No, she'd think he was stalking her. *Shoot.* Maybe he was, because last night he'd pulled out of her driveway, then turned off his lights and sat in the darkness, waiting until her house darkened for the night before driving the few blocks home. He hadn't realized she lived so close to him.

Delete.

"I can't believe you're coaching." Jack wrenched up the seat. "You tried that once, years ago, and said *never again.*"

Conrad took the bench from Jack, hoping his brother didn't see how he blanched as his lungs seized up.

"Things have clearly changed," said Harper, singing the last word. "Coaching, eating pizza with a bunch of kids. Next thing you know he'll be buying them new jerseys."

Yes. Bam.

Conrad carried the seat out and dumped it. Then pulled out his phone.

Conrad

Hey. Wondering if you want to go pick out hockey gear with me for the team. Tomorrow afternoon?

He waited, saw the message change from *Delivered* to *Read.*

Three dots . . . typing . . .

A moment later, the dots died.

Nothing.

He waited another minute, then pocketed the phone.

Probably better this way.

Harper came out of the bus, holding her car keys. "Jack and I are headed over to the house for Doyle's goodbye party. You're coming, right?"

He shoved his hands into his pockets, shrugged.

"What's that look?" She walked over to him.

"Nothing. It's just . . ." He shook his head. "She told me she wasn't going to fall for me, so I'm not sure why I'm even—"

"She got to you."

"No, just . . ."

"Don't let her stupidity scare you away. And don't believe her about not falling for you. She's got a huge heart—she's just scared."

He raised an eyebrow.

Harper made a wry face. "Okay, I probably shouldn't tell you this, but Penelope had a boyfriend years ago named Ted Whitey. He played baseball for the University of Minnesota, but what he really wanted was a tryout—specifically for the Detroit Tigers, in Florida."

She glanced at Jack, coming out of the bus, carrying his tools to his workbench. Back to Conrad. "Penelope was his biggest fan, and of course, when she found out that he wanted to go, she was all in. Except it cost money—he had to stay and train for six weeks and even needed a batting coach. Anyway, she sprang for it. Dipped into her trust fund, handed over thousands of dollars to get him to Florida for tryout season."

A sickness stirred in his gut.

"She waited until tryout week and then flew down to see him. Except—he wasn't there."

"What?"

"He'd gone to Florida, washed out the first week, hooked up with some girl, took the money and vanished. Sixty g's, which isn't a lot for a Pepper, maybe, but he took her money and ghosted her. Of course, her father tracked him down—in Vegas. He'd gotten it in his head that he might strike it rich and blew the entire wad. Oh, and he got married. Different girl. Elvis presided."

Conrad fought a terrible urge to hop on a plane to Vegas, have a little chat with baseball boy. Except, imagine if the kid *hadn't* lied . . . well, maybe Penelope would be hitched to the schmuck right now.

He released a breath.

"She swore off athletes after that. Said they were too in love with their success. Then again, she said that about a musician she dated, and even about a lawyer, the last year of college. But . . ." She sighed. "The only man she ever loved was engaged to her sister—and that's a story in itself. And then he was killed in a fire. Or was murdered. Either way, don't be too hurt, Conrad. Penelope has a deep heart. But I'm not sure even she knows what she wants." She put a hand on his arm. "I'm not saying don't try. I saw the pictures—you made her smile. That's a start." She patted his arm. "Besides, she really is working. She got another lead—she texted me this morning about a file that Beckett sent her before the fire."

He stilled. "What?"

"Yeah. Said she didn't check it until after she'd gotten home. It's encrypted though, so I sent her to Coco."

"Wyatt's wife?" His goalie had married a computer wizard.

"Yeah. They're probably trying to get the file open."

The phone buzzed in his pocket.

Harper walked back to Jack as Conrad pulled it out, thumbed open the text.

From Penelope.

Penelope

Send me the when and where.

He'd have to call Jones and get the equipment manager to hook him up with their supplier.

Conrad

Okay. We can probably get in tomorrow. I'll send you details.
It's a date.

He held his breath.

Dots . . .

Penelope
LOL. Good one. Yes, a date.

Weird response. Still, the words lit a little something inside him, and he couldn't help it.

Conrad
Are you okay?

Immediately.

Penelope
Fine.

He probably shouldn't ask, but,

Conrad
Did you get a bodyguard?

Blinking. Then,

Penelope
For the love, you're overreacting.

Apparently that was the theme of the day. Still.

Conrad
Did you not listen to anything I said?

Penelope
I was in a sugar coma. I'm fine. Working.

His thoughts went to her comment about forgetting to eat.

Conrad
The Ironclad has takeout. Want me to pick you up a cookie?

What? Oh, delete, delete—shoot.

Penelope
Sweet. No. I'll see you tomorrow.

Right. But the spark died. He sighed.
Jack had come over. "Everything okay?"
"I'm not sure . . ."
Jack clamped him on the shoulder. "Stop the obsessing. Let's go eat cake."
He pocketed the phone.
"Don't believe her about not falling for you."
Challenge accepted.

⬩————————————⬩

She supposed this was how the dating game was played.
Penelope sat in her car, the heat on, waiting for Conrad to pull up outside the entrance of the Ice Gear Depot, a warehouse set in a neighborhood of Bloomington, just off 494, in a tangle of industrial buildings.
Apparently, this was the Blue Ox supplier as well as a wholesaler of hockey gear. She was listening to callers' voicemail messages responding to her previous podcast, sorting through them to find any juicy theories.
"Hello, Penny. Love the show. Could it be a case of mistaken identity? Maybe the real target was someone close to Sarah, someone who looked similar or was connected in some way. The murderer could've gotten the wrong person by mistake."
She hit pause, her brain travelling back to the words she couldn't seem to dislodge from her brain—*"You, Penelope Pepper, are the connection."*
How? Why?
The next caller didn't help. "Hey, Penny. My thought is about silencing. Maybe the victim saw something she wasn't supposed

to and was about to talk to the police. Killing her would keep her quiet permanently."

Except the murder hadn't kept Beckett from sending Penelope the file, hopefully revealing whatever was on Sarah's computer. It hadn't come in until after she'd arrived home—but then again, she never checked her phone while driving, so . . .

Unfortunately, the file had been encrypted, and she'd spent way too many hours yesterday trying to open it until she'd finally reached out to Harper's friend Coco, the wife of one of the Blue Ox players.

She checked her email, just to make sure that Coco hadn't sent her a message, but nothing so far.

A car drove into the lot but continued through to a different warehouse. She pushed Play on the next caller. "Penny. This one is a bit out there, but what if this is all about a hidden treasure? Maybe the victim stumbled upon some clues to a valuable secret, and someone wanted Sarah out of the picture to claim it for themselves."

Hidden treasure. She shook her head and dropped her phone on the seat, scrubbed her hands down her face.

"Did you get a bodyguard?"

Conrad, back in her head.

And yes, maybe she should call Franco, the personal security her father usually assigned to her when they had public events. But she didn't love being watched.

Followed.

But maybe Conrad was right, so she'd activated her home security system for the first time in months.

She didn't need a bodyguard.

What she needed was answers.

Her phone buzzed and she picked it up, checking her watch. Conrad was officially ten minutes late.

Clarice. She swiped the call on. "What's going on?"

"It's working. You officially got four thousand new followers with that pizza post."

"That wasn't mine. Someone else took the shot—"

"And tagged you, I know. I had my assistant reformat it, add some sparkles and hearts, and repost it on a phantom account."

Oh brother. "Listen—"

"When's your next date?"

The man drove up, parked next to her in his Charger.

"Now, actually. We're getting sports equipment for the team."

"That's not a date."

"It's totally a date. He called it a date."

"Really? Good. I wasn't sure he was on board—I talked with Felicity, who said she'd talk to him, so . . . okay then. I suppose it could be cute. Take pictures."

Conrad had gotten out, leaned down, and knocked on her window. She waved to him. It wasn't a date—not really. But it didn't mean she couldn't appreciate those blue eyes, something warm in them as he smiled and gave her a thumbs-up.

He was too easy to like, the way he sent a warm hum through her.

"Fine." She hung up, then dropped her phone in her bag and got out. "Hey."

He wore jeans and work boots, a wool jacket, and a tuque. His dusty-blond hair curled out of the back, and he smelled a little like sawdust.

"Sorry I'm late," he said. "Jack roped me into helping him put down new flooring in his bus." He walked to the warehouse door and rang a bell at the back entrance.

"He got a new bus?"

"Yeah. Gutted it and is remodeling it. He has a vision for it I can't yet see, but I trust him."

The door opened, and a middle-aged man, dark hair, greeted Conrad with a handshake.

"Hey, Grant. Did you get my request?"

They walked into the back room, a space filled with racks and racks of equipment, from helmets, gloves, padding, breezers, sticks, and skates to protective gear, picks, goalie gear, and boxes and boxes of unbranded jerseys.

She stopped at a box of dark-blue jerseys as they walked to the front, feeling the material. "What might it cost to get new jerseys printed?"

Grant wore a pair of khakis, a jersey with the Ice Gear Depot brand on the breast. Short brown hair, a little paunch, he turned and walked backward, hand out. "Glad to help EmPowerPlay with a discount, Miss Pepper."

Oh. Conrad must have filled him in on who he was meeting. "Thank you."

He flashed a thumbs-up and glanced at Conrad, and *ah,* this was all about King Con and his involvement. Maybe even an endorsement.

Everyone wanted a piece of Conrad. Even her, apparently.

So maybe he wasn't the villain in this agreement.

Grant ushered them into an office, and on the table lay an assortment of gear—a couple helmets, sample jerseys, socks, two types of skates, padding, and composite as well as wooden hockey sticks.

Conrad walked over to the sticks, picked one up, seemed to weigh it.

"I wasn't sure what you wanted as far as gear, so I pulled some choices."

She picked up a helmet, this one without a cage. "Do they come with face protection?"

"We have combo helmets. It is cheaper to get the combo than to buy them separately, but not everyone likes a cage."

"They're kids. Get the cage," Conrad said. "No need to lose any teeth."

She noticed he had perfect teeth and suddenly wanted to ask. Instead, "I agree. Combo helmets. And mouth protection."

"Absolutely." Grant had pulled out a tablet, started to mark up their order.

She picked up the other helmet. "What's the difference?"

Conrad put down his stick. "The brain protection. That one has an impact foam liner for the harder hits."

She had seen his game while cooking, and her bones ached just watching the hits against the board. Now she studied him, just for a moment, as he picked up the padding and inspected it. Tall, yes, but he also possessed a chiseled form to his body that she guessed meant hours in the gym as well as on the ice. Tight core, strong legs, corded shoulders that filled out his jacket. Capable of giving—and taking—a beating.

What if this wasn't a fake date? What if it might be—

Aw. Stop. He'd set the rules.

Fine. She could play the game too. She put on the helmet, then pulled out her phone. "Can we get a selfie?"

Conrad's brows arched, then he lifted a shoulder. "Sure."

She smiled for the camera, wearing the ridiculous helmet, and he leaned down, made a couple bunny ears. Okay, that was cute. She snapped it.

Done. Date accomplished.

Conrad picked out protective gear—shoulder pads, elbow pads, gloves, shin guards, pants, and bags to store them. "Can we get the kit price for these?"

"Absolutely," Grant said.

"Throw in some socks?"

"Just tell me how many."

He glanced at Penelope, but she shrugged.

"I think we have twenty kids." He picked up the stick. "And two dozen wooden sticks. I'll teach them how to cut them down to size and wrap them."

He walked over to the skates. "You don't have any discontinued brands, do you? Maybe throw those in, write it off?"

"Probably. We might have some trade-ins too."

Conrad clamped a hand on the man's shoulder. "Grant, you're the best. Head to will call the next time you're hankering to go to a game. You'll find tickets."

Grant grinned. "We'd love to talk about a couple commercials once you sign on for another season."

Conrad's mouth made a tight line, but he nodded.

Penelope glanced at him as they walked out. "You okay?"

He nodded, said nothing, and headed outside.

Stood in the cold, his eyes closing.

"What's the matter?"

"Nothing."

She considered him, and in the quiet, her phone buzzed. She pulled it out. A text from Coco.

Coco

Decrypted your file. See attached.

The next text came through—a video. She cupped her hand over the screen and tried to open it. It buffered, taking its time.

"What's that?"

"It's a decrypted file Beckett sent me." She looked up. "Sorry—I forgot to tell you. Beckett sent me a file before . . ." She swallowed.

"I know. Harper told me yesterday while we were working Jack's new bus. She said you sent it to Coco."

What didn't he know? Or had he been talking about her—*stop. Stop!*

"Yes. I couldn't get it open—here it comes."

"Are you sure?" The voice came from the phone, a female, and Penelope tried to see the speaker, but the sun's glare blinded the picture.

Then Conrad walked over and put his big hand over the screen, blocking the light.

"That's Sarah Livingston. I think this is a Ring video." She squinted into the screen as another voice said, "Yes. I'm sure. I hired my own arson investigator—he recovered two bullets in the wall."

"I think that's Holden Walsh, Sarah's boyfriend," Penelope said, glancing at him.

He frowned, didn't move.

"So, was Edward shot?"—Sarah.

The question stilled Penelope.

"That's what the forensic report says."—Walsh.

"What forensic report?"—Sarah.

"The one that the police don't have . . . but I do." Walsh looked behind him then. "I think this isn't a conversation we can have on your doorstep."

Yes, yes it was! But they went into the house and the video ended.

"I knew it," Penelope said. She lowered the phone. "If this is what Kyle was going to give me, then . . ." Her eyes widened. "I was—"

"Right." His blue-eyed gaze had darkened. "Whoever burned down Edward's building also killed him."

"And maybe killed Sarah. I'll bet she didn't have this on her computer when it was stolen—it was probably something she added afterward."

"She might have had an entire slew of information on her computer—but this was on her Ring storage," Conrad said. "Mine gets deleted after thirty days."

"So this happened within a few weeks of the robbery." She looked at him. "One of my *Penny for Your Thoughts* callers suggested that Sarah had been silenced. What if someone—a.k.a.

Swindle—knew that his partner, Walsh, hired the investigator? Maybe even knew he was talking with Sarah."

"When's the last time you talked with Walsh?"

She stilled. She hadn't even thought about—"Over a month ago. Before the wedding. He left town." She shook her head. "I never liked him. His alibi checked out, but he had a history of violence, and I thought ... Well, I guess I was wrong. He's probably in hiding."

"After what happened to Sarah, that seems right."

She pocketed the phone. "Thanks for the date." She headed for her car.

"Wait." He wore a frown. "That's it? I mean—um ..."

Oh. "Did you ... did you want more?" She'd taken the picture, sent it to Clarice ...

"I guess not." He sighed, put his hands into his pockets.

She gave him a smile. "Listen, you're doing great. And I appreciate it. I just know you have a life, and I don't want to interfere."

He raised an eyebrow. "Interfere?"

She shrugged, her chest already tight. The last thing she wanted him to think was that she was throwing herself at him, hoping he'd actually *like* her. Besides, she knew athletes. The minute she started to actually like him, he'd blow her off for some swooning fan. And she'd aged past swooning long ago.

He stepped off the curb. "Listen. You're not interfering. I blocked the entire afternoon to, um, hang out with you. Maybe we could, I don't know ... get a bite to eat?"

She stared at him, almost hypnotized by those blue eyes, the earnestness in his voice.

"There's this great burger joint near my place. Fantastic burgers—all named after hockey guys. You should try the King Con burger." He smiled and winked, and she got it.

Endorsements. Felicity had probably given him a list of places to go—snap pictures, tag the place, and get some Blue Ox brand love. She might have even negotiated an ad fee.

"Not today, sorry. I think I'm going to go talk to Edward's old townhouse neighbors and see if they can remember anything from that night."

She might as well have dangled a piece of steak in front of a hound. Conrad's ears all but visibly perked up, and she could have predicted his next words—

"Have you lost your mind?"

Oh goody. They were right back to Friday night at the house of cookies. "No, Conrad. I haven't *lost my mind*. I'm a mystery podcaster. I solve mysteries—"

"Murder mysteries. Emphasis on the *murder*. Sheesh, Penny." He shook his head, his hand across his mouth as if he might be trying to hold something back. His next words emerged soft, controlled. "I'm going with you."

She cocked her head. "Conrad—c'mon—"

"Where is his townhome?"

She sighed. "St. Anthony Main."

"Great. Let's swing by your house, drop off your car, and you can ride with me."

He walked over to his car without her agreement.

"Bossy much?"

He looked over at her, then offered a slight grin. "You're not getting away that easily, Penny."

Who was trying to get away? Not her.

Definitely not her.

She pulled into the garage, then grabbed her bag, stepped out, and shut the car door.

"Nice digs," he said. "It looks vintage."

"It was built in 1927. The basement has low ceilings, but it's cozy. I redid the office—actually gutted the entire house. One bedroom up, another on the main floor, great room, new kitchen."

"Security?"

For some reason, she put a hand on his arm. Hello, muscles. "Yes, King Con, there is security." She held up her remote and clicked a button. "Activated. Happy?"

"I'd prefer twenty-four-seven close protection, but . . ." He lifted a shoulder.

He didn't look like he was kidding.

She slid into his passenger seat. Neat car, smelled recently detailed. He glanced at her. "Directions?" He turned on his display, and she read off the address. He keyed it in and pulled out.

Her father had a garage of higher-end sports cars. Not that the Charger was out of the ordinary, but it rumbled like her father's McLaren 720S.

Silence from her date beside her.

"Thanks," she said.

"We haven't found anything yet."

"Still. My sister thinks I'm obsessed . . . and maybe I am, a little."

He glanced at her. "Bullet holes in the wall. Doesn't sound obsessed to me."

"Right?" She sighed. "What I don't get is why she's *not* obsessed. It was her fiancé."

"Maybe she just needs to walk away from it." He'd taken a few shortcuts through the neighborhood, like he knew it, and merged onto the highway headed into the city. "My brother Doyle has been stuck for years since his fiancée died. He's finally moving on, so . . . Maybe it's her way of coping with her grief."

"I didn't know Doyle was engaged."

"She died in an accident on the way to the wedding."

Her eyes widened. "No."

"Yes." He blew out a breath. "It's a long story, but maybe letting it go is the best thing for your sister."

He left out anything about *her* letting it go, however. Still . . . "Edward wasn't my sister's fiancé but my best friend, at least growing up. We did everything together—he was the son of our housekeeper. My dad actually helped pay his way through college, and then he went to grad school at MIT on a scholarship. Really smart. Developed an AI system. I think he was getting some offers—high offers. Anyway, I . . ." She glanced at him. "I may have had a crush on him in high school."

Conrad's mouth made a grim line. He looked at her. "Sorry for your loss."

Oh. She hadn't expected the sweep of heat into her chest, the tightening of her throat. "Usually people say that to Tia."

"I'm sure." Then he took his hand off the wheel, reached out and caught hers. "You still lost someone you loved."

He let go, but his gesture lingered. She looked out the window. Nodded. Drew a breath. "It was more than that, I think." She drew in a breath, glanced at him. "Edward was the one who found me when I was kidnapped."

SIX

B Y SOME GRACE OF HEAVEN, HE DIDN'T REACT
to the word *kidnapped*. Mostly because the last thing Penelope
needed, probably, was him looking at her with what he knew
might be horror in his eyes.

But seriously, *kidnapped*?

She kept talking, and he managed to keep driving, his eyes on
the road, his hands on the wheel, instead of doing the one thing
he wanted to do—stop and maybe pull her into his arms.

Just hold on and steady the terrible thunder in his chest.

It was possible he was taking this harder than she was. Because
she was sitting next to him *just. fine.*

"I was nine. My parents were out of town—I don't know where.
Tia was two years older than me and had her own room, and that
night she was sleeping over at a neighbor's house. It was just me
and my nanny and, of course, Edward and his mom. They actually
had rooms in our house—he had a single mom, and she was with
our family until she died, not long after Edward. Cancer. Or grief."

She took a breath.

He swallowed the terrible boulder in his throat.

"Anyway, I was asleep, and woke up to someone putting duct tape over my mouth, and then, while I tried to scream, they taped my hands and feet and pulled me right out of my bed."

She spoke so differently than she did in her podcasts, without drama or sound effects. Like she might be giving a police report.

"They hid me in our house. We have an old house—built in 1887—and it has a creepy basement and a huge attic and even a dumbwaiter that moves from floor to floor, and that's what saved me. They put me in the basement—I'm not sure why. Maybe so they could tell my parents where to find me once they'd delivered the money. But we had this old cold-storage room where our housekeeper stored our apples and potatoes and other canned goods—she was from Germany and was this amazing cook—"

"Pen." *Oh,* he didn't know why he'd interrupted her. "Sorry."

"No—sorry. Not a podcast." She glanced at him and he caught her eye. She could steal his breath, and not just with her story but with the striking beauty she probably didn't know she possessed, wearing a white puffer jacket, leggings, and boots, that dark hair spilling out of her white hat. He still couldn't get the image out of his brain—her wearing that ridiculous helmet, lopsided on her head, grinning into the camera, her eyes glowing.

He'd gotten himself in trouble then, conjuring up things for them to do on their I-guess-not-a-date.

Whatever. At least he'd gotten her into the car with him, and now—

"So, anyway, they wrapped me up in a blanket and shoved me into the cold cellar, way in the back—"

"Who is they?"

She eyed him. "I'll get to that."

He huffed, a sort of laugh. "So it is a story."

"It has to be. Because if it isn't, I'll end up in therapy all over again."

Oh.

"So there I sat, all night. The next day, I had to go to the bath-room, really bad, and ended up . . . you know. At least it was warm."

"Aw . . ."

"I was mortified and really scared, but also had spent most of the night working off the tape on my mouth. They'd wrapped it around my head, so I lost some hair getting it off, but I got it free and then started biting through the tape on my wrists. Took me the better part of the next day, probably, although it was pitch dark in the room, so I had no idea. I finally got free, and then I realized that not only was I locked in but no one could hear me."

"You must have been terrified."

He crossed the Hennepin Avenue Bridge over the Mississippi, the waters gray, just a few boats on the river.

"I was. And then, after a while, I wasn't. I sometimes hid there when Edward and I played hide-and-seek, so I ate some apples and then opened a jar of pickles . . . To this day, the smell of pickles brings me back to that."

He nodded, his mouth tight. GPS spoke up and told him to take a left on University Avenue.

"Two days in, the door unlocked. It was Edward. He'd figured out where I was, but he said I wasn't safe, that I needed to hide."

"Why?"

"Because the person who'd kidnapped me was my nanny. And Edward knew it. He'd overheard her talking with one of the se-curity guys, Nicolai, who was in on it, and apparently my parents were negotiating the ransom, and he thought . . ." She sighed.

"He thought they'd kill you."

She nodded.

He pulled up to a sprawling block of brownstone condos that overlooked the river—grand buildings that appeared to have been built at the turn of the century. "Wow."

"I know, right? River view, and it's huge. He was going to be sad when he let it go . . ." She unsnapped her belt.

SUSAN MAY WARREN

He put a hand on her arm. Turned to her. "So you hid."

"Yeah. In the dumbwaiter. Edward sneaked me food until my parents got home, and then he told them where I was."

"Why didn't he call the cops right away?"

"He wanted to, but his mother didn't know who to trust—she thought security might be in on it, so she wanted to wait until my parents got home. She knew I was safe, and that was the important part. I think they were both pretty scared." She lifted a shoulder. "Anyway, that's why my dad started EmPowerPlay. Because he thought I needed to feel strong and capable and . . ."

"Really? What sport did you play?"

"Soccer. I was terrible. I think I even scored a goal for the wrong team once." She got out.

He followed her. "At least you scored."

"The goalie left the net." She pointed to a unit at the end of the row. Yeah, he saw it now—wood boarded up over the front door, windows blackened.

"The fire didn't catch the other units?" He followed her across the parking lot.

"They made them a little sturdier back then for exactly that reason. Brick walls, brick foundation." She stared at the unit. Took a breath.

He couldn't stop himself from coming up behind her, putting his arms around her. "We'll figure this out, Penny."

We. Yes, we.

She held on to his arms for a moment, then turned, wiping her cheeks. "Okay, so the fire happened around nine p.m. My guess is that there had to have been someone home that time of night."

He followed her to the townhome next to Edward's, and she knocked on the door. He checked his watch. Monday afternoon . . .

His team had a game in about four hours. He should probably watch.

The door opened and a woman stood on the stoop holding a

107

yapping poodle. Mid-forties, brown hair, she wore her eyeglasses on her head—so probably computer glasses and they'd interrupted her workday. "Yes?"

"My name is Penelope Pepper and this—"

"Oh my—King Con."

He gave her a tight-lipped smile, lifted his hand. "Ma'am."

"We're actually here because . . . well, we were hoping that you might know something about the fire next door."

The woman sighed. "Other than I wish they'd gut the place? It's an eyesore and dangerous to the neighborhood. Homeless sleep in it, not to mention the dogs." She met her dog's eyes. "Norm here is completely freaked out."

Norm didn't have any front teeth, so Conrad guessed she might be right.

"Were you here that night?" Penelope reached out to pet the dog, but he emitted a growl, so she pulled back.

"Don't mind him. But no, I wasn't. I was on vacation. Came back to this tragedy. But Janet Foster was. She's retired, doesn't go out much." She pointed to the unit on the other side. Lowered her voice. "Sees everything." *Everything* was a three-syllable word, accompanied by raised eyebrows and a nod.

"Thank you," Conrad said and took Penelope's hand.

"Hey," said the woman. "Don't you have an away game tonight?"

He nodded, then pulled Penelope away. "Don't you know not to pet strange dogs?"

"No. I never had a dog. My mom is allergic. But I always wanted one."

"I thought you'd be a cat person."

"Oh no. Give me a floppy, loyal, shedding golden retriever any day." She knocked on Janet Foster's door.

Nothing. The wind scurried off the river, into the parking lot, the sun hovering over the city, shadows creeping across the pavement and grimy snow.

Conrad reached over her and knocked again, harder.

The door opened nearly immediately. "I'm here, for Pete's sake!"

The woman wore a pair of jeans and a sweatshirt with the words *All You Knit Is Love* appliqued on the front. White fluffy hair and a few pounds turned her into a grandma type, except for the scowl on her face.

"Sorry." Conrad held up a hand. "We were wondering if you could help us—"

"You look familiar." Except she wasn't looking at Conrad. The woman narrowed her eyes at Penelope. "How do I know you?"

"Um—"

"This is Penelope—"

"Oh my—*Penny for Your Thoughts*! Goodness, come in!" A smile broke through, and even though she gave Conrad the side-eye, he followed them in.

Cozy place, right out of the eighties, with blue overstuffed sofas and end tables covered in doilies and a tangle of knitting on the sofa. The television played a YouTube video. Janet picked up the remote and muted it. "I just love your podcast. I intend to call in someday—really, I do." She moved the knitting. "I still think that Tommy Fadden, her nosy neighbor, killed Sarah."

Conrad had met Tommy when he'd been shot trying to help Harper find Penelope, so nope.

Penelope sat down. "Actually, Tommy is sort of a hero in the story, but that's still an upcoming episode. I'm researching a different, um, murder."

Conrad stayed standing, the smell of something baking lifting from the kitchen. His stomach growled and he pressed on it. He hadn't eaten, thinking, well, thinking this was a date.

Weirdest date he'd ever been on.

"How can I help?" Janet had seated herself on a nearby rocking chair.

"The night that . . . your neighbor's building burned, what do you remember?"

"Edward. Oh, he was such a darling." She leaned forward. "I loved his fiancée too. Such a pretty girl. What was her name?"

"Tia?"

"No . . . that wasn't it. Anyway, yes, I was here that night. Such a tragedy. They evacuated me, but of course, my unit was unharmed. And they got here so fast—well, you know, they were probably on their way anyway after I called them." She leaned forward. "I gave my statement that night, but they never came back. I'm not sure why. I could probably describe him if they wanted to hypnotize me."

Conrad frowned.

"Describe who?" Penelope said.

"The man who killed Edward."

Penelope visibly froze.

"He came into the apartment, and I heard shots. Three shots." She held up her fingers, just in case. "So I called 911. And then I saw him leave. He ran right out the front door and into the parking lot, and I tried to see where he went, but it was dark and . . . well, about five minutes later, the entire building rumbled and the windows exploded—terrifying. I stood out in my housecoat for three hours while the firefighters hosed it down. Insurance put me up in a hotel for a week before they'd let me back in. Oh, sweetheart, are you okay? Don't cry—"

Oh no, he hadn't noticed, given the fact that he'd turned and looked out the window, trying to decide if Janet could be telling the truth. Not a huge picture window, but enough to make out a fleeing suspect.

Now he spotted Penelope grabbing tissues, Janet sitting next to her on the sofa. She pressed the tissues to her eyes. "I just feel so sorry for his fiancé."

"Oh, I know it," said Janet. "Such a pretty girl. Blonde hair.

Drove a really sweet orange Volkswagen bug. Those things are expensive—I mean, back in my day, they were dirt cheap, but now—"

"Do you remember her name?" Penelope's voice shook, just a little.

And he got it. Penelope knew very well the name of Edward's fiancée. Except he'd *met* her sister, Tia, who had dark hair. And probably didn't drive a bug, and—Penelope was faking.

Oh. Wow. She was very, very good at the fake. Should probably teach a few of his wings.

"I think he called her Sarah. Anyway, they were so cute together. He'd sometimes cook out on the grill facing the river. Not that I watched them or anything, but oh, they seemed so in love."

Penelope covered Janet's hand with hers. "Thank you for telling me. Do you really think you could describe the shooter?"

"Absolutely. Tall, dark hair, big build. Looked like a tough guy, you know?"

A tough guy. Yeah, that described the majority of Conrad's team.

Penelope got up. "Do you mind if I get your number? You know, just in case I have any questions?"

Janet rattled it off, and Penelope put it into her phone.

Conrad watched as she hugged Janet, gave her a warm smile.

He thanked the woman as they left. He walked out to the car, a clench in his gut.

"We already knew that Sarah knew Edward, right?"

"Right." She opened the door, her expression unreadable.

Ho-kay. He slid into the driver's seat and turned to her. "It doesn't mean he was cheating—"

She held up a hand. "It doesn't matter. Maybe Tia escaped tragedy." She looked away, her jaw tight.

Oh no. Especially since he didn't exactly know how to fix it. "Cookie?"

He got a laugh. Not a big one, and maybe it wasn't even a laugh but an expulsion of breath that also loosened the tension in the car. "No, thank you. But . . . it makes me think about what Harper said to me." She turned. "Two weeks before Sarah was murdered, someone broke into her apartment and stole her computer."

"Yes."

"Tommy saw him—tried to stop him. Lots of reasons, but in the tussle, he tore his pocket and ended up with a box of matches from Turbo."

"Turbo—wait, the nightclub?"

"Yeah. Tommy and Harper went there to talk to the security, but it was closed. They ended up at the offices of S & W but then got carjacked and . . . Anyway, what if this so-called 'tough guy'"—she finger quoted the words—"worked for Turbo?"

"Why Turbo?" He'd turned on the car to crank up the heat.

"The building is managed by S & W—so it's possible the security works for the building, not just the nightclub."

He put the car into Drive. "They should be open by now."

"What are we going to do—ask around for a big guy?"

He looked at her. "No, PI Penny. We're going to take some shots of the security guys, and you're going to text them to our friend Janet. See if we get a hit. And while you're doing that, I'm going to eat something."

She laughed. Put a hand on his arm. Squeezed.

Yeah, this date was so not over.

◆————————◆

Conrad clearly had more power than just a few thousand social-media followers. Apparently, the guy had friends tucked away everywhere, or at least fans everywhere, because although Turbo was closed to the general public, Mr. King Con sat with a plate of wings and a Diet Coke, talking with Rex Dalton, the owner of the nightclub, a man in a pair of dress pants and an untucked fitted dress shirt.

Rex, the superfan who'd invited them in and bought the story Conrad had fed him about needing some publicity photos.

Felicity would go wild. They selfied in front of the black dance floor under disco lights, and in one of the round white-leather booths that circled the floor, and at the media console that looked down on the masses, the DJ giving them peace fingers, and even in the private balcony, where Rex got into the picture.

Penelope drew the line at the dance platforms, thank you. But this was clearly not a wasted date, and she had to admit, Conrad was clever. And hungry.

Now, while Conrad chatted, she wandered around and took "publicity" shots, which conveniently included the security.

She counted seven men, not all of them fitting Janet's rather loose description, but maybe the woman would recognize one. Because of course she'd recognize a man from three years ago that she'd seen running from a building in the shadowy night, his back to her. *No problem.*

Penelope slid onto a high-top chair beside Conrad, and he glanced over his shoulder. "Hey. Get what you needed?"

She grabbed a wing. "How hot are these?"

"It'll take the roof off your mouth," said Rex. He wore his dark hair short and had a shade of whiskers, and rings on his fingers.

"I think I'll wait until dinner." She set her chin on Conrad's shoulder, just in case someone might be a social-media follower. "Where are we going? Or are you too full?"

He hadn't even jerked at her intimate gesture, so game well played. Instead, he wiped his fingers with a wet wipe. "Are you kidding?" He stood up. "Thanks, Rex."

"You should come by when we're actually open," Rex said. "I'll put you in the VIP stand."

"You too. You ever want tickets, reach out. I'll set you up." Conrad shook Rex's hand, then held his out to Penelope. *Oh,* they were still onstage. She took it, let him lead her outside.

"Get the shots?"

"Already sent to Janet. We'll see if she gets a hit."

Outside, the night had started to pitch the streets, lights puddling the icy sidewalks. Her breath caught in the cool air despite the nearly above-freezing temperatures. She needed a vacation, pronto. Probably someplace in the Caribbean. She could follow Tia to her remote-island gig.

"Were you serious about dinner?" Conrad asked, leading her around the back to the parking lot.

"You're actually hungry?"

"I'm a hockey player. I'm always hungry."

They emerged from the alleyway into the lit lot. When they'd arrived, a delivery truck had blocked the back entrance, so he'd parked away from the door, on the other side.

Now, he slowed as he came up to his car.

She saw it too ... Glass speckled the pavement, and as they drew closer ...

"Someone vandalized my car."

The driver's-side window had been shattered, the steering wheel sheared off the mount. The front windshield, too, bore a spiderweb.

He dropped her hand. "What?"

She stepped closer, and her foot crunched glass. "Who would do this?"

"C'mon." He took her hand, pulled her away, back toward the club, nearly running.

"Conrad—what—"

"Listen." He pulled her into the alleyway, turned to her, almost pushing her back against the wall, his gaze fierce on hers. "I don't know, but this feels ..." His jaw tightened.

And right then, she heard his words, the ones that now formed in his eyes, the ones he'd spoken just a couple nights ago, brutal and sharp inside her—*"You, Penelope Pepper, are the connection."*

Her mouth opened.

His gaze dropped to it, back to her eyes, and for a second—a terrible, confusing, magical second—her fear dropped away, and all she could think was—

Yes.

Please.

He backed away, took her hand, breathing a little hard. "Let's call the cops."

Probably *that* was the right answer.

An hour later, she found him standing in the lot as a tow truck backed in to trolley away his car. The air had turned bitter, with two police cars lighting up the lot, the area roped off. She'd given her statement—which filled about three sentences—and he'd given his, and no one had asked why someone would do this. Apparently, the catalytic converter had also been stolen and he'd sported a designer steering wheel, and the cops took pictures and packed up the crime scene and attributed it to vandals.

Bummer for King Con.

She didn't take any selfies. She did, however, call an Uber XL because she thought maybe he wouldn't want to be shoved into an economy car on the drive back to her place.

Indeed. He sat in the SUV, head back, eyes closed. So maybe this was the end of their date.

Poor guy. He'd clearly gotten in over his head saying yes to this game.

"Please tell me you have other wheels," she said.

"I do. A truck."

Of course.

He lifted his head. "But this can't be the way this date ends."

Her eyes widened.

He sat up. "I'm sorry about the vandalism—"

"That wasn't your fault last time I looked."

"That was sort of a cosmic, blanket *sorry*, the kind that meant I'm sorry that the world occasionally sucks and that people do bad things, and I'd really like to end this night on a positive note."

"Are we talking cookies?"

"Actually, I'd prefer a steak." He stretched his arm over her seat. "My place? I cook a mean ribeye."

Oh. His place. Which meant . . . no paparazzi. No King Con sightings.

No fake-dating game.

Crazily, she was about to nod when her phone buzzed. She pulled it out, thumbed open the text. Stilled. "Shoot."

"What?"

"It's my mother. I forgot—Sunday-night dinner." She closed her eyes. "It's a thing. I'll text them and tell them I'm busy—"

"No." He looked at her, his voice kind. "Family is important. It's fine. Drop me off at home."

Oh. And it was something in his tone—defeat, maybe—that made the words emerge from her mouth. "Come with me."

He raised an eyebrow. "To dinner?"

"Yeah. It's fine. Casual. Sort of. Okay, not at all, but our chef is amazing, and . . . you did say you were starving."

"I managed to pack away a dozen wings. I think I'll survive until I can get home and order a pizza."

"It's beef Wellington night. Garlic potatoes. Homemade bread. Crème brûlée—"

"Yes."

She laughed then, and he smiled, and it took the sharp edge off today's events. The Uber drove them to her house, and she picked up her car and he wedged himself into her passenger seat, and forty-five minutes later, she pulled up to her parents' lakeside home.

Er, estate.

She entered the code at the gated entrance, drove up the long drive, and seeing him sit up as he took in the house elicited a pride she hadn't felt in ages.

The house rose, striking under a starry winter sky. It looked like something out of time that always made her pause, consider the generational wealth that had gone before her. The Georgian-Tudor style, with the steep, slate gable roof, gave it a stately aura, and why not?—the entire house spanned over thirty-thousand square feet. Lights arrayed over the front revealed the half-timbering of the exterior, especially along the wing, the rest of the house a herringbone brick. A two-story portico jutted out from the house into the cobblestone driveway, and electric candles flickered in the tall, narrow windows.

"The main house was built in 1887, with the wing added right after World War I. It's old and beautiful, with tall windows that overlook the lake, and sleeping porches off every bedroom—of which there are eleven—and a great room that my entire house would fit inside. A three-story zinc fireplace and even a third-floor ballroom, sort of like your parents' inn.

"This is nothing like my parents' inn," Conrad said as they pulled up. "But it is gorgeous and reminds me a lot of old money. What does your dad do?"

"Now—he manages our investments. But my great-great-grandfather was in lumber. And then, of course, paper. We're the Paper Peppers."

They stopped under the portico and she got out.

Conrad came around. "I feel this might have been a bad idea. I don't think I shaved today."

She glanced at him. "You haven't shaved in ten years."

"What do you know? I shave every year after the Stanley Cup."

Felix came out of the building in his usual suited attire, hair freshly cut, a dark expression aimed at Conrad.

"Keys are in the ignition."

"I'll park it in the garage, ma'am." He got in.

Conrad shot him a frown. "Valet?"

"Security. My dad went a little crazy after the kidnapping. I had a bodyguard in college."

She opened the scrolled-oak door. "Usually we use the side entrance, but . . . it never hurts to show off the entry."

"Holy cannoli," he said as he stood in the two-story vaulted entrance. It led straight through to the great room and then beyond, to the solarium.

Yes, it was impressive to the first-timer. On either side, a hallway lined with black brick led to the living areas and the bedrooms respectively. "When I was a kid, I would ride my bike in the hallway. It's nearly the length of a football field."

"I feel like shouting or something, seeing if my voice echoes." He took off his jacket.

A man, blond hair, well-built, always reminded her of a Nordic Viking, walked up. "Ma'am."

"Geoffrey. This is Conrad Kingston."

"Yes, ma'am, we know." He took Conrad's coat.

Of course they did.

"Thanks," Conrad said as Geoffrey collected hers as well.

"Ma'am, your family is gathering in the small dining room." He offered a tiny bow, then moved away to stow the coats in the nearby closet, secreted behind an oak panel.

They walked into the great room. "Okay, when Harper said you were . . . you know . . . *rich* . . . I thought maybe one of those nice homes on the lake. I didn't realize it was"—he cast his voice down—"like, own-your-own-country rich."

"And that is why I don't tell anyone. Don't act weird."

"I'm not."

"You totally are."

He'd stopped at the Postimpressionist painting that hung on the wall opposite the fireplace.

"Yes, that is a Cézanne original."

"My mother would love to see this place. She's all things vintage." He ran his hand along the scrolled built-in bookcase, then stood behind the creamy white sofa that faced the fireplace. Puddles of light fell from the sconces on the walls.

He walked over to the solarium, heavy with the scent of plants. Terra-cotta tile led to the floor-to-ceiling picture window and doors. Beyond, in the darkness, the expansive lawn led right down to the lake.

He turned to her. "Do I need a tie?"

"Stop talking. I'm starved." She pulled him toward the smells of the dining room.

So maybe she was hungry.

Except, in the room papered in gold tapestry, the chairs were empty at the twelve-foot dining table, although candles flickered in the candelabra in the middle and places were set. The smell of garlic and a hearty roast came from the kitchen.

She pressed a hand against her growling stomach.

"This is the *small* dining room?" Conrad arched a brow.

"Fine. Follow me." She gestured back to where they'd come from and crossed through the great room to the dining hall.

An eighteen-foot walnut table, coffered ceiling, a custom-made Turkish rug, and gold-framed pictures of her greats, most of them with family gathered on the lawn.

"Now *this* is how to have a family dinner. We could fit the entire Blue Ox team."

"My dad has a big party every year, brings in his board. We usually use the small dining room for family."

"Pep! I didn't think you were coming."

She turned and Tia came into the room, wearing leggings and a gold blouse, UGG slippers. "Is this . . . wait—Conrad Kingston? You were at the gala, right?"

Please. Penelope managed not to roll her eyes.

He had to bend over to give Tia a hug, and she rose on her tiptoes as she looked over at Penelope and winked.

Aw. Don't get crazy, Penelope mouthed. She needed a word with her sister.

"Sadly, despite the great smell, the gas went out on the stove," Tia said. She turned to Conrad. "In this old house, we aren't connected to city gas or water or sewer, so we have our tanks delivered." She put her hands on her hips. "Our house manager, Charles, was out last week, and Chef Taylor didn't think to order it. Anyway, Mother is the kitchen and . . . I think we might be having peanut butter sandwiches."

Conrad did a poor job of hiding a smile. "Back to steaks at my place?"

"Fine. But first, I need a minute with Tia."

He held up his hands. "I'll be in the great room looking for a first-edition Dickens."

"It's on the top—" Tia started.

Penelope grabbed her arm and pulled her away, into the hallway and down toward their mother's office. Their father had a study on the other side of the great room.

She pulled her inside the room with plush white Turkish rugs, deep blue sofas, and pictures of their family gallery-style on the walls. A Queen Anne desk her mother rarely sat at faced yet another fireplace, this one in white marble.

"What?" Tia said, rounding on her. "And what is Conrad Kingston doing here? And by the way—he is still smokin'—"

"Stop talking and listen."

Tia held up her hands. "Wow. Hangry much?"

Penelope wrinkled her nose. "A little. But that's—" She took a breath. Maybe . . . shoot. This might be a bad idea. "I got the forensic arson report from Edward's apartment."

"Yeah, so did I." Tia folded her arms.

"No—a different one. The *real* one. The one that found two bullet holes in his wall."

Tia's eyes widened.

"I went there today and talked with one of the neighbors, and she saw a man run from the townhouse right after hearing three shots."

Tia reached out, backed up and hit the sofa. Leaned on it. "So he was dead before the fire."

"Yes."

She breathed out, bent over, gripped her knees. "Oh, thank God."

Penelope stilled. "What?"

"I was so worried that he'd burned to death." She stood up, her eyes filled. "That he'd suffered in the flames, but . . ." She swallowed. "Thank you. It's like a gift, knowing—"

"Tia. I've been saying for years that someone *murdered* him and set the house on fire to cover it up."

Tia's eyes widened. Her mouth opened, and Penelope could almost see her brain working. "I know. I just . . ."

"Loved him. And you didn't want to think that someone could murder him."

A tear trekked down her sister's cheek. "But the alternative— that he burned to death—was just as horrible."

Penelope stepped up and wiped it away gently with her thumb. "I know I've asked this before, but I need you to really think. Did Edward have any enemies? Anyone who would've wanted to hurt him?"

Tia shook her head. "No. Everybody loved him. He was so smart and brilliant and . . ."

Cheating on you. But Penelope kept that to herself, not quite sure she could believe it.

"That's it, then," Tia said. "I didn't want to believe you, but I guess . . . now we know. We give the evidence to the police and walk away. Let them handle it."

Penelope blinked at her. "Tia. The police know—they *have* to know. Or . . ." She frowned. "Okay, yes, but . . ."

Tia put her hands on Penelope's shoulders. "Give them what you found. Then you need to let him go too." She pulled Penelope into her embrace.

Huh. Her heart thumped, not sure . . .

Tia pushed her away. "So, I heard things are going well with EmPower. Lucas called—said the photo shoot went spectacularly. We already have pictures on the website."

Really? But Conrad's words about Tia's way of grieving rounded back to her, so, "Yeah. I bought equipment for the team today." It felt like a thousand years ago. "Conrad helped."

"Uh-huh. You two a thing?" She looped her arm through Penelope's.

"No. I mean . . ." *Shoot.* What *did* she mean?

They had exited the room, walking down the hall into the great room. Voices.

She slowed, listening.

Her father's voice.

And Conrad's.

"I don't know," she finally said to Tia.

"Mm-hmm. I'm checking on the sandwiches." Tia left her there, in the room, listening.

"Nice boat." Conrad's voice. He was probably looking at a picture of her father's pride and joy, moored in their boathouse—a Melges 24 sailboat.

"She's a beauty. Been sailing since I was kid." Her father, his voice deep, warm. He had a way of making everyone in the room feel like they might be the only one.

"This is a good picture." Again, Conrad.

"That's one of the boards I sit on. Quantex Dynamics. Had our meeting in Barbados a few years ago."

"I invested in crypto stock about three years ago. Totally tanked. I lost about a hundred K." Conrad's voice.

"That's rough, Conrad. You've got to learn how to find the right stock." The sound of a bottle opening. Except Conrad didn't drink.

Or at least, she thought not.

"Thanks," Conrad said.

"That's a glass of Macallan Dalmore 62. Try it."

"Actually, sir—"

See?

But silence, and then her father laughed.

Her throat tightened.

"Son. You need to learn how to enjoy the finer things in life if you want to be with my daughter."

Wait—what?

"The fact is, investing is always a gamble. You can make an educated guess, but you never know how it's going to pan out. But you can't get scared when things look like they're going to take a turn. Stay in the game. Have a little faith."

"I'm working on something, sir, that I hope pans out. We'll see."

Right. His contract with the Blue Ox.

The one her father could influence.

So, they were back in the game.

And she had an answer for her sister. *We're nothing.*

She took a breath, then walked into the office. Opulent, with a bookshelf floor to ceiling behind the massive mahogany desk. Another fireplace, the photographs assembled in gold frames along the mantel.

Her father stood with a highball, holding court at the fireplace.

Conrad's hands were in his pockets. He looked over at her. Smiled.

She took a breath. "The gas is out in the stove. No dinner tonight, Dad. C'mon, Conrad, I'll drive you home."

Conrad frowned, then reached out to shake her father's hand. Turned and walked over to her. "Did I do—"

"Date's over, Conrad."

He stiffened, swallowed, his mouth tightening. Then, quietly, "What date?" He shook his head and walked out the door.

———•———

Of all the places for Emberly to run back into Steinbeck Kingston, a cathedral in Catalonia seemed the most improbable.

Unless you factored in fate, and the fact that the man had a magnetic pull on her—even from the moment she'd met him (that had nearly been tragic)—and of course, their shared target.

Declan Stone.

Too-handsome, too-smart, too-arrogant, too-freakin'-charming Declan Stone, who didn't remotely resemble an international or even a domestic terrorist in his khaki pants, black rain jacket, and baseball cap, wearing the pedestrian earphones and headset handed out by the group tour guide. *Sheesh,* he practically blended into the group of tourists wandering around the interior of Sagrada Família, his gaze heavenward at the windows that were currently turning the nave of the church a bright orange.

Honestly, if a girl slowed down and actually listened to the guy talking in her own headset, she might admit that Gaudí's nature-forward cathedral mesmerized her, with its attention to gathering the shifting daylight to stream down lavender, teal, gold, and fuchsia into the corridors of the space. That and the pillars carved to resemble massive sequoias jutting to the ceiling of the church gave the place almost a fairyland spell.

Nimue would love it. If Emberly could drag her sister out of the darkness of the deep web. Although, right now, Nim might be sitting on the bow of her restored fishing boat, moored in a private harbor in Geiger Key, just outside Key West.

Yeah, clearly Emberly was the one who needed a vacation from her life.

Stone sat on one of the pews in the middle of the cathedral, staring at the crucifix hanging in front, listening to a boys' choir sing some hallelujah-type chorus. Emberly pulled the headphones from her ears and merged into the crowd, standing in the shadow of one of the tall sequoias.

And just to confirm that her disguise worked, she glanced at Stein.

He stood away from Declan, but only a few feet, not even trying to hide his stun power, the dark, burnished hair that seemed unruly and long for a former SEAL, his stance less than casual, the way he stood, legs apart, arms folded. He wore a black jacket, black pants, and a black baseball cap—could anyone say private security? *Hello.*

But maybe that was the point. Akin to a giant Do Not Disturb sign across his chest.

No earphones for him. He'd wandered in seemingly almost uncaring at the grandeur of the place.

Which made it a little hard to complete her mission, *thank you.*

She dug out her earwig and pressed it into her ear. "There's no way I can grab him." Her voice, low, was answered with a sigh.

"We'll need to get creative." Her boss on the other end. Emberly could picture her, pacing in her apartment in Montelena, the one that overlooked a small alpine town with a castle embedded on a mountainside and one of the most secure crypto vaults in the world.

One that required the blood of the vault holder for access.

Whoops. Should have figured that out during her last go-round with Stone, back in Minnesota.

"You just need to get close enough to poke him."

"I need more than that. I need three cc's—that's a teaspoon—which means I actually have to get him alone, secured, and still for a good sixty seconds."

She had the entire kit in her sling bag. Just in case fate decided to, maybe, send an earthquake through Barcelona, separating Stein from his client and maybe rendering Stone unconscious. Yes, that would be überhelpful. And maybe God should listen, because she was one of the *good* guys.

Had sort of thought Stein was too. She still hadn't sorted out how and when he'd switched sides. Or really, why it irked her.

"If you don't get him today, then he goes back to the conference, and only three more days until he heads home, back to his fortress."

"He might go to his retreat in Mariposa."

"You think you'll have a better chance of getting near him on his *private island*?"

"He doesn't own the entire thing—"

"Okay. Listen. You're creative—that's why we tapped you for this. Get it done." Her voice softened, and frankly, Emberly didn't hate her new boss. She spoke with a slight British accent, had lived around the world, and had a sort of compassion about her. Code name: Mystique. "I checked into Stein, like you asked. He survived the bombing in Singapore, got shipped out to Tripler in Hawaii, spent a year in rehab, and tried to rejoin his team. Didn't go well. Got out and sort of wandered around for the last three years. Fell off the radar. I'll keep checking, but I don't think he's a threat."

Yeah, well, Mystique hadn't seen how said Not Threat had looked at her across the room Saturday night like he'd wanted to devour her. Shock, then a sort of fierceness, as if he might have been trying to place her, and the sense of it burrowed under her skin.

No way could he have recognized her, right? She'd worn a different wig, contacts, pants, a white shirt—completely different presentation than the woman she'd been on the dance floor a month ago.

Except, the way his gaze had changed to almost a hunger . . . She'd downed her vermouth, and when he turned away, fled.

Shoot, he'd gotten into her head, clearly.

"I'll get creative," she said now to Mystique. "You can count on me."

"I know." She hung up.

Emberly pulled out the earwig, pocketed it, and then watched as Stone got up, the choir having finished, and followed his tour group out of the cathedral.

They stopped outside, where a light rain drizzled, and she pulled on her own baseball cap, sunglasses (just because), and her black rain slicker. Even managed to sidle up to the group and hear the guide talk about the brutal modernist sculptures on the back of the cathedral, depicting the Passion, the final days of the Gospel.

Around them, tourists stood in a line, waiting to enter, and across the street, buses splashed through puddles. Bicyclists pedaled, heads down, along bike lanes, barely looking up.

"The facade is intentionally severe," said the guide. "Designed to depict the suffering of our Lord, the severity and pain of the crucifixion."

It did appear cruel, the sculptures almost austere, bare stone, with relief in places to represent body parts, faces. A stark, grim contrast to the Renaissance paintings that hung in the Louvre and other art houses around Europe.

These people got it—no romance in death. It was ugly, horrid business, and she turned away from the depiction.

A scream lifted and Emberly held in her own shout when a bicyclist slammed into one of the tourists who had stepped out from the line to capture a picture. The woman flew, hit a bus, thankfully stopped, and more people started to scream.

Blood ran into the street, the drizzle turning it into watercolor.

Declan and Stein had turned, along with others, and of course, Stein stepped up to his man, put a hand on his back.

Maybe he thought this was a distraction.

And it hit her then.

Yes, a distraction. Something that would make Stein think Stone was in trouble. . . .

Maybe even an accident of his own.

Take out Stein, and she got to Stone.

The thought put a fist into her gut, thickened her throat, but she couldn't help it that he'd changed sides.

All was fair in . . . war.

And love could have nothing to do with it.

SEVEN

OACH JACE WAS RIGHT—CONRAD JUST needed to get out of his head. Which meant a good sweat or, in this case, a cold plunge.

"That's nearly three minutes, Con." This from his trainer, a man named Ethan Parker, who stood near the tank in the Blue Ox training room with a watch. He pointed to the next tank, where Wyatt Marshall shivered. "And you have another four."

"I can't feel my body," Wyatt said. He sat, teeth gritted, his head back on the stainless-steel surface, eyes closed. "I love it."

Conrad, also shivering, laughed. "Why?"

"My hip doesn't hurt, my knees aren't swollen, and just maybe by Sunday, I'll have my racing body back."

"I get you," Conrad said and held out his fist. Wyatt met it. Third day back to practice had him feeling like an eighty-five-year-old man. But the pain made him focus, get his head in the game, and frankly, he needed the distraction.

Off the ice, he simply spent too much time dissecting Penelope's crazy end to their nondate.

Maybe he needed to put in some time in the weight room, purge her from his brain, again.

But her dismissal sat under his skin, and maybe a little in his chest, the way she'd gone from warm and friendly on their drive to her house, to downright arctic during their drive *back* to his place. She'd dropped him off, barely a goodbye. And no amount of dissecting the disastrous Blue Ox games or working out in his home gym or even pushing himself in practice could dislodge the questions.

He just didn't like to fail.

Aw, maybe that was the problem—he'd seen it as a personal goal to get her to trust him.

"Okay, three minutes are up," said Ethan, and Conrad pushed himself out of the plunge and grabbed the towel the trainer offered.

He ran it over his chest, his shorts, and then draped it around his neck.

Coach Jacobsen walked into the room. He gestured with his head, and Conrad followed him out into the locker-room area. Most of the guys were still around, some of them changing after showers, a few in the massage room—Conrad might have preferred that. He spied Justin on the exercise bike, cooling down, his EarPods in.

Jace folded his arms. "Time-out is over. You ready to get back in the game on Sunday?"

"Always."

Coach nodded. "You saw the last game."

"Disaster."

"Justin doesn't have your instincts yet. He hesitates at crucial moments, second-guesses himself. Thankfully the Idaho games weren't ranking, but we need to win against the Omaha Outlaws."

"I'll bring it home, Coach."

Jace nodded again. "How's it going with EmPowerPlay?"

"Good. We have that tournament tomorrow. Got the kids new equipment. They were crazy excited." The memory of the kids opening the boxes, suiting up in their gear, pressed a smile to his mouth. "We might not win, but we'll look good losing."

"Great job. After this weekend, I need your focus back on the Blue Ox. We have a cup run, and I want to look good *and* win."

"You got it." Conrad had started to shiver under his towel.

"Go get warm. See you Sunday."

Conrad headed to the showers, his body still numb, and stood under the spray, his hands braced on the tile for a long time, his muscles loosening. *Date's over, Conrad.*

Aw.

He turned off the water, got out, and headed with his towel to the locker room. The problem was he didn't know what he'd done. Maybe it'd been his conversation with her father. Except Oscar Pepper seemed like a nice guy, and sure, he wanted the man to like him—had nearly stepped over his personal boundaries to taste the whiskey the man had poured. But he'd circled that conversation through his head over and over and couldn't figure out what he'd said that had turned her cold.

Maybe he'd been too verbally impressed with her parents' house. Sure, the Pepper estate was magnificent, and he'd been a little knocked over at her family's wealth, but he'd been around money, and frankly, it only caused headaches.

And stress, thank you. Because he had lost a painful chunk of investments last year. And Oscar Pepper's words had prompted him to come home and check his stocks, even slide some over into an S&P 500 account.

He got dressed almost on autopilot, threw his towel and soiled clothes into the hamper, then headed out to his truck. Practice had gone late—the sun was already down, the stars blinking overhead. The crisp air filled his lungs.

"I'm not saying don't try. I saw the pictures—you made her smile. That's a start."

He shook Harper's words away. He was done trying. Penelope Pepper was just too . . . mysterious. Complicated. Maybe even high-maintenance.

Too much relationship math to keep track of in his brain. Besides, she hadn't texted him. And he wasn't going to text her. He recognized the boot end of a goodbye.

No more Pepper in his brain.

He went home, fried up a ribeye with butter, garlic, and fresh rosemary, added some baby smashed golden potatoes, and watched the latest Outlaws game. Took a few mental notes on the signals the center dropped to his team right before a face-off. Their starting center also tended to stay high in the zone to cut off the passing lane. And he was aggressive.

He also kept the puck longer than he should, maybe.

Conrad paused and rewound a couple of the goalie snatches—the man was strong on his glove side, but had given up two goals on his stick side.

He could use that.

Overall, an intensely physical team, although by the third period, they lagged. So, he'd have to conserve his energy, exploit that.

Conrad went to bed after three whole hours without Pepper in his brain. And then promptly returned to that moment in the alleyway outside Turbo when the urge to kiss her had nearly possessed him. Still did, because when he closed his eyes, she was right there, staring up at him, her golden-brown gaze wide, words in her eyes, as if—

No. He sent a fist into his pillow, enacted a few breathing techniques, and managed to grab hold of sleep.

But he was up at five for a workout, eggs, and bacon, and had a stiff black coffee in hand when he pulled into the North Star Arena.

Simon met him, parked in front of a school bus with the team's name and logo, holding coffee and a clipboard. Kids were milling around the lot, their gear bags in a pile. The forecast had suggested a storm on the way, but blue skies arched overhead.

"Hey," Simon said. "You going to follow us or ride in the bus?"

Why not? "I'll ride."

"It's two hours away, nearly up in Brainerd."

"We'll talk strategy." He grabbed a couple bags and walked them around to the back, opened the door and threw them in. Shouted at the kids to load up, then turned back to Simon, who had followed him. "I haven't seen Jeremy at any of the practices." He probably shouldn't ask—especially since not having the kid around had kept him from having an episode.

In fact, he'd managed to keep his cool for every practice. So maybe the nightmares wouldn't win.

Simon closed the back, gestured to the kids to get in. "Yeah. I called him. Said his dad got an infection, was in the hospital. He needed to stick around and help."

Conrad frowned.

"His mom works full-time, and he has a couple younger siblings. He helps out a lot. Good kid, tough lot."

He walked around to the entrance of the bus.

Conrad stood there, his chest tight. *Breathe.*

He finally followed Simon onto the bus, sat down on one of the seats in front, turned, and glanced back at the team. They were playing on their phones, many of them plugged in with earbuds.

"Different from our road-trip days when we just threw things at each other," Conrad said.

"Hey. I had that Game Boy," Simon said. "You were the one who couldn't sit still."

Conrad grinned. "I was a little hyper back then."

"No, you were intense back then." Simon raised an eyebrow as they pulled out. "I don't think much has changed. You were a little hard on the kids this week."

"We want to win, right?"

Simon shrugged. "We play to learn and grow. And yes, win, but losing doesn't have to be failure."

Conrad narrowed his eyes, took a sip of coffee. "I have some ideas on how we might win." And then he spent the next two hours outlining his game plan, starting with identifying the opposing team's key playmakers during the first period and assigning defensemen to shadow them, implementing a trap neutral zone strategy to slow them down during a turnover, and taking as many shots on goal as possible.

"We want to tire them out, keep them guessing."

"They're kids. Most of them are thirteen."

"By the time I was thirteen, I was playing in the Quebec International Pee-Wee Hockey Tournament, had scouts looking at me, coaches inviting me to the juniors."

"You had parents who were involved. Who showed up—"

"But that's the point of EmPowerPlay, right? To show the kids that they can do this on their own."

Simon raised an eyebrow. "I think that is exactly *not* the point, Con. We're a team, and we need each other—"

Conrad held up a hand. "I know. But I mean . . . no one is going to succeed for you. You need to figure it out and play your best game if you want to win. You can't depend on others to play your position. Man up."

Simon considered him for a moment, then nodded. "Spoken like the Duck Lake Storm team captain."

"We won state in our division." He leaned back, noticing that they'd left the highway, were working their way through plowed country roads, the forest shaggy, the occasional road cutting through from houses buried deep in the woods, maybe seated on the shores of nearby lakes. This area of northern Minnesota was lousy with vacation getaways. "Is this an outdoor rink?"

"The Frozen Lakes Youth Cup semifinals. We win this, we advance to the finals tournament in St. Paul. It's a recreational league, nonofficial, but it's still a big deal."

They drove up to a large parking lot jammed with trucks and SUVs and kids hauling gear. The words *Crystal Lake Ice Circle* were painted on a Quonset warming house with glass doors. The shed faced a rink that glistened under the sun, bleachers stretched out on either side. Kids skated, shooting at the goals, warming up their puck handling. He spotted at least five different jersey colors.

"It's going to be a long day," he said as the bus stopped at the warming hut.

"C'mon," Simon said, getting up. "This is going to be fun."

Fun.

Hockey had ceased being fun over a decade ago, really. But he piled out of the bus, got the kids moved into their section of lockers in the warming building, and then walked out with Simon to watch the first game, a fresh cup of cocoa in his hand.

He pointed out a few weaknesses of the other teams, but frankly, the entire gameplay felt like a collision of small bodies scampering over the ice, scrabbling for a wild puck. Not a glimpse of strategy in sight. Simon kept laughing at him too, so *whatever.*

But he eventually found himself cheering for the peewee goalie who kept nabbing the shots that came near him—most went wide, into the net behind the cage.

"He's not bad," Conrad said. "But he needs to keep his body square to the puck, not the player."

"For the love, Conrad," Simon said, but grinned at him. "We're up next. Let's go gather the team."

Conrad listened as Simon briefed them on the upcoming game strategy, managed not to butt in when Simon told them to have fun out there. To his credit, the coach had adjusted the strategy to match Conrad's suggestions.

Maybe they wouldn't get annihilated.

When he took the ice with his team, slapping the puck to the wings in warmup, he realized he hadn't thought of Penelope all morning.

Bam.

The kids huddled up on their bench, and he gave a pep talk to the first line, nothing too intense. "Remember, keep your heads up, support each other, and play smart. We've practiced hard to get here, and now it's time to bring that practice onto the ice. Pass the puck, communicate, and stay alert. I want each of you to give it your all." He looked up at Simon, took a breath. "But most important, I want you to enjoy every moment. On three."

He held out his hand, and they added theirs to the middle, and okay, this *was* fun.

They took the ice, skating out for the face-off.

That's when he spotted her. Lined up on the other side of the boards, dressed in a dark-blue hat, a silver-and-blue jersey, her long dark hair down, loose in the wind, clapping wildly.

Aw. She looked good. Too good.

The kind of good that could derail a guy trying to focus on the peewees.

Nope. He shut her away and turned to the game.

Face-off—the Ice Hawks scrambled after the puck, and for a second he lost her in the action. *Good.* Except the other team, the Maple Falls Polar Bears, scored, and when his team skated in to change lines, he spotted her on their side, seated on a bench.

He ignored her.

Simon crouched in front of the line. "Listen up! That goal— they earned it, but it's just one goal. We've been down before, and we know how to bounce back. Let's shake it off—"

Conrad stepped in. "Focus. Nab your passes, stay sharp on defense, and communicate out there. Let's go out there, take control, and play our game."

Simon lifted his fist. "We've got this! Let's go show them!"

They spilled out, and he barely noticed her in his peripheral vision.

They scored, and the team erupted on the bench. They switched lines and kept the puck moving—

They weren't terrible. And by the time the period ended, he had some new strategies. He gathered the boys in and appointed the defensemen to watch a couple of the Polar Bears' players.

No goals in the second period, and Simon huddled up with the kids.

She stood on the outskirts, her gaze like a burr under his skin.

The crowd had dispersed, parents leaving to get hot cocoa or to warm up. He'd barely noticed the chill.

A motor fired up, and he looked up to see the Zamboni enter the rink. It rounded the outside, a smooth layer of ice freezing in the crisp air.

Simon was still talking. "We're not defined by one goal or one game. We're defined by our resilience and our teamwork—"

"Oh no!"

Penelope's voice, and of course, it zinged right into his brain. He looked up, saw her moving toward the open gate to the ice.

Then he spotted the trouble.

A kid, maybe three years old, had toddled onto the ice from the opposite side, now stood in the middle, holding a puck. He dropped it on the ice.

The Zamboni had rounded the far edge, heading toward him.

And Conrad didn't think. He dove through the door, slipped, caught himself, and then ran, flat-footed, short steps, scampering in his boots toward the kid.

The Zamboni roared in his ears, but he didn't look. Even if it stopped, it would slide at least a few feet on the ice.

He pushed off and slid, scooping up the toddler as he skimmed across the surface.

He reached the new ice, still forming, and his feet zipped out from under him.

He held on, angled himself and landed, *bam*, on his hip, rolling to his back.

Heat flashed into his bones, shaking out his breath, and he lay there groaning, the kid screaming and writhing in his arms. Players from the other side skated out, and the coach of the Polar Bears grabbed the kid from his arms.

"You okay, King Con?" This from one of the youngsters. Of course they'd recognize him. He sat up, breathing hard.

Glanced over at the Zamboni.

It had slid into the path, right where he'd plucked the kid.

"That was amazing," said a voice behind him, and he spotted a couple of his kids also out on the ice. "Way to go, Coach!"

He nodded and rolled to his feet, his hip on fire, but glanced over to where the toddler's mother held him, shaking, nodding at Conrad.

He shooed away help from his team and picked his way back toward the bench. Crossed in front of the Zamboni.

And maybe it was the exhaust from the engine souring the air, or the crisp smell of the fresh ice, even the rumble of the engine— or maybe just the near tragedy—but his heartbeat jumped into overdrive, and a sweat broke out along his spine.

No, not now—

His throat started to close, his chest tightening. *Breathe— breathe—*

He made it to the bench, sat down.

"Wow, Coach, that was cool!" One of the players—he couldn't recall his name at the moment—

"Okay, guys, let's give Coach Con some room. Focus on me—"

On the ice, the Zamboni fired back up.

Conrad's stomach started to roil. *Not here. Not now—*

He got up and shoved through the players to the edge of the bleachers, then out and around to the back—

There. A garbage drum. He gripped the sides and bent over, and just in time, because he lost it.

Not a lot to lose, but still—not his finest moment. He spat, wiped his mouth, completely grossed out now, and then turned to find a place to hide—

"Conrad? You okay?"

There she stood, concern in her beautiful eyes, hands in her pockets.

Aw ... So much for purging her from his brain. Especially when she came over, put her hands on him, and said, "C'mon. Let's get you out of here."

———•———•———

She probably deserved the cold look he gave her at her suggestion that he escape prying eyes, but the man clearly had something going on.

Conrad shoved his hands into his jacket, shivered suddenly—and why not? The temps hovered just below freezing a crisp day with blue skies and brilliant sunshine. A glorious afternoon for a hockey tournament in Minnesota, so maybe the forecasters had been wrong.

No dark storm clouds huddling on the horizon.

Unless she counted the ones in Conrad's expression.

"Conrad. Really. People are watching. Let's get you inside."

She reached out for him, but he drew in a breath, glanced at the game now resuming on the ice, then closed his eyes, shook his head as if in pain.

"You're breathing funny—"

"I'm fine," he snapped.

"You're clearly *not* fine." She'd dropped her voice, leaned in. "You nearly got run over by a Zamboni."

He opened his eyes, emotion sparking in them, and then his mouth tightened and he nodded.

Okay then. It felt a little like bringing a buffalo to heel.

She made to take his arm, but he stiffened, so she just walked with him around the rink, toward the Quonset hut. Except a crowd gathered there, watching them, so she gestured toward the parking lot. "I have water bottles and sandwiches in my car."

"You brought sandwiches?"

"I called Simon—he said the kids would need lunch after their game, so yeah." She dug her fob out of her purse and unlocked the car.

He walked over, got in, and she opened up the back hatch and retrieved a couple water bottles. She'd wait on the sandwich, given the tragedy over at the garbage can.

Clearly a response to the adrenaline, the near miss.

She got in and handed him one of the bottles. From here, they could see the game, although the boards hid most of the action. Still, his gaze stayed on his team even as he cracked the top of the water bottle and guzzled it.

"Go easy there—"

He lowered the bottle and looked at her.

"Sorry. Just . . . you know."

"I'm fine." He leaned back, closed his eyes, his breathing hard. Almost looked like . . . "Are you having a panic attack?"

Nothing. Not even a muscle moved in his jaw.

"I mean, I get that—you were nearly pancaked. So yeah, just breathe."

"Thanks, doc."

But he didn't follow with a smile, so *ouch.*

"I used to have them, and my therapist said to focus on something—"

He held up a hand.

Right.

She turned on the car, then upped the heat. Watched the game.

The Ice Hawks clearly scored, because their sticks went into the air and they huddled up, hitting one of the players on the helmet in congratulations.

"We're ahead."

"Mm-hmm," he said, and she glanced over. His eyes were open, watching the game, wearing almost a fierce expression.

And she was right back in her father's study, hearing Conrad's low—pained?—voice. *"What date?"*

She'd barely stopped herself from crying the entire wretched ride home.

Especially since after he walked out, she spotted his full glass of whiskey on a side table, untouched, so *way to jump to conclusions, Pep.* And not that she would care—but . . .

Maybe he hadn't been trying to wheedle into her world, earn her father's favor.

But she didn't know how to say that. Maybe the cold front turning him into a dark and grumpy Roy Kent version of King Con was for the best.

The last thing she needed was to fall for a guy whose world was sports. Conrad was all hockey, all the time, pro or otherwise. He hadn't even noticed her when she arrived at the rink.

Good thing he'd noticed the toddler, however. "That was brave—what you did."

He glanced at her. "It required no bravery, Penelope. Just instinct, and maybe a little familiarity with ice and Zambonis. I was in the right place at the right time—"

"With the right skills."

"Sliding. Hardly a skill."

"How did you know that Zamboni wasn't going to be able to stop?"

He capped the bottle. "Physics. It's putting down fresh ice, which is slippery, and even going as slow as it was, it was going to slide. Ice, big machinery . . . not hard math."

A muscle pulled on his jaw, however, as he looked away.

The man had a tell.

"That's not all. What am I missing here?"

A beat. He sighed. Looked back at the game. "I saw a Zamboni accident, years ago. The machine slid and pinned a guy to the boards. Crushed his leg. He eventually lost it."

"That's awful."

"Yeah, it was. Young guy. Had a kid—one year old. He was in the hospital, then rehab for months." He shook his head, swallowed. Glanced at her. "Actually, you met his son Jeremy at the gala."

She frowned, trying to recollect. "The Ice Hawks kid."

"Yeah. His dad was the security guard at North Star Arena in Duck Lake. He was working late one night—hockey schedules are crazy late and brutally early to get all the ice time in for the teams. A peewee team had just cleared out."

He drew in a breath. "A bunch of high-school players had hung around, hoping to slap around the puck, and one of them got on the Zamboni, started driving on the ice, goofing around. When they spotted Joe, they piled off, and the Zamboni just kept going. Joe ran out to try to stop it, fell, and couldn't get away in time."

Her hand covered her mouth.

"Terrible accident." He took another sip of water, then stared out at the game, his face hard.

Wait . . . "Oh, Conrad—you were the high schoolers."

His jaw tightened.

"You weren't the one *driving*—"

He looked at her, the answer in his tortured eyes. "I'd driven the Zamboni a few times, part-time job, so I had keys, I knew how to run it. It wasn't off-limits, at least to me. But a buddy of mine got the keys, started it up, and lost control. I tried to take over, but . . .

I panicked. I hit the brakes, put the Zamboni into neutral . . . and bailed. I never meant . . ."

He shook his head. "It was deemed an accident, a malfunction of the Zamboni. I was found guilty but only of negligence and was given community service. I spent a summer cleaning the local parks, coached the peewee hockey team, and had to work as the janitor at the arena for an entire year."

He finished the water. "I never played hockey there again. Thankfully, I was already playing in the juniors, so I'd moved on. But . . ." He looked at her then, his blue eyes thick with pain. "I relive it over and over. I made the news in my small town, and it was humiliating. I felt so stupid. So . . ." His mouth tightened. "Naked."

Oh.

"I don't know what I was thinking. I knew better—but I was with my buddies, and we were in our senior year, had just won state, and I just didn't *think*. It was impulsive and stupid and . . . and I wrecked someone's life."

She simply didn't care if he shrugged her away when she put her hand out and touched his forearm.

He looked at her hand, back at her, met her gaze with a slight frown.

"I'm sorry I was rude on Sunday night. I was . . . I . . ." She drew in a breath.

He cocked his head.

"I read into . . . Never mind. Clearly I misjudged you, Conrad."

He gave a small huff. "It happens." He lifted a shoulder. "Don't believe everything you read on the internet."

She raised an eyebrow. "Clearly."

He turned, his blue eyes holding hers, what looked like a question in them.

On the ice, the buzzer sounded. The kids erupted, hugging on the ice, and it broke his gaze. She released her hold on his arm. "I'll get the sandwiches."

He got out also, dropped the bottle into a nearby trash can, and then helped her carry the loot to the Quonset hut.

The team traipsed in, and he high-fived them, grinning, and it seemed he'd rebounded, back in his element. Simon came in too. "You good, bro?"

Conrad nodded, gave Penelope a quick glance. "Yep. Sorry—"

Simon held up his hand. "No problem. Great coaching today. On to the finals, boys!"

Shouts, which was her cue to get out the sandwiches.

The team descended like wolves and scooped up the food, some of them still in their new gear. A few parents came in, and she posed with some of the players. She noticed that Conrad didn't try to get into any shots, although a couple players cornered him.

He didn't suggest even one with her.

The team finished the meal, and she gathered up the debris while they changed out of their gear. Conrad and Simon had gone back outside to watch the next game.

She joined them, standing at the boards. They were pointing out players and different gameplay. Conrad seemed revived—she noticed he'd downed a sandwich and another bottle of water, and the color had returned to his handsome face. The sun shone down into his beard, the red highlights turning him into some warrior Norseman, and all she could think of was the pain in his blue eyes.

Yes. She'd misjudged in epic leaps and bounds.

One of the teams scored, and the period ticked down. The rest of the team had trickled out, some throwing snowballs at each other, others watching the game. A few remained inside, playing on their phones.

Conrad caught her eye. "Simon wants to head back." He shoved his hands into his coat pocket, his mouth a line.

Oh. Um . . . and then—*wait.* "Do you want to ride back with *me?*"

He narrowed his eyes, glanced at the sky. So maybe the forecasters hadn't been all wrong. A few darker clouds hovered to the west, blowing in from North Dakota. "I don't want you driving alone."

She cocked her head.

He held up a hand. "I know. You can take care yourself. But . . . you have a couple sandwiches left. I might get hungry." He smiled.

Oh, wow, she simply had no defenses against Mr. June's smile. No wonder they'd doubled their sales this year.

"You can catch me up on your research," he added.

"Research?"

"The pictures you sent to Janet?"

"Oh, those. She said that none of them were the guy, so . . ." She lifted a shoulder.

"Sorry."

"That's okay. I had to prep for my podcast anyway."

She waited for him to suggest that he'd listened to it, but he just nodded. *Oh.* A small ding landed in her heart. Not that it mattered, *hello.*

The team had started to gather their gear. He walked over to the bus and she followed. He helped Simon load the bags, then shook his hand and turned to her.

And maybe the ding in her heart healed a little when he said, "Let's listen to your podcast on the way home."

"I'll recap," she said. "I can't listen to my own voice."

"Right? I hate my interviews." He got into the car and moved the seat all the way back to make room for his legs. Funny, he hadn't done that before.

The bus pulled out, but she needed gas, so she took the route into the town of Crystal Lake and bought a couple coffees while he pumped gas. Like they might be on a road trip.

She got back in and handed him a coffee as he climbed in the passenger side.

Snow had started to peel from the sky, fat snowflakes that melted against her windshield. She pulled out.

"So, you met my dad." She didn't know why she'd started there, but . . .

Okay, she wanted to know if her heart was right about Conrad. *Please,* let her father not be part of the game.

"Nice guy. Interesting. Smart, clearly. We talked about investing. I looked up the company he sits on the board of. Quantex Dynamics. They're up over 44 percent just this year. Crazy."

"Yeah. Apparently it's some sort of AI software company—"

"Software, hardware. They develop GPUs that are used in AI research for deep learning and computations. They're big in the gaming world. They had a big competitor a few years ago—an electric car company developing AI autonomous-vehicle technology. But their AI software is years behind Spectra and they're struggling." He took a sip of coffee. "This is like tar."

"Don't be such a diva. At least it didn't cost a kidney."

He laughed. The entire car filled with the robust sound of it, and it seeped right into her, warm, smooth, sweet, like chocolate. "I've never heard that phrase before."

"I had a friend in college who said it."

She turned onto the two-lane county road back to the highway, noticed that the snow had started to stick, turning the road a little slick.

"I personally like kidney-costing coffee. Give me a latte at Caribou any day."

"I got used to the cafeteria coffee at the U, and there's a perverse sort of joy in the suffering. It offsets my clothing budget."

"Is that an issue?"

She sighed. "It should be. I barely make ends meet with the podcast. But of course . . . there's the trust fund . . . I'm so weak."

"I think it's fantastic that you want to make it on your own."

Sweet.

"Except, why is it so important? Your dad seems like a generous guy."

She didn't know why Conrad's words hit with such force. She probably winced, because he frowned.

"Did I say something?"

Shoot, her eyes suddenly burned—where had that come from? She'd made peace years ago with—"No. Yes." She glanced at him. "My dad refused to pay the ransom on me when I was kidnapped."

There, it was out. And her chest eased. "He told me it was because he knew who took me, that he knew my nanny wouldn't hurt me, but . . . I don't know. It's always made me feel like . . . you know . . ."

"You needed to be on your own. Take care of yourself."

She lifted a shoulder. "I never know when someone is going to betray me."

He went silent, and she winced again when he said, quietly, "That explains a lot."

She looked at him then, probably for too long, because he jerked, slammed his hand on the dash.

"Pen!"

She righted them into the lane a second before the other car passed. But she slightly overcompensated and their car swerved.

Yanking her foot off the gas, she resisted hitting the brakes, let the car slow on its own, and straightened them out. She blew out a breath as she eased them up to speed again.

"Wow. That was . . . pretty good."

"I took a defensive driving class in college."

"Sexy."

She smiled, glanced at him.

"Eyes on the road!"

"Sorry."

Night was descending, twilight sparking through the trees. Headlights beamed on the road behind her.

"Sorry about your dad," Conrad said.

"I forgave him long ago. He is pretty smart with money—he's

managed our family's investment holdings since he was out of finance school."

"At the U?"

"Cornell. I was the only one who went to the University of Minnesota."

"I never went to college."

"Really?"

"Drafted when I was eighteen. Made it to the NHL by the time I was twenty. But I've taken some business and investing classes. And I've done okay."

"Given your digs, more than okay."

"Trying to stay in the game."

"That seems to be your specialty." And she didn't mean it as a dig. She glanced at him to see if he might have—

He smiled back.

Lights burst into her rearview mirror. She winced and adjusted the mirror. "Sheesh."

"Brights much, buddy?" He turned in his seat.

The car did seem to be too close. It pulled out as if to pass, and she eased up on the gas. *Go ahead, pal—*

The car moved parallel with her, kept speed.

In the distance ahead, she spotted headlights. "C'mon, pass me."

The car stayed even and then—

"Hey!" She swerved to avoid it as it crowded into her lane. She tapped the brakes.

"Get behind it—"

Not fast enough. The car jerked into her lane right in front of her, clipping her hood—

The Nissan spun, slamming her against the door as she hit the brakes. Too hard. She worked the wheel, but the car slid across the road, flying into the shoulder—

Airborne.

They touched down and rolled. Down into the ditch, beyond,

into a tangle of pine and scrub brush, her seatbelt pinning her as the car pitched into the snowy woods.

And her scream echoing into the night.

EIGHT

H E FELT INTACT. SURE, HIS HIP BURNED, sending spurts of pain down his leg, exploding into his bones, but as Conrad tried to adjust his eyes to the fading light, to get a handle on the state of the car, at least he knew he wasn't dead.

Just upside down, the seatbelt slicing into his shoulder and waist as he hung.

"Penny?" He didn't know why he kept calling her that, but it's what emerged. "Penny?" He turned to her, found her also hanging.

She groaned, stirred. "Conrad?"

The terror flashed inside him—spinning, rolling, the chaos, her screaming—but he shook it away, put his hand on hers. "I'm okay."

She gripped his back. "Me too. I think." Her voice shook.

"Okay, listen, let me unbuckle, then I'll help you out."

"I can—"

"Just wait!" He didn't mean to shout, so maybe his adrenaline was burning a little hotter through him than he'd thought. "Sorry. Just . . . let me figure this out." He reached for his buckle before she could object, then braced himself against the roof of her now painfully cramped car as he dropped.

He landed on his bad hip, the pain a flare. He grunted, bit back a shout. But he ignored it and sat up. Put his hands on her hips. "I got you. Brace yourself on the roof and then unbuckle. I'll catch you."

"Don't let me hurt you."

Probably too late for that, given the fact that he'd completely ignored common sense and told her about his Zamboni disaster. Talk about letting her inside his soul—see, this was what happened when he led with impulse and maybe his hopes and not his brains.

But she'd told him about her dad, and the story simply made sense. No wonder she had such a tragic history with men. And it had nothing to do with him being an athlete—*hello,* he saw right through that.

It had to do with him being another human being who could let her down. Betray her—at least in her mind.

"Ready?"

"Let 'er rip."

She released the buckle and made a tiny noise of panic as she fell. He caught her weight and eased her down into his arms.

"See? Gotcha."

She sat there for a moment, just holding on to his arms around her. "Sorry."

"For?"

"Um . . . hello? We're in the ditch."

"I think this is more than the ditch. I think we've careened into the forest like a snowball."

"Then I'm super sorry." She looked up at him. He could barely make out her face in the darkness, but he'd guess tears edged her eyes.

"Not your fault, Pen. I'm not sure if that guy was trying to force you off the road or was just an überbad driver, but totally not. your. fault."

She nodded then, and he had the craziest urge to—

No. "Are you hurt?"

"Just bruises." She pushed away from him and crawled over to her door. "It won't move."

He turned and tried his. It creaked open, a crack. He ground his jaw against the pain and kicked it.

It scraped against the snow, but he managed to wedge an opening. Snow billowed in, the wind brisk, casting in flakes.

"The blizzard is catching up with us."

The dome light hadn't come on. "Can you find your phone?" he said.

She searched around her seat and then in back. "No. I don't know. I don't see my purse either. And it's too dark to see anything."

He too had lost his phone, his hands finding a few sandwiches, bottles, but nothing to call for help.

"Okay, let's see if we can get up to the road, and maybe we can flag down a car."

"We're on a county road—I took a shortcut. But we're still a good ten miles away from the highway."

He rolled over, pushed himself out of the opening chest first, crawling. He turned, held out his hand. "We're going to be okay."

She took his grip and he helped her out.

In the darkness, he didn't have a clue the damage to her car, but it seemed they'd mowed a swath off the road, because he spotted a dent in the darkness, a shadow that led up to the road.

With the blizzard moving in and the stars gone, they had little time to get to shelter. Maybe they should stay in the car . . .

She took his hand, squeezed.

"Okay, let's go." They'd rolled maybe thirty feet into the forest, enough to be hidden, so maybe this was the right move. He scrabbled up, gripping broken tree branches and fighting his pulsing hip, and helped pull her up the hill until they hit the pavement.

The road sprawled out in both directions, darkness in the darkness.

"Now what?"

"I think we passed a mailbox about the time the car came up on us. I remember his lights shining on it." He glanced either way—as if a car might be coming? *For Pete's sake.* Then again, if it were, he might stand out in the middle of the road.

Okay, maybe not, given the slickness as they crossed to the other side and headed back toward where they'd come from. On this side, any car coming would see them.

And with luck, they'd run right into the mailbox.

"You think the car was really trying to take us out?"

"I don't know, Pen." He hunched his head down, the snow finding his cheeks, burning. She couldn't be much warmer in those leggings, fancy boots, the jacket made for looks rather than warmth. But she kept moving beside him.

C'mon, God, send a car.

Hopefully the Almighty still heard the prayers of the desperate.

But the night seemed deserted, the wind picking up into a moan, the flakes now turning to ice, the edges biting.

Conrad nearly walked right by the mailbox. If it hadn't been for it catching his jacket arm as he brushed by, he would have kept going into the yonder for who knew how long. Rounding, he stopped, and Penelope nearly banged into him.

He'd noticed she'd gone quiet, probably trying to endure the storm. "I think this is a driveway." The snow seemed to dip here, as if it might have been shoveled, perhaps earlier in the season.

"To what—a lake home?"

"There are plenty of closed-up cabins in this area. Let's see if we can find it." As he started down the path, the snow up past his ankles, he thought he spotted a clearing in the darkness ahead, maybe the lake reflecting the snow.

They trudged down the trail, his hand tight on hers. She tripped once, and he caught her. "Hang in there."

Please let this not be a mistake. There it was, another prayer. He didn't *not* believe in God. On the contrary.

He just feared that God didn't believe in him.

Thankfully, the path didn't turn, just a straight shot, and yes, he'd guessed right. The drive opened to an expansive view of some tucked-away lake, the surface glistening with white even in the storm.

And situated beside the lake, a cabin. It looked like it might be two stories, with a porch and gabled windows.

"How are we going to get in?" Penelope's voice trembled.

"Good question. I don't want to break a window—"

"Maybe you should try them. Sometimes people forget to lock them." She wrapped her arms around herself, openly shivering. "You'd be shocked how many houses are broken into that way."

Apparently he was going to add breaking and entering to his record. But rather that than perish. He climbed up the porch steps, less snow here, and tried the door. Locked. He went to the main windows beside the door—also locked. A massive window overlooked the lake—no opening there, but in the back side, near the propane tank and a boathouse, he found a small double-hung utility window.

It slid open. Except, no way could he fit into the small twenty-four-by-eighteen-inch opening.

Penelope had walked around behind him. "Boost me up."

He wove his fingers together, and she stepped into his hands. He lifted her and she wedged the window open the whole way, then worked her way in, headfirst. He helped her navigate into it, and she disappeared.

Grunting.

Then the side door unlocked and opened. "And Bob's your uncle!"

"At least we won't freeze to death." He walked inside a small entry and tried the lights.

They worked, and he guessed the place had some heat that ran year-round to keep the pipes from bursting. As they walked into a great room, the temperature seemed a balmy mid-fifties. A river-stone fireplace rose against one wall, with a worn coffee-leather sofa facing a wooden table. An overstuffed chair faced the sofa, anchored by a round braided carpet.

A round oak table held four chairs, and a small U-shaped kitchen with stools at the counter anchored the far wall.

Like God had planned it, firewood and kindling lay stacked in a wood hoop near the fireplace. *Okay, thank You.*

"I'll see if they have a telephone," Penelope said.

"My guess is no, but have at it." He went to the fireplace and opened the flue. Then he laid the logs in a log-cabin pattern, kindling and paper shoved inside, and lit it. The flame popped to life and started to crackle.

Penelope returned carrying a couple comforters. "No phone, but two bedrooms—one on the main floor, and there's another upstairs in the loft." Dropping the bedding on the sofa, she headed to the kitchen. "We should have brought the leftover sandwiches."

He picked up a blanket, draped it around himself, felt warmth finding his bones. "Right?"

She had found something, and he heard the clanking of dishes. He went to the counter. "What are you making?"

"Oh, it's totally gourmet." She had opened a bag of—

"Are those saltines?"

"Absolutely. And"—she reached into the cupboard—"peanut butter."

"Wow, protein!"

"I even found gummy worms. Still packaged, and I checked the date. All good. And . . . for the finale"—she pulled out a box from behind her back—"unopened Christmas Crunch cereal!"

She had pulled out a large bowl and now dumped the entire contents inside. "It's a party."

Oh, he liked her. He really, really liked her. And as she stood there, grinning, he just . . .

Yeah, he was in big trouble. Because his brain kept shouting, *Slow your roll there, sport.*

But his heart—his stupid, impulsive, get-him-into-trouble heart—said, *Let's go.*

She carried the bowl of Christmas Crunch to the coffee table, along with the gummy worms, and sat on the sofa. He grabbed the saltines and peanut butter and a couple spoons and brought them over, took the chair.

"It's like an after-school snack."

"Right? Except . . . I'm not sure what an after-school snack is—"

"It's the snack your mom has out when you come home from school. You know, like frosted graham crackers or peanut butter apples or even Rice Krispies bars?"

"You lived a different life than me. First, I went to a private all-day school and we got meals. And second, my so-called snack was takeout that our driver bought us."

"Oh."

She had donned the blanket, something suddenly wan and broken in her expression.

"Penny?"

"Thank you, Conrad. I . . . I would still be out there freezing to death if you hadn't . . ." She looked at him. "You're a nicer guy than I deserve."

He frowned. "I don't think so."

"I *know* so. I mean . . . you sort of got roped into all of this, and now you're eating saltines with me in a cabin that we broke into."

Roped into . . . oh, right, EmPowerPlay.

"Best voluntold gig I've ever been assigned to." He winked.

She frowned but picked up a saltine and a spoon. "What do I do with this?"

"Dip it in the peanut butter."

She opened the jar. "By the way, I sort of like it when you call me Penny." The spoon came out with a gob of peanut butter. "Edward called me Penny. It made me feel normal." She passed him the jar and he dug in.

"You didn't feel normal?"

"Would you, growing up in that house? And after the kidnapping, I had protection all the time. Dad still has a guy who is assigned to keep an eye on me. His name is Franco. He doesn't follow me around anymore, but I have a panic button on my phone. It goes off, he appears, like Superman."

"Too bad he didn't follow you to the hockey game." He spread his peanut butter onto a saltine. "But yes, I get it. I wouldn't have felt normal either."

He paused. "So, I get needing to find justice for Edward, but if everyone else thought Edward died in the fire, why did you believe he was murdered?"

Her eyes widened. "I . . ." She looked away.

"You don't have to tell me—"

"It just didn't feel right. He wasn't reckless. And he wasn't a drinker—didn't do drugs. I just couldn't wrap my brain around it. And I thought, if I could find his murderer, then maybe it would all make sense."

"What would make sense?"

She sighed then. "Why he picked Tia." She looked back at him. "I mean—I get that part. Tia is . . . she's perfect. Smart and beautiful. But Edward and I . . ."

"You were in love with him." The statement issued out, took a piece of him with it.

"Of course I was. He saved my life. But he was four years older than me, so I get that he never thought of me that way . . ." She drew up her knees, wrapped her arms around them, looked so forlorn that he nearly reached out.

Nearly.

"And my sister is always so put together. She's not a mess like me. She's easy to love."

A mess?

"I guess I just thought maybe if I could understand what would make someone want to murder him, then maybe he wasn't as perfect as I thought he was. And if he wasn't perfect, then maybe it wasn't me."

She looked away.

And he didn't get it. "What wasn't you?"

She turned, met his eyes. "If he wasn't perfect, then maybe I could understand why he didn't pick me. Why he didn't love me. Because all I can come up with is that there was something wrong with me."

Oh, Pen.

"Maybe I was too much of a mess."

She said it again and . . . "No—"

"I mean, it makes sense, right? My dad doesn't pay the ransom, Edward doesn't pick me . . . Whatever. Clearly I'm"—she lifted a shoulder—"unlovable."

"That's—are you serious?"

She'd made a sandwich out of her saltines, took a bite. "Oh, my mouth is glue. I need water."

He still had the bottle he'd taken from the car and handed it to her. Held on to the bottle as she took it. "Penelope, look at me."

She shook her head.

"You are not a mess. You're smart, and brave, and a man would be crazy not to fall in love with you."

Yeah, he'd said that. And now she lifted her eyes to him. "I told you not to fall for me."

Too late, maybe.

She smiled.

He narrowed his eyes, let go of the bottle.

She opened it, took a swig. Then picked up a gummy worm and wiggled it at him. Laughed.

The sound was fairy dust, turning the room magical after the darkness had descended.

Yes, he was clearly in big trouble.

"What's so funny?"

"This is my first ever gummy worm."

He picked one up. "Seriously? I'm not sure that's a bad thing."

She sighed. "All my life, I just wanted to be normal. Only, I didn't really know what normal might be. That's why I went to the U of M, why I had a roommate—I lucked out to get Harper. But even then . . . I knew I was different. I just saw the world through a lens of abundance."

"Maybe that's the right lens. Maybe abundance isn't about money but well-being." He had taken a handful of the Christmas Crunch. "When I was younger, my grandpa had a small sailboat."

"You mentioned that."

"He was this great guy. Had spent his entire life in the town of Duck Lake, managing the King's Inn. He loved to fish and sail and tinker on his antique cars, but on Sunday afternoons, after church, we'd take out the sailboat, just him and me. Sometimes we wouldn't even talk. He had this life verse—2 Chronicles 15:7. 'But as for you, be strong and do not give up, for your work will be rewarded.' It felt so simple." He sighed. "I wish it was simple."

"It's not?"

He considered her. "You look at life as abundant. I look at life as a game with options and plays I should make."

"And when you get them wrong?"

"I might let it sit in my brain and tangle me up." He looked at the fire, now crackling, warming the room. "I'd like to figure it out, maybe not spend so much time caught in a power play."

"A power play?"

"The odds against me, just trying to defend the net."

She smiled. "Always hockey with you."

"I've been playing hockey since I was two years old and my dad bought me skates. We'd play out on the lake, and there was just something about the camaraderie of competing with my brothers. They got me into organized hockey when I was three—"

"Wow."

"I loved it. The game is fast—you gotta be always alert, always looking for holes and opportunities. Like basketball, except on skates. And it's tough, like football. And teamwork, like soccer." He lifted his shoulder. "It's the perfect sport."

"You still love it, after all these years."

Her words pinged inside him, swept up the feeling of watching the kids play today. "Yes. I was born to play hockey. I guess that is the one thing I know."

She smiled at him, her eyes reflecting the fire, her hair down in soft waves, long lashes against her skin, and it hit him.

He could fall for this woman. This woman—the one who ate saltines with him and listened to his life and kept his secret . . .

So perhaps that was two things he knew.

A log fell in the fire, sparks hitting the hearthstone, the burning wood rolling to the edge. He got up to push it back and groaned.

"Are you okay?"

"Yeah. I landed on my hip. It's fine. I've had harder falls before."

She joined him as he braced his hand on the mantel and grabbed the poker. Now she took it from him. "Sit down." Using the poker, she moved the log back onto the pile, then drew the metal screen across the opening. Set it back.

He hadn't sat down. And she was right . . . there. So close he could reach out and pull her to himself . . .

So easy. So right. No questions, no tangles . . . and his thought was probably written across his gaze because her eyes widened and she swallowed . . .

"What's happening here?" she asked softly.

"Whatever you want to happen," Conrad said, his heart thick in his chest.

"Oh, this is a bad idea," she said, and stepped up to him.

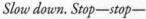

Slow down. Stop—stop—

She heard the words in her head, but they had nothing on the pull of Conrad's devastatingly blue eyes, the way he searched her face, the desire that flickered deep inside his gaze. And she might not be a professional PI, but she could certainly unravel his intent.

Maybe this *wasn't* a game.

It certainly had stopped feeling like a game when he'd looked at her, his gaze intense, and said, *"You are not a mess. You're smart, and brave, and a man would be crazy not to fall in love with you."*

Terribly, she'd wanted him to say, *Like me.* A guy like him could fall for her.

But he hadn't. Because he'd made promises not to fall for her, right?

She, however, had broken her side long ago, maybe. But right now, she didn't care. Not with the fire flickering behind her, the fact that he'd saved her from a blizzard, that he'd made her feel like he'd taken off the body armor, let her see his heart.

"Whatever you want to happen . . ."

This. This was what she wanted to happen. She put her hands on his chest—his amazing, sports-built chest—and then slid them around his neck, clasped her hands behind him, her heart banging, her breath held.

He smiled up one side, then the other, and it lit his eyes, the sun bursting forth from a storm. "Okay," he said, put his arms around her, lowered his mouth to hers.

Softly. Sweetly. Touching her lips like a whisper, his beard a little scratchy on her skin. She just sank into the touch of him, the way he pulled her in, increasing his ardor. She tightened her arms around his neck, and he pulled her closer, diving in, nudging her mouth open, deepening his kiss.

Of course kissing Conrad would be like being swooped up, captured, taken away, her breath caught, her heart leaving her body to reach for his. He was heat and power and light, and then she simply stopped thinking and gave herself over to his kiss.

It had been years since she'd kissed a man—her last boyfriend a boy, really, trying too hard to get it right.

With Conrad it just *felt* right—

She pulled back, breathing hard, met his eyes.

He frowned. "Are you okay?"

"This isn't . . . I mean . . . yes. But are you okay? Are you sure this is what you want?"

His gaze ranged her face, and a soft rumble left his chest. "Yes," he said almost in a groan. "But yes, maybe . . . just . . ." He drew in a breath. "Maybe we take a break in the action here, because . . ." He leaned away. "I don't want to get carried away."

Carried away. As in straying too far from the pretense of their relationship?

He touched her hair, drew his fingers through it, grabbed a lock of it. "You are way too beautiful to be in my arms."

Oh . . . What was that? But she laughed, and it sounded like she was twelve.

He cupped her face. "I can't turn off my brain here, Pen, or I'll get in over my head."

Right. And there it was, wasn't it? Reality.

She nodded, was about to step away, when he looped his hand around the back of her neck.

"Then again, maybe I already am."

He kissed her again. This time with the passion, the intensity, of the man she saw on the ice—all in, skilled, determined, in control, but playing with an edge of danger.

Yes. And maybe she'd been lying to herself to think that she wouldn't completely, hard and swiftly, fall for this man. That she could keep it just fake, no strings, shallow, and professional. She'd probably known it in her heart from the day over a month ago when he'd taken her in his arms.

She trusted him.

The truth of that filled her veins, made her take a breath, relax. Enjoy.

And then she just held on as he kissed her, and kissed her, and kissed her.

Her comforter had fallen off her shoulders, but the room had heated and her entire body turned to flame. He finally lifted his head, breathing a little hard, and met her eyes.

"Okay. You should sit down on that other sofa, and don't move, no matter what I say. Or want to say."

Her eyes widened. "Oh?"

He actually pushed her away, then bent and grabbed her comforter, wrapped it around her, tucking it into itself like a burrito. Then he picked her up and brought her over to the sofa. Set her down.

Kissed her forehead.

"What is this?"

"This is me behaving myself." He put distance between them, picked up his comforter, and draped it over his shoulder like a superhero.

Oh. It was sweet, really, because no, she hadn't thought he'd pushed her too far. He'd left her wanting more.

He sank down onto the chair.

"This is silly. Come over here," she said. "There's enough room."

He cocked his head.

"The fire will die. It will get cold...."

His eyes narrowed.

"I might have nightmares."

He rolled his eyes but smiled.

She struggled and sat up. "And I refuse to let you sleep on a chair. Or the floor."

"There are two bedrooms," he said.

"I already feel like a criminal. I'm not climbing into their beds."

Maybe the word *criminal* sat on him, because he nodded. But he still didn't get up.

"You'd make a good bodyguard with that resolve."

"Don't give me that much credit." No smile, but the flames of the fire flickered in his eyes.

Oh. Okay then. "I fell for my bodyguard when I was fifteen. He was twenty-eight, so way too old for me. And for his part, he didn't know. It was all in my head. But I had dreams of him rescuing me—"

"Were you lost?"

"No. I was Veronica Mars."

"Who?"

"Oh, it's this old television show about a high-school girl who becomes a PI with her father. But she has this nemesis named Logan who turns out to be the hero of the show. He's a rich kid but troubled, but being with her sort of straightens him out. And whenever she gets in over her head, he's right there to help pull her out." She folded her legs inside the comforter. "Although, she rescues him plenty of times too."

"I'm sure she does." His gaze held hers. "In more ways than one."

"He just needed someone to focus all his energy on. And Veronica needed someone who had her back, even if she didn't want to admit it."

He smiled then. "Sounds like a good team."

A beat, and the quiet settled between them. It was all she could do not to get up, walk over, settle herself in his lap.

He ran his hands over the arms of the chair. "When I was ten years old, I went through the ice."

She frowned.

"It was in March, late in the year, when the King's Inn closes for a month—shoulder season—so my parents can take a vacation. Usually we went with them, but that year, they were celebrating twenty years, so they left us with our grandparents. We'd been told not to play on the ice, but we were a little obsessed with broomball, so Stein talked us all into playing. Doyle shot the ball into the snow outside the boundary, where the snowpack warmed the ice—and when I went to get it, I just went through."

"Oh wow. Terrifying."

"Yeah. I thought I was going to die. Jack was super coolheaded. He told everybody to make a chain out to me, and they laid on the ice—all of them holding on to each other's feet—and then Jack crawled out to the edge and grabbed me. He held on to me while they all pulled him back."

"You could have all gone in."

"I know. It's a sort of recurring nightmare. Thankfully, the distributed weight kept the ice from breaking. My grandfather was there with a ladder when they dragged me in—he saw me go in and grabbed it to rescue me, but they'd already hauled me out. I'd never seen him so upset, the way he held on to us. And me. But he called them all heroes."

"They were."

"Yes. And we realized that we were braver and stronger together than on our own."

"Are you trying to make a point here, King Con?"

"Just saying that you don't have to sit in the cellar alone, Penny."

Silence fell, his words landing. *What? Because . . . wait.* Was he saying . . .

He stilled. "Do you hear that?"

"Hear—"

He held out his hand, got up, the comforter falling off his shoulders. "Shh."

The wind moaning and—"Voices."

He walked over to her, pulled her up. "Into the bedroom."

"The—why?"

He had already started to move her toward the door of the main-floor bedroom. "Because what if it's the guy who tried to mow us down?"

She rounded on him. "C'mon, Conrad, why—"

The front door banged open, the one by the kitchen, and then—"Get away from her!"

Conrad spun, put her behind him. "Back off!"

Her eyes widened at the two men who barreled in wearing warm jackets, hats, and boots, and holding weapons.

She put her hands up.

Conrad didn't. He took a step back, pushing her toward the bedroom.

The first of the men held a gun on him. "Step away from Miss Pepper."

What?

Oh . . .

And then her gaze fell to the second man. Blond hair, big—*aw.* "Geoffrey—what are you—"

Except Geoffrey wasn't listening. He came in, took two steps, and grabbed Conrad, pushing him away from her.

But Conrad spun away, disentangled himself, rounded.

Geoffrey slammed a fist into his sternum. Conrad huffed out a sound that hurt even her bones, and slammed into the wall.

"Stop!" She jammed up between them, her arms wide. "Stop!"

The first man—*oh,* and now she recognized Franco under all that body armor—held a gun on Conrad. "Step away from him, ma'am."

"What—everybody calm down!"

Geoffrey grabbed her, pulled her away.

And then Franco stepped up, and just like that, swept Conrad's feet out from under him. He landed with a grunt, started to roll, but Franco pounced on him, shoved him down.

"Don't move," he growled.

"Leave him alone!" She shoved Geoffrey, but he stepped in front of her again.

"Ma'am, just calm down—"

"You calm down! Leave him alone—" She moved toward Geoffrey, and this time he held up his hand, let her pass.

She ran over to Franco. "Get off him!"

Probably unnecessary, because Conrad had rolled and, exhibiting his years playing tough hockey, landed a fist in Franco's face, enough for the man's hold to release. Then he tackled the security officer, slamming him into the kitchen floor before rolling away.

Geoffrey had stepped in front of her. "Back off."

For. the. love. "He's my boyfriend!"

Even Conrad stopped, looked at her, his eyes wide. But that was the game, right? Even if it felt true.

Franco bounced up, blood in his eyes, breathing hard. "Are you all right, ma'am?"

"Of course I'm all right—sheesh—"

"Your car went off the road." He glanced at Conrad, who still wore something fierce, almost dangerous, in his expression.

No, *definitely* dangerous. Clearly not at all rattled by her close protection team showing up at a remote cabin in a blizzard.

"Yes, it did. We got into an accident." No need to make them even more crazy with the suggestion that someone had tried to run them off the road. "But we're fine. Conrad found us this cabin . . . Wait. How did you know?"

Franco gave her a look. "We are always monitoring your GPS. An alarm activated, indicating your vehicle had been damaged. Although, we were already on our way," he said, sighing.

"Why?"

His mouth made a tight line. "Because someone broke into your house and set it on fire."

And if she'd ever wondered if it was real, if Conrad was really on her team, if he might be playing a game . . . He walked over, pushed past Geoffrey, and pulled her into his arms. Held on tight, his big embrace enfolding her. And lowered his mouth to her ear. "Don't be afraid, Pen. I'm right here. And I'm not going anywhere."

* * *

As usual, the explosion hit Steinbeck's chest, cut off his breath, pinned him to the bed even as it played out in his nightmares.

A lucid dream. One where he could scroll back, rewrite events. A technique that his counselor at Tripler had taught him.

So, yeah, he calmed his breathing, told himself that he could rewind, replay. Recast.

And maybe take another good look at what had gone wrong.

He scrolled back—way back, twenty-four hours—to the moment they'd sieged the embassy, taking it back from the Russian special-ops team that had locked down the ambassador and, most importantly, their cybertech asset, Luis Sousa, who'd been taken hostage.

Get in, liberate the hostage, get out—a simple mission with a not-so-simple operational plan. Step one, rig the consulate's security alarm to trigger a false perimeter breach, drawing the guards into the yard. Step two, use the chaos to rappel from the roof, breach the rooms upstairs, and work their way to the consulate director's office via the secure escape route built into the seven-story building.

Step three, escape with Luis and his cyberencryption program to the safe house.

His brain landed in the middle of the chaos, his team separated,

John and him trapped in one of the back offices, pinned down at the—

She appeared. Seemingly out of nowhere, but through a bookcase passage he hadn't seen on the blueprints.

She rolled, came up with a handgun pointed at him. "Stand down. I'm here for him." Short dark hair, dressed in canvas pants, a vest, dark hat, dark shirt—as if she might be part of her own commando team. The Minnie Mouse variety, because she stood maybe five-six, a hundred twenty pounds soaking wet, but clearly a team that included women who could handle themselves.

He nearly dropped her. Except she flashed an American patch from a velcroed pocket, and it stymied him enough to pause.

Then there were pops in the hallway and his chief, Trini, shouting at him to evac, and he met her eyes.

Green. Piercing, bold, focused. "Who are you?"

She wore a scrape on her chin, as if she'd encountered trouble.

"Call me Phoenix. Let's go." She gestured to the open door of the bookcase, then took off for it, holding the door open as he grabbed John by the collar and scurried the smaller man over to the opening.

"Where'd you come from?"

"I've been here for two days. Thanks for screwing up my mission—"

He had nothing to say to that and followed her inside the tunnel.

The corridor trekked behind the walls of the building, cement-lined and dark. She flashed a light down the corridor, and he lit his own torch, and they flanked Luis as they descended two flights, then into the basement room with monitors and a steel door.

"Safe room," she said, and he spotted his guys engaging with the Russian Cobras on three of the four monitors.

The other showed an empty yard outside a different embassy. "That's the Brazilian Embassy. We'll be safe there—"

An explosion fuzzed out the picture, and even the Portuguese building shuddered.

Silence as dust shivered from the ceiling.

"We need to get out of here," he said. He keyed his mic, but the comms had gone down. The other screens, however, showed his team still engaged.

"Clearly not through Brazil." She pulled out a small tablet, studied it. "We're going to need to get creative."

He glanced at John. The man stood less than six feet, skinny, all brains, no body. A cut over his eye had dried, and he'd been banged up, limped. "He can't move fast."

She repocketed the tablet, velcroing it into her vest, and picked up the handgun. "I found a way out, but you have to trust me."

"I don't even know who you are."

"I'm one of the good guys." She winked then and gave a hint of a smile, more of a smirk, maybe, her green eyes almost daring him. "Are you with me?"

He should have trusted her. The sense of it sank through him as time slowed, as memory dissolved through him, into his bones, left her smile imprinted in them.

Phoenix.

His eyes opened, and he stared at the coffered ceiling of the deluxe room. Early sunlight streamed in through the gauzy curtains, and he got up, stared out the window at the red-tiled roofs, the ornate buildings, the boulevard that stretched through the city.

Four more days and they'd be moving on to Declan's resort-like estate on some Caribbean island.

Four more days, and no trouble so far, so maybe he could stop letting the nightmares find him.

He made coffee—an espresso shot, because, you know, Europe—and took the tiny cup outside. His balcony butted up to

Declan's next door, and he stepped out in his pajamas. The temperature hung in the low sixties, balmy for Minnesota but maybe nippy for Barcelona. Traffic moved four stories below, and he leaned on the cement railing, staring down at the city.

The trees were still prebud, and the air smelled of winter—crisp, bearing a hint of chill. He preferred the cold, frankly, his breath caught in the morning air, his body waking with the chill.

"You too, huh?"

He looked over, and Declan sat on one of the wooden outside chairs in his plush hotel bathrobe, also drinking an espresso, a tablet on the round side table. He had bedhead and a five-o'clock shadow. A regular guy. Could be a friend, if he wasn't his boss.

"Sir?"

"The brisk mornings. I thought about going for a run, but I didn't want to wake you."

Stein raised an eyebrow. "I can be ready in five."

A moment. "Your knees up to it?"

Gauntlet thrown. He smiled.

Ten minutes later, they were garnering a little attention—not threatening, just curious—as they ran down sidewalks along the Passeig de Gràcia, past closed high-end shops, a few open bakeries and cafés, the intricate, old-fashioned streetlights flicking off as the sunlight bathed the city. Their feet slapping on the pavement, in rhythm.

"Maybe we should have stayed in the gym," Stein said as they waited at a stoplight. He wasn't breathing as hard as Declan, but he kept his fist pump internal. A woman with a tiny white Havanese on a leash eyed them even as the dog snarled.

Declan shook his head. "I've been trapped in there for three days. No, thank you. I need to clear my head for my talk today."

The light turned, a green man icon flickering to let them walk. They took off, landed on the other side, and ran the length of the block, stopped at the next light. "What talk?"

"It's an interactive workshop called 'AI-Driven Decision-Making in High-Stakes Environments.' It's all about how artificial intelligence can help make quick, smart decisions during intense situations, like in military or defense. I'm going to show that these AI systems have actually been used to do things faster and more accurately than humans could."

"Maybe. But AI can't consider all the variables to human emotion, human panic." Stein didn't know where that'd come from, but . . . okay, he'd blame the dream.

The memories.

"Agreed. I'm working on those nuances. But you're right. A back door is always needed—something to override the AI programs, interject them with the human element."

Like instincts? Experience?

They took off again, and when they reached the next block, Declan checked his watch. "We should cross and head back."

Traffic had picked up, and as they crossed to the other side, heading back, Stein spotted a few Vespas lined up, threaded between the cars, a number of bicyclists also, in the skinny lane.

They hadn't been out in the city much since the trip to Sagrada Família, and frankly, he'd like to keep it that way. Too many variables.

They ran back, passing Gaudí's Casa Milà with its seaside exterior, the balconies made to look like waves, the wrought-iron railings like seaweed. Passed another ornate street lamp, this one with a heater and bench built into the foundation. Stein had read about that in one of the large coffee-table books in his suite.

They stopped at the light, and traffic lined up with more Vespas and he glanced over.

Wait. Maybe he'd seen that Vespa—blue, vintage-looking, the driver a woman with a retro blue helmet to match. She wore mirrored aviator sunglasses, black jeans, a puffer jacket, and Converse tennis shoes.

She turned her head and met his glance.

Smirked.

He stilled.

The light turned, and Declan took off toward the hotel. Stein caught up fast, his heart thumping. *No . . .* His brain was playing games with him.

He focused on the hotel, his gait. Not even a hint of a limp, given his reflection in the glassy storefront mirrors.

They slowed the last twenty yards, Declan's hands on his hips, breathing hard. Stein stepped in beside him. "It's more than just nuance, sir. It's memory and interpretation and even instinct."

"The God factor." Declan looked at him. "I know, Stein. There will never be a replacement for God's creation in human beings. But maybe we can get a head start with the right AI assist." He pushed into the building.

Stein frowned, the words working through him. But before he followed, he spotted a blue Vespa in the reflection of the windows that angled out toward the street.

He turned and froze, seeing the woman drive by. No, couldn't be the same woman.

But a fist formed in his gut, the same feeling he'd had three years ago when he'd retorted to Phoenix, "I don't think so, honey."

He should have listened to his instincts then.

What had Declan said? *The God factor.*

He pushed inside. Four days to go. For the first time since joining Declan, he couldn't wait to get to the Caribbean.

NINE

HE NEEDED TO GET HIS HEAD IN THE GAME.
Conrad skated into the bench, breathing hard, undid his chin strap, and refrained from throwing anything—so *see*, he didn't have to unravel. But—"C'mon, guys. That's the second power play they scored on!" He stared down at his line, the guys breathing hard as the second line went in and tried to recover.

The board had them two goals down at the end of the first period, and the Blue Ox fans roared in frustration, pounded the plexiglass, shouting insults and name-calling.

Yeah, he got that. They'd played like first graders, missing passes, surrendering the puck, and landing sloppy penalties against the Omaha Outlaws. He blamed himself.

Conrad leaned on his stick, watching as Justin snatched up the puck at the blue line from an Outlaw. Admittedly, the kid had skill. And speed as he weaved through the neutral zone, a hot knife through butter. He picked up speed at the opposing blue line, a defender on his heels. His stick handling had improved too, so maybe Conrad's time-out hadn't been a terrible move for the team.

Except—Justin wound up and fired a blistering slap shot—it

went wide of the left post. The crowd roared. One of the Outlaws' defenders grabbed the puck behind the net.

A few players launched to their feet, shouting, banging on the glass as the line fought off the attack of the Outlaws. The game exploded, the players a blur on the ice.

Conrad lost track of the puck, his jaw tight. He'd missed five shots on goal, had been outgunned down the ice twice, missed a couple crucial back-checks, and he ached a little from an into-the-boards shot that'd sent fire into his hip.

Which only turned his thoughts toward Penny and last night's craziness and the early-morning attack by her bodyguards—maybe she didn't need him to protect her after all—and then the solemn drive back to Minneapolis to her burning house.

Not the house, but the garage, and it had been burned to cinders. The fire chief at the scene, still mopping up when they arrived, had suggested an electrical fault—bad, ancient wiring igniting a stack of paint supplies.

Yeah, right.

Conrad had taken Penelope's hand, wanting to tell her that everything would be just fine, that they'd figure this out, but her father showed up with his team to take her home, and with the night waning, Conrad went home to get some shut-eye before the game.

Right.

Her words circled his head, round and round. *"He's my boyfriend!"*

Really?

The crowd roared, bringing him back as the puck shot loose at center ice. Justin picked it up, breaking free, barreling toward the Outlaws' goal. Conrad took to his feet, banged on the plexiglass. "C'mon!"

Justin shot across the blue line, mano a mano against the goalie, faked left—*good move, kid*—jerked right, and the goalie bit.

Open net, right upper corner—*shoot!*

Justin let it fly, a scorcher, toward the net.

It ricocheted off the post in a heart-wrenching clang.

No score.

The first-period buzzer sounded, razing through the audience, and the line skated in. Conrad grabbed his blade guards, put them on, and headed back to the locker room.

The guys walked in, a couple of them pulling off torn jerseys, one walking to the equipment manager to tighten his blade.

Conrad sank down on the bench.

Coach Jace came in, his expression dark. He stood, his arms folded over his chest, legs braced, scanning his team.

This wouldn't be good. They were better than this.

Coach drew in a breath, clearly trying to school his voice. It came out low and almost lethal. "What's going on out there? Did you guys forget how to play hockey? Or maybe you think this is some pickup pond-hockey game?"

Oh.

A helmet had landed on the ground—the emotional outburst of one of their rookies. Coach picked it up, set it on the bench. Sighed.

"This is a disgrace. It's not just about losing the puck, it's about losing our pride."

Conrad might prefer shouting from Jace, but Jace had never been that kind of coach. Now he walked the length of the locker room.

"We need to take control back. No more sloppy passes or half-hearted checks. They are in *our* house. Let's not let them forget that. Get aggressive, get smart, and let's show them who owns this ice."

He looked at Conrad then, his gaze dark. "If you're not ready to step up, you'll find yourself watching from the bench."

What? Except, maybe.

"Now get out there and fight like your season depends on it—because . . . it does."

Again a look at Conrad. His jaw tightened. *Got it.*

Jace disappeared into the coaches' office with the others, and Conrad got up, grabbed a water bottle, hydrated, and then grabbed his towel and wiped his face.

He followed Justin out onto the ice—but right before they hit the ice, he grabbed him. "Hey."

Justin rounded. "What?"

"You're playing with your gut out there. You gotta slow down, think—"

"Step back, Conrad. I don't need a lecture. I'm here because I don't freeze up, thinking about ten different things. I'm fast, I'm sharp, and I'm not playing chess on the ice. Try trusting me—"

"I do trust you—"

"You say that, but every time I get the puck, I can feel you waiting for me to screw up. You overthink everything. Let me play the game."

"I only want you to think a step ahead."

"Or maybe you should stop thinking and just play." He pushed away from Conrad.

A couple players bumped past him, out to the bench. A Zamboni rumbled on the ice, finishing its pass. Conrad stood, stretching, trying not to let Justin get under his skin.

"You overthink everything."

Whatever.

Okay, maybe, because his thoughts rounded back to Penelope and the conversation with the arson investigator who'd asked her who might want to hurt her.

She'd shrugged and Conrad had wanted to jump in with the fact that someone had—maybe—forced them off the road. And maybe the investigator should take a closer look at this crime, and Edward Hudson's arson case.

And it all circled back to his words to Penelope over a warm cookie—*"You, Penelope Pepper, are the connection."*

It still didn't sit right inside him, and *shoot,* now he wished he'd invited her to the game just so he could keep an eye on her—

"He's my boyfriend." Maybe he wanted that too, more than he could admit. Because he couldn't hear that without sinking back into the memory of kissing her.

She'd tasted like peanut butter and saltines and hung onto him, kissing him back like she'd meant it, like she wasn't going to walk away this time.

So yeah, maybe he *was* her boyfriend.

There was banging behind him on the glass, and he thought he heard his name. *Fans*—they went a little crazy during the period breaks—but he turned to wave and—

Penelope. She stood in the seats above him, waving, wearing— wait, *his jersey.* She even turned and pointed at his name on the back. King Con—

What?

"Is that Penelope Pepper?" said Kalen Boomer. "She's wearing your number."

And she looked good doing it too, her dark hair tumbling out of a pom-pom hat, her golden-brown eyes shining. She seemed recovered from the trauma of the past twenty-four hours, but then again, she always seemed to be able to show up with a smile.

He walked toward her, climbed up on the bench, holding onto the plexi. "Hey."

She leaned over, standing on her seat. "Thanks for the ticket! Do you like my jersey?"

Ticket? Maybe he'd misheard her. But, "Yeah—it's great." He gave a thumbs-up, and the crowd roared. She looked up, grinned, and he followed her gaze.

They were on the jumbotron for the world, or at least twenty-thousand arena fans, to see.

She waved and then, as he watched, she blew him a kiss.

What?

He turned back to her, and she winked, then climbed down and banged on the glass. "Go get 'em, King Con!"

Huh. He banged back and then climbed down to where his team had congregated. Jace came out, said a few words, and Conrad let them galvanize him.

Stop overthinking. Penny was here, safe, and this game was his.

He hit the ice on fire. Won the face-off.

It clicked. His passes sharpened, he connected with his wingers, and he moved the puck down the ice. A shot banged off the pipes, but he picked it up, looking for gaps.

Another shot, and an Outlaw nabbed it up.

Conrad beat him down the ice, checked him, and the puck went loose.

Kalen picked it up and slapped it back to Conrad at the center line. He brought it down, the crowd a hum around him.

He shot it off to a wing, then skated behind the net to grab a rebound.

Another missed shot, but he caught it, brought it around—

Tucked it into the goal.

The siren sounded, and the team rushed him, caught him up.

Bam.

They switched lines, and Justin won the face-off. He might have listened to Conrad after all, because he seemed less reckless, passing off the puck, working it toward the goal.

Shots, the play relentless, the rebounds fast, a scrum of players fighting—the crowd hit their feet, fans shaking the glass.

Justin shot—

Siren. The red light flashed, and Conrad pumped his stick in the air.

He caught a glimpse of Penny as they headed back into the locker room after the second period. She waved, grinning.

Yeah, he had this.

They came out just as hot in the third period, the velocity of the game brutal. They changed lines four times before they landed a power play, the Outlaws attempting a poke check. Instead, the stick came up high and caught Kalen in the face mask.

And that was it. A minute left, and the puck rebounded off the boards right to King Con at the blue line. He nabbed it, spotted the goalie out of his zone, beyond the post—

Fired.

The puck sliced through the air, power and precision, a classic King Con shot, and slipped past the goalie's outstretched glove, stick side, into the net. The goal horn blared as the red light flashed, almost surreal, just barely drowned out by the roar of the crowd.

His team descended, flattened him on the ice, the buzzer sounding. Hands pulled him up, and he lifted his stick to the crowd, the fans, and even caught eyes with Justin, who lifted his fist.

And that's how it was done.

He skated in, more slaps on his pads, and even Jace congratulated him.

He finally glanced up to Penny's seat.

Empty. He frowned. Maybe he'd missed her in the chaos.

He'd see her afterward—would text her when he got back to the locker room.

Of course he got delayed by reporters already milling in the designated area. He gave an interview, something short about teamwork and keeping your mind focused on the win—Felicity ran them through a PR course every preseason.

Then he stripped off his pads, his skates, his breezers, and found his phone.

Conrad

Lost you in the crowd. Post-
game cookie?

He even added an emoji. *Oh brother*. But why not?

She was, after all, his *girlfriend*.

He showered, checked his phone—no answer—then returned to the bullpen for more conversation and the after-game press conference. Felicity met him outside the room, wearing her Blue Ox gear. "Good game, Con."

"Thanks." He glanced inside the press room. Spotted Ava shooting questions at Justin, grinning, so maybe that was still on.

"You're up next," she said. "And great job with the jumbotron shot with Penelope. I wasn't sure you'd be up for it, but I'm glad you said yes—never hurts to get some positive PR from the ladies. You're trending."

He frowned at her. "What?"

"Did you like the jersey? I left it at will call for her, along with the ticket. I wasn't sure she'd wear it, but clearly she's all in too, just like her manager said. So good job, Con. Nice to see you on board for once."

He just blinked at her. "I don't—"

"Okay, Justin is done. You're up. Remember—play nice." She all but pushed him into the room.

But all he could hear was *She's all in too . . .*

All in for what?

He sat at the desk, the Blue Ox logo behind him, and fielded questions.

"Can you walk us through the moment you scored the game-winning goal during the power play? What was going through your mind as you saw the opening?"

"As we set up for the power play, I knew we had a great opportunity to take the lead. My teammates did an excellent job of moving the puck around and drawing their players out of position. It's all about precision in those few seconds. But scoring goals like that, especially in a tight game, is what you play for. You have to trust your instincts and your teammates. We've been building up to these moments all season, and to see it pay off feels incredible. It reaffirms that the hard work and the focus on our power-play strategy are making the difference."

He glanced at Felicity, and she gave him a thumbs-up.

Ava stepped up, identified herself. "You seemed to really step up as a leader tonight, especially after the incident with the rookie earlier. How do you balance your roles as a mentor and a key player on the ice?"

He wondered what Justin might have told her. "As a veteran, I aim to lead by example—staying calm under pressure and making smart plays. I support the rookies by sharing insights and encouraging them, but I also focus on my game to ensure I contribute effectively. Balancing these roles comes down to communication and experience."

He didn't let her respond, just called on another reporter. "There was a noticeable increase in physical play tonight. How did this affect your game plan, and how do you adjust to a more physical game without crossing the line?"

Maybe he'd crossed a line with Penny. It didn't feel like it, but . . .

He found an answer. "The physicality definitely ramped up, which required us to be more focused and resilient. We adjusted by emphasizing solid positioning and smart puck play to avoid penalties while still responding strongly. It's about maintaining our intensity without compromising our discipline. One more."

Ian Fletcher had bounced up, and Felicity pointed to him.

Great.

Ian grinned at him. "During the game, we noticed Penelope Pepper in the stands wearing your jersey and really getting into the spirit of the game. How does having her support in the crowd impact your performance on the ice?"

He looked at Ian, words leaving him. Swallowed. Glanced at Felicity, who grinned at him, nodding.

What?

"Um. It's always great to have support from the stands. It definitely adds to the motivation to perform well. I appreciate everyone who comes out to cheer us on."

Ian gave him a look. "C'mon, Conrad. You can do better—your social media has been flooded with pictures of you and Penelope. Are you two dating? What's going on?"

He stood up, his heart banging. *What—what?* His social media? He braced his hand on the table. "Thanks, everyone. That's all for today." He headed toward the door, the world suddenly narrowing at the edges.

Now? Why now? But his gut roiled and he barely made it to the door.

Felicity followed him out. "That was brilliant. Keep them wondering—oh, your Instagram is going to explode!"

He braced his arm on the wall, a slight sweat breaking down his back.

She had caught up to him. "Are you meeting her after the game? Take a video—something candid, as if it might just be for yourself. You can send it to me—I'll put it up and tag Penelope, and her manager can handle it from there." She held up her fist for him to bump, and he stared at her.

"What?" She lowered the fist. "Okay, no video. I just thought—"

"What are you talking about?"

She recoiled. Glanced past him, then frowned and shot her voice low. "I'm talking about you and Penelope Pepper. And your agreement to . . . you know." She whispered the last words.

"No, I don't know. Our agreement—wait." He frowned. "Is this about my coaching EmPowerPlay? I thought that was Coach Jace's idea, not Penny's—"

"Cute. You're calling her Penny. I like it. I'll use that—"

"For what?" He didn't mean to roar, but—"What are you talking about?"

"Your fake relationship. Sheesh." She had lifted her hand to get him to lower his voice. "What did you think I was talking about?"

He stared at her, trying to sort the words through his head. "Fake . . . what?"

She stepped up to him, her voice even lower. "You know—you pretend to date her and she pretends to date you, and you use each other's fame to grow your followers?"

Even with the full sentence, he didn't grasp it.

Not for a full five seconds. Then, "It's *fake*?"

Oh . . . oh no. Because her mouth opened, and he winced, and now his heart really thundered inside him, the room nearly spinning—

"Conrad—I thought . . . oh no. I thought you knew. I mean— yes, I was supposed to ask you, but you didn't go to the last game, and I haven't been to practice and . . . Conrad?"

He pushed past her, already wearing his jacket, his keys in his pocket, and ignored her as she called out his name.

Then he thundered out into the night, to the stars and the chill and the open air and the truth.

Penelope had been playing her own spectacular game. And clearly was every bit the pro.

Talk about playing like a first grader. *What. an. idiot.*

And then, because he didn't know what else to do and it was better than throwing his brand-new phone, he pulled it out, opened his imported contact list, and deftly blocked Penelope Pepper from his life.

———•———

She should have stayed at the game.

Penny turned off the post-game radio show and sat in the silence of the parking lot at Theodore Wirth Park, the looming beach house quiet and cold under the stars. Snow blanketed the playground, and the ice of the frozen lake spread out ahead of her, dark yet glistening under the moonlight.

She shivered. Oh, she should have waited for Conrad. The memory of his embrace as she'd stared at her charred garage swept through her, settled. It was probably what had pushed her to go to the game today when she'd gotten his direct message through her Instagram account. She might have ignored it—it'd felt weird that he hadn't texted her—but then again, he hadn't found his phone after the accident, so maybe he didn't have a new one yet.

Her father had secured a new phone for her, her data transferred, her phone number intact, and all of her contacts imported. And of course, her GPS locator app installed.

The locator also worked on the car he'd loaned her, a super inconspicuous Audi A8, so there was that.

She should probably thank him instead of feeling stalked.

Instead, she'd let herself settle on the memory of Conrad trying to protect her at the cabin. It only added to the sense that . . . this might be real. He'd certainly been excited to see her at the game, grinning at her like it might just be him and her, not a show for the entire world.

And then he'd gone out and scored a goal.

Her phone buzzed, and she lifted it. Not Conrad, of course. Holden Walsh.

<u>Holden</u>
Sorry I'm late. You there?

She texted back.

<u>Penelope</u>
Yes. Waiting.

If it hadn't been for the period break in the game, she might not have gotten his initial text at all. Frankly, she hadn't heard from the man in over a month, and she'd feared he'd gone the way of Sarah Livingston or Anton Beckett or . . . Edward.

She was turning up the heat when her phone rang.

Again, not Conrad.

"Harper. 'Sup?"

"Was that you on the jumbotron? Good night, girl—are you and Con a thing now?"

Right. "You saw that?"

"We're at Jack's parents' house, and yes, we were watching the game. So, the fake dating"—she'd lowered her voice—"is working?"

"I'm not so sure it's fake," Penelope said. "Or maybe it used to be and isn't anymore. I don't know."

"I called it. Bam. From the moment he introduced himself at the wedding, I saw that coming. You two are perfect for each other."

"What? How?"

"Conrad's always been the guy you can depend on. The one who shows up, who gets it done. And you, Pen, need a guy who watches your back, makes you feel safe. Case in point—him carrying you up the stairs at Boo's wedding."

"I could have walked. It was a little overkill."

"Or exactly what you needed. Of course you could have walked. But there's no sin in letting a guy try to protect you. It's how they're built. Or at least, it's how Conrad is built."

Penelope didn't have any trouble remembering his arms around her, at the wedding, at the gala, at the cabin. "He is . . . strong."

Harper laughed. "By the way, I saw you in his jersey. That's a pretty big sign of commitment. When did you get that?"

"Today. He DMed me on Instagram and said to get a ticket at will call. The jersey was with it."

"Cute. Except why did he DM you?"

"Long story. The short is that we lost our phones last night in a car accident."

A beat. "You okay?"

"Yes. He found a cabin, and we did a little B & E, and my security located us a couple hours later."

"What happened?"

She paused. "I don't want to tell you."

"Why?" The word came out soft, low, with some reproach, as if Harper knew.

"Because Conrad thinks we were forced off the road. I don't know—it was slippery, and it was a tiny two-lane road . . . Anyway, it's all good. Or it was until they told me my garage was on fire."

Another beat. "*Fire?*"

"My garage burned down last night. They think it was an electrical short—"

"You've got to be kidding me. Pen. What is going on?"

"I don't know. But I'm about to find out. I'm sitting at Theodore Wirth Park, waiting for Holden Walsh."

Silence.

Then, "With Conrad, right?"

"No, I had to leave during the game—"

"Are you out of your everlovin' mind? What—okay." And now the voice on the other end turned muffled. "We're on our way."

"What? No. Harp. I'm fine." Except, yes, here she was, sitting in an abandoned, snowy parking lot too late at night, waiting for Sarah's ex-boyfriend and the one man linking them all together— Edward, Beckett, Kyle, and Sarah—to show up.

Headlights scraped by on the road behind her, then disappeared into the night.

Maybe this wasn't just a bad idea but an epically bad idea.

"You're right—okay, I'm outta here."

"Good. Call me when you get home."

Yes, she should have waited for Conrad. She picked up her phone, and on the off chance that he might have already gotten a new one, she texted him.

———————————— Penelope
Sorry I had to leave. Got a lead
on Walsh. I'll fill you in after
you get back.

She thought for a moment and then added—

———————————— Penelope
XO

Okay, yes, that felt right too.

Because maybe, possibly, she could fall hard for Conrad Kingston.

She was putting her car into drive when more lights flashed in her rearview mirror.

Walsh. Finally.

Keeping her car running, she got out, letting the dome light bathe her, and lifted her arm. She'd only met Walsh once, although she'd recognize him anywhere, given the images on her crime wall. But maybe he wouldn't know her.

The car—a late-model Ford Escape—stopped thirty feet away, and she closed her door, shoved her hands into her pockets, started to walk toward it.

The trees surrounding the lot creaked in the wind, and she ducked her chin into her jacket. Why couldn't he have asked to meet at a coffee shop? Or a *cookie* shop—

The Escape revved its engine and she paused . . .

It lurched forward, skidding a little on the ice, gathering speed—

What? She stilled, then turned and took off, running hard for the edge of the parking lot, her feet sliding on patches of ice.

The engine roared behind her, but her feet found pavement and she launched forward, propelling herself into a snowbank. She scampered up, then rolled over the edge, down the backside, found her knees . . .

And kept running.

The Escape plowed into the snowbank in an explosion of ice and grime and dirt. Lodged there, the engine burning.

She kept running, the beach house ahead of her. It sat mostly encased in snow, but a trail ran down to the lake from the house, which was clearly used as a warming hut.

She scampered up the steps of the porch, tried the door—*locked*. Glancing behind her, she spotted a figure getting out of the car. *No—no—*

Running to the far edge of the porch, she leaped off it, landed in the snowy darkness, and kept running.

And running.

The park flattened out near the playground, but she edged around it, staying in the shadows, thankful now for the dark-blue Blue Ox jersey she wore over her white parka. She hit the far edge of the park, with the towering oaks and maples, and zigzagged through them, finally secreting herself behind one.

Her breaths puffed out hard as she flattened herself against the tree, her heart in her throat.

Maybe she'd imagined it, but . . .

No. She'd just nearly been pancaked. Peeking around the tree, she spotted the headlights of the Escape, still lodged in the snowbank.

And her car, still running.

But she could hardly go back . . .

Or could she? Because she'd taken her key fob with her, so that probably meant the car had locked behind her.

If she could sneak up, she could unlock it, dive in, and lock it behind her.

It might be preferable to freezing to death.

At the very least, she needed her phone.

She crouched, then peeked out from behind the tree. No movement, and in the distance, the lights on the snowbank suggested he might still be stuck.

This could work.

Edging out from behind the tree, she threaded her way back to the edge of the forest and then moved out to the parking lot, creeping behind the snowbanks as she sneaked back toward the cars. Light puddled in places, but she hugged the darkness, now ruing her jersey against the white snow.

From here, she made out the driver of the assailant car pushing at the front end, the front wheels off the ground. Shouting and cursing lifted into the night.

Yeah, well—seemed like what he got for trying to *run her over.*

She waited until he got in front of the car again, ducked down, and then she scampered, low, over to the edge of the lot, nearly crawling her way back to her car. The other car sat thirty feet away, wedged in.

But her father's Audi continued to rumble, unfazed.

Pulling out her fob, she nearly pushed it—then paused.

It would beep. As soon as she pushed the button to unlock it, her assailant would hear.

Which meant she had to be fast.

She crept up to the car, all the way to the passenger side, crouched at the door, and took a breath.

Here went nothing.

She pushed the button and the car alerted, but she wrenched the door open, flung herself inside.

Pushed the lock button.

Of course she missed and hit the panic button—which maybe she should have thought about before—but they were in a secluded lot, so of course all it did was alert her attacker to her sudden return.

She lunged for the driver's-side door lock. Smacked it, climbed into her seat, and slammed her foot on the brake to put the car into reverse.

Her window shattered. She screamed and floored it.

She jerked back so fast that it threw her forward against the steering wheel, but she hung on, then turned the car. It screeched.

"Penelope!"

She jerked at the voice, turned, and saw the man standing in the shadows.

Holden Walsh?

This man wore all black, including his stocking cap, and she couldn't make him out in the darkness.

But she wasn't sticking around. Not when he held a tire iron in his hand. So—she jammed the gear into drive and again mashed the gas.

She skidded out of the lot onto Glenwood, her heart hard in her chest, her breaths hot, and kept the accelerator to the mat.

C'mon, police, pick me up!

But no cops as she followed Theodore Wirth Parkway, turned south, and didn't slow. No headlights in her rearview mirror either.

She crossed under 394, and her brain clicked in as the road changed to Cedar Lake Parkway. Her heart was leading the way to Conrad's house. The dark, mid-century-modern million-dollar home with security, and the man inside who could wrap his muscled, hockey arms around her, help her breathe again, and maybe ... after a while ... sort this out.

Pulling into his driveway, she turned off her car, her face frozen, aware now that glass littered her lap, her jacket, her hat.

Her body shook as she climbed out.

Light burned in the small windows along the front edge of the house, and around the back that faced the lake, more glow.

He was home. Maybe he'd gotten her text.

Her knees nearly buckled as she walked up the steps to his elevated front door. She pushed the bell, heard it ring deep and long in the house.

She stood, brushed off her jacket, and glass shuttered off her.

Nothing.

She pressed the bell again. Waited.

He was home, right?

The door opened. Conrad stood in the entry, changed into faded jeans, a flannel shirt, wool socks, looking very northland Viking with a little lumberjack thrown in.

She couldn't stop herself. She barreled inside and clung to him, her arms clasped around him. "Oh good, you're here. You're here."

He didn't return the gesture. His body seemed to shudder, then stiffen.

She let him go. Stepped back. "You okay?"

"Fine." He wore a frown, his face dark, his jaw tight.

What? She glanced outside. "Can you shut the door?"

His mouth tightened. He shut it.

What was wrong with him? Maybe, "I'm sorry I left the game."

He shrugged. "No big deal."

No big. deal?

"What are you doing here, Penelope?"

No Penny. The chill in his tone made her step back. "I didn't know where to go. I was . . . I was scared, okay? And I thought—" She sighed. "Clearly this was a bad idea."

Turning, she waited—hoping he'd stop her.

Instead he opened the door.

Opened. the door.

"Clearly it was," he said.

She looked up at him and couldn't stop tears, the way her throat thickened, and she sucked in a breath. "I don't know what I did, but . . ." Then she shook her head. "Never mind."

"Okay then." He nodded and then reached to flick on the outside light.

She stepped outside, her legs again rubbery. What had she been thinking? Of course this was . . . too much.

She'd read too much into the jersey thing, the tickets, the jumbotron.

The kiss.

"What's on your jacket?"

She was nearly down the stairs and now turned. He stood in the doorway, arms folded akimbo, a barrier to his heart.

"Glass."

He frowned.

She swallowed. *Why not?* "I got a text from Holden Walsh. He asked me to meet him."

That bombshell barely flickered on his face. Or in his voice when he said, quietly, "I see."

That was it?

After a moment. "And did you?"

"No—yes—I don't think so. No. It wasn't Holden." Her voice started to shake again.

His eyes narrowed.

"He broke my driver's-side window."

A beat, and his voice darkened. "*Who* broke it?"

"The man who wasn't Holden—"

She didn't get any further. He stepped outside, grabbed her arm, and pulled her back up the steps.

"Inside. And then you need to stop lying to me and tell me what is really going on."

TEN

THE LAST THING HE SHOULD BE DOING WAS letting Penelope Pepper back into his life, let alone his house. But she'd looked scared. And he just couldn't be the guy who left her on the doorstep or shoved her back into the night with glass on her jacket and trauma in her eyes.

Even if he wanted to simply leave her in the entryway and escape back to his kitchen, where an ice pack for his hip waited along with a nice rare steak and an unfinished sailing show on YouTube.

"Can I get you something?" He turned on the overhead light, chasing away the puddled luminescence from the kitchen hood. He'd sort of preferred sitting in the dark.

"How about a reason why you called me a liar?" She had shed her jacket and now came in hot behind him.

Yeah, he'd left that exploded bomb in the entryway, rattled by her gape, her wide eyes. Maybe actually moved, curious, and painfully hopeful that Felicity had been the one lying about the fake-dating agreement.

But he didn't want to stick around to see if hope won, because his chest already hurt. And he only had so much ice for the aches.

He opened the refrigerator and stared into the light, effectively hiding his face from her as he tried to school his response. "Water?"

Silence, and he grabbed the chilled water and closed the door. She stood, arms folded, at the end of his kitchen island, her jaw tight.

As if she might be trying not to cry.

He set the bottle on the counter. "So, even now you're going to act like it wasn't all a game?"

"A game?" She took a breath. "Of *course* it was a game."

Her words punched him, a straight shot to his sternum, and he couldn't breathe.

"Of course it was a game."

He shook his head, pushed the bottle toward her. "I'm such an idiot." But he could hardly kick her back into the night, not in her current state. "Do you need me to call someone? Maybe the police?"

She just stared at him. "Why are you an *idiot*?"

He held up his hand. *No.* He wasn't going there. Wasn't going to admit that she'd completely duped him.

That he'd swallowed whole the *he's my boyfriend* comment, let it sit in his heart.

Let it seed ideas.

"Who was this man who broke your window?"

His question played on her face for a long moment, and then she shook her head and reached for the water bottle. Opened it. "I don't know." She took a drink, set it down.

Her hand shook.

He looked away.

"He tried to run me over in the parking lot, but I got away, and when I snuck back to my car, he chased me down again and broke my window with a tire iron."

Her words made him want to walk over, pull her to himself.

But stupid impulses got him into trouble. He needed to take his own advice to Justin and think.

"Why?" he said instead. "Who would want to hurt you?"

"The same person who burned down my garage?"

He nodded.

"Who might be the same person who burned Beckett's house, and Edward's house."

He folded his arms. "Right."

She took another drink, tried to cap the bottle, missed, and the cap flew out of her grip.

Shoot. He walked over, picked it up from where it had landed on the floor, then touched her arm. "Let's sit down."

He swiped the ice pack from the counter.

"No."

He turned.

"You can't call me a liar without calling yourself one. That's completely not fair. You *agreed* to play the game."

He didn't mean to roar, but, "*What?*"

"You said yes. And frankly, I would have been fine with no, but you started it, that day with the team. So of course I was in. And sure, I probably got the most out of it—but this goes both ways, King Con."

His mouth opened, his mind trying to sift through her words. "That day with the team—wait, do you mean the EmPowerPlay practice?"

"Yes. And the 'date.'" She finger quoted the words. "And even the photo shoot at the Ice Hawks game. Please—you were all in."

All. in? "Of course I was—my coach practically ordered me to do it. Sheesh, have you not met me? When I say I'll do something, I do it."

She swallowed, and what looked like hurt flashed across her face. Then it vanished. "Right. So you can stop calling *me* the liar here." She picked up her bottle, turned away from him, and finished it off. Then walked over and threw it in the trash. "This was a bad idea."

His mouth tightened. "Clearly."

He might have been imagining it, but her eyes glistened. *Tears.* He looked away. *Don't be fooled.*

"For the record, it stopped being fake for me after . . ." She swallowed. "After you kissed me."

He couldn't help it. "*You* kissed *me.*"

She gaped. "Okay, fine. But you definitely kissed me back. And then again. And that didn't seem one bit fake—"

"Of course it wasn't fake!" He held up his hand as if to school his own voice. "I'm not sure what you're thinking, but *nothing* I did was fake. And that's the problem, isn't it? One of us is playing a game, and the other isn't."

She blinked at him. A beat, then, "Wait. Are you suggesting *I'm* still playing the game?"

He shoved the ice pack against his hip. "Unless I'm mistaken, you're the only other person in the room."

"I just told you it stopped being fake for me—"

"And I told you nothing about that kiss, about *us,* was ever fake. I don't know where you got that idea."

"From you!" She pressed the heels of her hands to her forehead. "You agreed to this whole thing from the very beginning!"

"To what whole thing?" And he was back to roaring.

Her eyes flashed. "To the fake dating! So we could grow our followers on social media! What did you think I was talking about?"

Her words sliced through him, all the way to the bone. "You thought I was faking too?"

A thundering beat. Her voice fell. "What are you saying?"

"What are *you* saying?" His breath thickened.

"I thought you were . . ." Her eyes widened.

"Faking everything," he said softly.

"That was the agreement."

Her broken tone, the light shake of her voice shivered through him. He set the ice on the counter. "I made no such agreement, Penny. I thought I was agreeing to coach the Ice Hawks. I had no idea that . . . this"—he gestured between them—"was a setup."

She swallowed, caught her lip, then, "And I thought it was the only reason you wanted to be with me."

The only reason? The fist in his chest loosed, and seeing her standing there, a tear hanging on her lashes, hurt in her eyes . . .

He forced himself not to move toward her. Instead, softly, "I don't need a reason to be with you."

Aw, but the words just slipped out.

Her mouth opened. Then closed. And she wiped a fallen tear from her cheek.

And that was just *it*. He stepped up to her, touched her face, wiped the other tear with his thumb. "Penelope, you're smart and beautiful and brave and funny and . . . no man needs to be coerced into a game to be with you."

His heart banged against his chest as she looked up at him, those golden-brown eyes big.

And he kissed her. Completely without thought, just instinct and impulse and desire. His hand behind her neck, pulling her up to him, kissing her with a sort of possession, a force.

A truth.

She hung her hands on his forearms as he took her face into his other hand, cradling it, deepening his kiss.

Tasting the mystery, the intoxicating person of Penelope Pepper.

And any cold left in his body turned to fire, swept over him as she relaxed, softened her mouth, and kissed him back.

"He's my boyfriend."

Yeah, he was.

He finally lifted his head. "That wasn't fake."

A smile touched her mouth. "No, it wasn't."

He tightened her against him, and she held him back, her arms around his waist as if they belonged together. "No more secrets, okay?"

She nodded. "Do you mind if I stay here? Just until I can figure out who is after me?"

He let her go. "My house is your house. My security system is your security system."

She laughed then, and it loosed the final hold anger had on him. "And your computer system?"

He nodded. "What are we searching for?"

"Why someone would want to kill Edward. Because I might be the connecting piece, but Edward is the flashpoint."

"So, we figure out who killed Edward, and we find our arsonist."

"That's the hope." She looked at him. "You don't happen to have anything besides water, do you?"

"I'll make you a steak." He met her gaze again, then pressed his forehead to hers. "For the record, I like seeing you in my jersey."

"For the record, I'm keeping it, so don't think you're ever getting it back."

He kissed her forehead, shaken suddenly at how close she'd come to being seriously injured. "And next time you go meet someone in an abandoned, dark parking lot, you take me with you." He let her go and went to his fridge. Found a ribeye and pulled it out, then headed to the stove and pulled out a cast-iron pan. Heated it as he seasoned the steak with salt and pepper. "Did Edward have any enemies?"

She'd slid onto a counter stool. "I asked Tia—she said no. He lived a very quiet life. Was a nerd, really. He was working on a highly sought-after AI program. I remember him talking about it to my father at dinner one night. He was hoping to sell it to a tech company—I think he was even entertaining a bid."

"Quantex Dynamics?"

"No. I think they wanted it, but another company had bid for it. I can't remember who the other company was."

He put the steak in the pan, letting it sizzle, then grabbed his laptop from the counter, opened it, keyed in the password, and pushed it toward her. "Do you remember the name of the AI program?"

"Axiom?"

The word nudged a memory in him. "I've heard of that before." He glanced at the steak, turned on his hood fan, then headed into his office just off the kitchen.

The night pressed through the high windows, and he flicked on the light. It splashed over his computer desk, the credenza behind it. He headed to his files and pulled out a thick folder. Opened it.

Yes. He still had the prospectus, the word *Axiom* across the top. He took it out to the kitchen, set the paper on the counter, and returned to the stove. Flipped the steak.

"Where did you get this?" she asked.

"It was a stock offering I was considering through a cybertech company I invested heavily in." He went to the fridge, pulled out butter. "MetaGrid. They specialize in defense technology and, more important, AI applications." He slathered the butter on the steak. "I lost my shirt on it."

"Really?"

He covered the steak. Turned. "Over a hundred thousand dollars. They acquired Axiom, and then the offering went south, dropped in value so much that MetaGrid lost millions."

She was typing. "Axiom is now owned by Declan Stone, as a part of his bigger company, Spectra."

He raised an eyebrow. "He was at the wedding."

"Yes. And he's a friend of my father's."

Another memory slid in. "Now I remember why I noticed your dad's picture on the mantel, the one with his fishing trip to Barbados."

"He loves that picture. They caught a blue marlin, nearly a thousand pounds."

"I remember the fish." He turned and plated the steak. "But what I really remember is Declan Stone standing in the group. Is he on the board?"

She took the plate from him, and he added a knife and fork. "I don't know. But"—she turned the computer toward him—"Axiom *was* owned by Edward. I'll bet this was his company, and after he died, the deal with MetaGrid tanked. And then Axiom was acquired by Stone's company, Spectra. Quantex has shares in Spectra." She dug into the steak.

"That was probably why Declan was on the fishing trip." He pulled the computer toward himself. Did an internet search for Quantex, clicked on the picture for the current board. No Declan Stone.

"Do you think Stone would kill Edward to get his company?"

"This steak is delicious, and I don't know." She got up and helped herself to another bottle of water from his fridge.

He smiled at that, her making herself at home here. He could get used to this, someone hanging out with him in his kitchen, tossing ideas around.

No, he could get used to her, hanging out with him in his kitchen. In his life.

"We could ask Stein. He works for Stone."

She slid back onto the chair. "That's a start." She took a drink. "The other start is to find out where Walsh is and why he sent someone else to meet me in the parking lot."

"Are you sure the text was from Walsh?"

"It was from his phone number, the same one he used before to text me."

"Maybe someone got ahold of his phone. How long has it been since you've heard from him?"

"Since before the wedding."

"And then he just texts you out of nowhere, the day after your house is torched?"

"Garage, but . . ." She pushed her empty plate away. "I hadn't thought about that."

He folded his arms over his chest. "I think the bigger question is, did Walsh and Edward know each other?"

"Walsh owned the apartment complex, so it's possible."

"Do you think Edward told him about Axiom?"

"Why would it matter? Walsh was in real estate, not cybertech." She pulled back the computer, turned it.

Frowned at the screen. "What is this picture?"

"It's the Quantex board. I was checking to see if Stone was on it. He's not."

"I found the connection." She turned the computer back around and pointed to a man in the back, sandy-brown hair, in a blue suit. "That, right there, is Derek Swindle, Walsh's partner at S & W Management Group. I always thought he killed Edward, I just couldn't put together why. But if Edward told Walsh, he might have told Swindle."

He leaned in. "He's in the same picture on the mantel. He was on the fishing trip, with Stone."

She leaned back. "What if they knew about the offering, decided that Quantex needed it instead?"

"But that would be too suspect. So they had to launder the transaction. Swindle killed Edward, and Stone swooped in to pick up the bankrupt company, Axiom, to merge into his own."

"Or Stone killed him," she said.

He stilled. "Or neither. We have twelve people here who could be culpable, if we're going that direction. Including, and I hate to say this—your father."

She cocked a head at him. "Are you suggesting—"

He held up a hand. "No. I like your dad. But I'm asking the question—who might benefit from this?"

"Anyone who invested in Quantex." She'd been typing and now pulled up a chart. "This is the Quantex stock price before and then after they acquired the Spectra stock." She turned the computer. "They had a stunning 209.9 percent, fifty-two-week rate of return last year. Their monthly rate averages over 21 percent."

"Wow. That's life-changing."

"Maybe life-ending, for Edward," she said. She closed the computer.

"Here's the thing," Conrad said. "We can't connect Swindle to any of this motive without proof that he knew—or someone else knew—about the AI program. And that doesn't prove murder. We need proof that he burned down Edward's place and proof that connects him to the ballistics report. Which the police don't seem to have, let alone the right forensic report."

"Which brings us back to the argument that Sarah and Walsh had on her doorstep. Didn't Walsh say he had the forensic report? How would he have gotten that—and why?"

Oh no. A dark swirl had started in his gut. "Penny—"

"We need to get into Walsh's office—probably his home office—and see if we can find the report. Maybe that's even why he texted me—"

"Unless he's dead and someone else texted you!" He didn't mean to raise his voice.

Okay, maybe he did. He picked up her plate and put it in the dishwasher. Closed it with more force that he'd planned.

She said nothing. But she was smiling, almost conspiratorial.

"I don't like that look."

"Like I said. We need to get into Walsh's house."

He closed his eyes. "No, Pen."

"Yes. If Walsh has a different forensic report than the police, we need to know why . . . and who has the power to suppress evidence with the police."

He should call Stein, because only one person came to mind. A guy with power, money, and his own security force.

"Whoever can do that is behind the murders of at least four people." Her gaze hit him hard. "And the attempt on me."

Aw, and that was the twist, wasn't it? If he wanted to keep her safe, he needed to find out who was chasing her down, setting her home on fire, and trying to run her over. "That is a very bad idea."

She leaned forward. "But you still want to do it, don't you?"

"If it means keeping you safe . . ." He shook his head. "How much trouble are you going to get me into, woman?"

Her eyes glowed. "Thanks, King Con. You're my hero."

And what was he supposed to do with that?

———————•———————

It'd bothered her all night—the scream into the air as she'd pulled away in the parking lot. She *knew* that voice.

Or maybe she simply feared she did because Conrad's question about who would benefit by killing Edward had stuck inside her like a burr.

Her father. Who helped run the board of the major stockholder of the company Edward had helped build.

Had he known that Edward planned on selling it to MetaGrid, Quantex's competitor?

Except he'd loved Edward, right? He'd paid for Edward's schooling, been supportive of the man's engagement to Tia.

It didn't make sense, and she'd tossed the night away in Conrad's spare room, in his überluxurious king bed, staring at the beams in his slant-vaulted ceiling, their conversation lighting up inside her.

And not just the speculation about Edward's killer or the anticipation of breaking into Walsh's home, but the words from Conrad when he'd accused her of lying.

Of faking their relationship.

"Nothing about that kiss, about us, was ever fake." And she had

nothing for his soft words, the way they'd crept inside her, found tender, raw soil. *"I don't need a reason to be with you."*

The man could make her weep, especially when he'd made her the extra bed and told her to not be afraid. The way he'd stood in the hallway, an outline of safety and protection, when he'd mentioned that his bedroom was right down the hall, and if she got scared, to just shout.

Since she'd promised no more faking, she couldn't suddenly scream just to test his words, right?

So she'd stared at the ceiling instead, also trying to figure out how to get into Walsh's house. She'd pulled up his location in a western suburb—he lived in an older house, remodeled, but the windows looked original, which meant the locks could be old . . .

Now she'd turned into a cat burglar.

What if Walsh was simply home, and she knocked on the front door?

She turned that what-if over in her head for a long time, trying out the scenario where he would have texted her, set her up like bait, then sent a henchman to do her in.

That nearly made her send out a real scream, but by then it was five a.m., so she sent a text to Clarice.

> Penelope
> **Back off the social media posts.**
> **It's over.**

That should make Conrad happy. No more faking for the public.

Penelope finally smelled bacon frying and rolled out of bed. Probably needed a shower, but she settled for clean teeth (he'd left her a new brush and paste in the bathroom), pulled back her hair, and emerged feeling a little edgy, hungry, and ready to commit crimes.

The first might be stealing pieces of crispy bacon from the tray on the counter. Conrad stood at the stove, wearing faded jeans, a Blue Ox T-shirt that stretched over his chest and his muscled biceps, and wielding a pancake spatula.

Eggs sizzled in the cast-iron pan.

The barest shimmer of sunlight cast across the lake, the night still heavy around them even in the wee hours of the morning. She glanced at the clock.

"Six a.m. You always get up this early?"

"It's not early. And I like my first workout to be before break-fast." He gestured to a French press on the counter. "You'll find cream and sugar in the containers."

She fixed herself a cup of coffee in a mug that said *Coffee, the official power play,* and slid onto a stool.

"Scrambled? Or over easy?" He held up a couple eggs.

"Scrambled."

He broke them into the sizzling pan.

"It's like sitting up at the counter in the kitchen, having Edward's mom cook for me. She used to make me pancakes with chocolate chip faces."

"I'm fresh out of chocolate chips, but I could whip up a cake for you." He looked over and winked.

And there was nothing remotely fake about the way her heart just took off, soared inside her. Yes, she could very much love this man.

Might already be halfway there.

"So, I did a search and found Walsh's address on his formation documents for S & W Management," she said. "I pulled up his house on maps and did a walk around. It's a pretty old house. And it looks like he's in the middle of the remodel project. I went onto the city website, and he's pulled a permit for a bathroom and kitchen remodel."

He plated the eggs. "So, you're still thinking a B & E?"

"No. I have a better idea."

"One that doesn't end with us in the clink?" He handed her the plate. "I also did a check—he has a security system. It's not a fancy one, just an internet company. I think if we take out his internet, we at least have a chance of getting in before we get detected." He grimaced. "I can't believe I'm saying any of this."

"So, you're still in."

"If it means keeping you out of jail, or worse, a coffin, yes." He took a sip of coffee, then set the mug back down. "But the first hint of sirens, we're gone, okay?"

"Okay."

He dove into his eggs.

She'd sort of lost her appetite. The last, *very* last, thing she wanted was for him to end up compromising his career. "Maybe this is a bad idea. . . ."

"We're not going to steal anything, right?"

"In theory."

He sighed. "Fact is, what's been going through my mind is simply that Walsh might be in trouble. Who knows that he's not lying dead in his home right now?" He drained his orange juice, then he slid off the stool, put his dishes in the washer, and headed to his office.

She, too, finished. "What are you doing?"

He returned with his tablet, the digital map pulled up. "Okay, he lives on a dead-end street, so there won't be much traffic. I think we do a drive-by and then figure out how to get in."

"Perfect." She took the paper. "If my hunch is right, this might be easier than we think."

He eyed her, but then swept up his keys and jacket, pulled on a wool hat, and donned his gloves. Led her down the stairs to his garage. He opened the garage door, and there sat her pitiful car, the front driver's window destroyed.

He surveyed the wreckage. "Yikes."

"Yeah." She'd pulled on her jacket, her boots, hat, gloves. And now seeing the damage sent a shudder through her.

"I don't suppose you called the police?"

"And let them take the car into the impound? No. Besides, my dad is freaked out enough."

"He's not the only one." He glanced at her.

Oh?

And then he put his arm around her, pulled her against himself. "C'mon. The sooner we get answers, the sooner we solve this, and the sooner you're safe."

Maybe they should go back inside, forget this crazy idea.

She climbed in, and he set the GPS and headed west.

Darkness still sat around them in the early-morning hour, and he'd flicked on his headlights, a few cars negotiating the icy pavement as he pulled out onto Highway 7.

"Thanks for doing this."

He wore a dark hat, a black jacket, and almost looked like a burglar. Except they weren't going to burgle anything, really. He glanced at her. Winked.

Oh boy.

He slowed and turned off his lights as they pulled into the man's neighborhood. The house sat at the end of a long drive, all black with wooden accents, clearly remodeled and updated, at least on the outside. The kitchen-remodel permit he'd pulled was dated only two months ago.

"He's home," Conrad said as he slowed. A late-model Acura MDX sat in the driveway, its roof covered in an inch of snow, the windows frosted over.

"Maybe. Or maybe he just has to park outside because his garage is full of appliances and remodeling supplies."

He glanced at her. "That's your hunch."

"Yes, and . . . pull into the driveway."

"So we can be caught on camera?" He raised an eyebrow.

"Listen, we can say we were doing a welfare check."

He shook his head but parked behind the Acura. She got out and looked in the car. There, on the visor—the garage-door opener.

"Let's knock first," Conrad said and headed up the steps to the front door. She followed him, stood under the porch, and listened to the bell chime. Darkness bled through the sidelight window.

He rang again and waited. "Just in case he's in bed."

And not dead. But she didn't say that out loud.

"I think he's not here."

She turned and headed down the steps, past the Acura, to his truck. "Can you pop your hood?"

He frowned but reached into his driver's side and opened the hood.

"I need to borrow your hood stand." She held the hood open.

"Why?"

"It's a trick I learned from a previous boyfriend. He used to lock his keys in his car all the time."

Conrad loosed the stand from the base, then gently closed the top.

She'd reached into his car and grabbed a snow scraper.

Then she peered into the Acura. It had a simple lock tab above the door handle. She just needed to flip it.

"How—"

"Watch and learn." She worked the edge of the scraper into the door, pushing the top of the door open and wedging the scraper in to crack open the top of the door. Then she fed the hood latch inside, angling it down to the lock tab. It took a couple attempts, but she hooked the tab and flipped it forward. The door unlocked.

"You can't use a regular wire hanger because it's too flimsy." She pulled out the hood stand and opened the door. Then she reached in and deployed the garage-door opener.

"You scare me."

"Murder podcaster. You learn stuff."

She closed the door and handed him back the hood stand. He stuck it in his front seat, then they headed to the garage.

Sawhorses, cabinets covered in tarps, new appliances in boxes . . . "I remember this mess when I remodeled my kitchen."

He glanced at her. "Are you sure you grew up in that giant house I saw?"

"I just wanted to see if I could do it." She made her way to the inside door. "Fact was, yes, I had the money to hire it out, but where's the fun of that?"

She made to push inside, but he held out his arm.

"Let me go first."

Her hands went up in surrender. "Knock yourself out."

He gave her a look and stepped inside. "Mr. Walsh? Are you here?"

The basement entry held a few work jackets and boots, sawdust, and the scent of oil and age. Conrad pushed open the inner door.

The basement had survived the passage of time, resting soundly in 1967, with an orange shag carpet and an old soot-blackened fireplace. A black leather sofa sat on the floor facing a massive flatscreen propped up on a couple end tables.

"I'll bet he was house hacking this," said Penelope.

"What's that?"

"Where you buy a home, live in it, flip it, and sell it within two years to avoid paying capital gains."

"Smart," said Conrad.

"You do investments, I do real estate. I'm an HGTV junkie."

He smiled and then headed to the stairs. The first riser creaked and he stilled, then held out his hand to her.

"You shouted his name. My guess is that if he was here, that might have alerted him more than a little creak in the stair."

"Right."

They headed upstairs into the main area.

The kitchen—or where there might have been one—sat gutted,

the floor ripped up, walls studded in, electrical wiring running between the joists. The scent of paint ripened the air.

A wall had been removed between the living room and the kitchen, just a beam running across where the load-bearing wall had been, a couple posts holding it up.

"It'll be nice once it's finished," Conrad said. He glanced down the hallway. "What do you think?"

"Let's try it." She opened the first door. "Storage."

"I got something here," he said, sticking his head into the next room. "Table, and a printer and a computer."

She joined him, and in the room, with stained Berber carpet, sat a table with a straight chair, and on top, a closed computer. She opened it and woke it up.

"We need a password," she said.

Conrad looked through the papers on the table. "Nothing here but receipts. One is for a ticket to Barbados, for over a month ago."

"Yeah. I talked to him before then, and he dodged my questions and said he was leaving town. I'll bet that's where he is."

He picked up a business card. "This is a PI's card. Didn't he say he hired an arson investigator?"

"Yes."

He pocketed the card.

"I can't get into the computer." She looked at him. "But why would he leave his computer if he was going out of town?"

He stared back. "Maybe he came back and really did contact you last night."

"So . . . who tried to run me over?"

He frowned. Sighed. "Good question."

Then he stepped out of the room. She followed.

He opened the last door. And his arm flew out.

She stopped, peered over his arm. Stilled.

A bedroom, and a man lay at the foot of the bed, clearly dead, lying in a puddle of rusty blood, a hole in his chest.

She put her hand to her nose, the smell faint, so clearly he hadn't been dead long.

"Walsh?" Conrad said.

She leaned past him to look, and everything inside her froze. "That's Derek Swindle."

Conrad turned and pushed her from the room. "Don't touch anything."

"I'm wearing gloves!" She went in for the computer, but he grabbed her. "Leave it!"

"What—"

"We're at a *murder* scene. We broke into Walsh's house, Penny! Let's move." He pushed her down the hall.

"But what if it has something on it?"

He rounded on her. "Whoever killed Swindle clearly wasn't interested in the computer. So whatever is on it doesn't matter. And I don't want to be charged with theft too. What *does* matter is—"

A siren. Deep in the neighborhood, lifting, and he stilled, his eyes widening.

"C'mon." She grabbed his hand, pulled him across the kitchen to the stairway, then down and out through the garage.

The whining grew louder. She closed the garage door on their way out.

He was already in the truck, engine on, when she climbed in. He pulled out, nearly without looking, put it in gear, and drove up the road, glancing in the rearview mirror.

No cops. But the siren still blared.

"Just drive normal."

"What's normal when you're fleeing from a crime scene?" He glanced at her.

"Normal is not running stop signs." She pointed at an upcoming sign, and he slammed the brakes.

Just a neighborhood intersection, but the tires slid on the pave-

ment, and he had to pump the brakes to keep the truck from ca-
reering into the ditch.

Ahead of them, on the next road, a police car screamed past
them.

Penny put her hand on Conrad's arm, the sinewed muscles tight.
"Just breathe."

He gave her a look.

"What?"

"I never want to do that again."

"Find a dead body?"

He shook his head, then leaned it back against the seat. Closed
his eyes. He looked a little pale.

"Conrad, are you having another panic attack?"

"I think this might be a cardiac arrest." He put his hand on his
chest.

Oh my. Yes, this had been a bad idea. She turned in her seat.
"We're fine. We didn't really commit a crime. We could call it a
wellness check."

His mouth tweaked, a tiny smile.

"You're having fun."

"I'm not. For the love. In the world I live in, it was a crime,
Penny."

"Then why are you grinning?"

He opened his eyes. "I'm not."

"You're totally grinning."

"Yeah, well, it's better than panicking!"

She raised an eyebrow.

He sat up. Turned to her, his eyes wide.

"What?"

"You. Wow."

"What? I don't—"

"You're the answer."

"To . . . world peace?"

He sat up, holding on to the steering wheel, staring ahead. "I got my first panic attack when I made the Duck Lake paper after the Zamboni accident. It was just a police report, but I was horrified. I'd been this sports hero and then . . ." He shook his head. "I felt naked, and exposed, and then I had a full-out episode. My sister Austen was there—saw the entire thing. I started seeing a therapist after that, and mostly it went away. But it's still there whenever—" He blew out another breath. "Whenever those feelings of helplessness, or maybe even embarrassment, show up."

He made a wry face. "Or, of course, when I think I'm going to be arrested."

Right. "So hanging out with me triggers panic. That's beautiful."

He wore a small expression of horror and she laughed.

"No, Penny, that's the thing. I've been living with panic my entire life until . . . you."

"Me?"

"You . . . you make me, I don't know—forget it, I guess. Or maybe focus on something else."

"Like my craziness."

"Like you." His gaze held hers.

Oh.

A beep behind them, and she looked back. They were blocking the road, halfway in the intersection.

He put the truck into Drive and pulled out. Seemed to nod to himself. Glanced at her with a look that turned her entire body warm.

"You."

"I need a cookie."

"Me too." She sighed. He was heading west, out of town. "Where are we going?"

"We're going to Duck Lake. I need to talk to Jack and figure out how much trouble we're in. And to get a cookie."

•———————————•

Emberly caught up with Declan and Stein on the corner of Rosselló and Gràcia, the blue sky arching overhead, the dawn bleeding in through the whitewashed buildings, the greening parkway, the temperatures brisk as Barcelona woke up.

This would work.

Four days of surveillance, and she realized it didn't have to be that complicated. Could be easy, even.

As long as Stein didn't recognize her. But really—three years and a lifetime ago, the world in chaos and the trauma of their disastrous escape should have knocked her out of his brain.

Except, of course, her exit from his life—as he lay in the rubble and bled out—must have imprinted on his brain.

She'd have to take her chances.

"Good morning." She wore her short blonde wig from the reception, had donned a pair of leggings, a running bra, a pullover that suggested she worked out regularly.

Yes. Just not on the streets of Barcelona. She might as well be holding an American flag above her head. But it seemed no one noticed this morning, and the sidewalks felt almost empty.

The traffic, however, had started to build on the streets, bicyclists whizzing by in the bike lane between the sidewalk and the street.

She grabbed her knees as if breathing hard, waiting for the light beside Declan. She didn't spare Stein a glance. Better to pretend he didn't exist.

"Mornin'," Declan said. He hadn't shaved yet today, wore a hint of an exotic aura about him, his pale gray eyes casting on her as she stood up. It didn't feel unusual to him at all that a woman might smile over at him, hope to catch his attention.

He smiled back. "Are you at the conference?"

She jogged in place. "Yeah. I caught your seminar on AI-Driven Decision-Making in High-Stakes Environments. I appreciated you adding the human element. Computers can make mistakes too—"

"Only when they don't factor in the nuances of human personality," Declan said. Stein glanced at her, but she didn't meet his eyes.

"They run scenarios based on outside factors—weather, tactics, mission success—but they forget the unpredictability of the human heart," she said.

"Precisely. Who are you?"

"Avery McMillan. From the University of Illinois at Urbana-Champaign. Department head of computer science."

He considered her for a moment, then nodded. "Right. I heard about your research into predictive analysis."

"Absolutely. It's about mapping the right factors, from health care to global threats."

The light changed and they headed out across the street.

One more block, then they'd cross the street and—well, hopefully by then, Declan would trust her enough to want to save her.

"You submitted a paper on ethical concerns," Declan said.

Well, Avery had. But poor Avery had gotten a severe case of food poisoning right before getting on a plane to Barcelona, so . . . "Of course." They hit the sidewalk, kept running, stopped talking as she kept up with him.

Although he slowed a little, probably for her sake.

Stein ran behind them both. His gaze burned into the back of her neck. *Calm down, sailor.* She just wanted a little blood and she'd be on her way.

It still irked her that he'd chosen Stone for his comeback into the security world.

They slowed as they reached the next light, to cross over the double-lane road and head back to the hotel on the other side.

This felt too easy, really. "It's not just about the efficacy of the prediction, but again, the human factor. Nuances and life events, the human heart. We can't base our decisions on what might be, according to what AI says. Otherwise, we find ourselves in *Minority Report,* only with a computer deciding our fate."

"*Minority Report?*"

"It's a movie, sir. Starring Tom Cruise." This from Stein, standing behind them.

She ignored him. "In it, people are targeted for the crimes they might commit in the future and jailed for those future actions."

Declan raised an eyebrow. "Yes, I see the problem."

"You can't blame people for something they haven't done."

And just like that, her words pinged against her. Through her. Touched her bones.

No, this was different. Declan was a . . . well, he'd already sold dangerous technology to the American DOD, and she'd been privy to a conversation he'd had with at least two global leaders, from Germany and Ukraine.

He couldn't be trusted. Frankly, no one with this kind of powerful technology should be trusted—

She turned to him, standing on the edge of the curb, and that's when she did it—lost her balance, her arms pedaling—

Screamed—not a lot, but enough to enact whatever latent hero gene Declan had.

He reached out for her as she nearly dumped into the bike lane. She turned, as if trying to catch herself, and *bam,* just like that, brought her elbow up into his face.

He jerked back, one hand on her waist, the other to his face—

Blood spurted out of his nose.

"Oh!" She turned, wore horror on her face.

The traffic whizzed by. He stumbled, holding his nose, blood pouring down his face.

"I'm so sorry—" She stepped up to him, grabbed the cotton handkerchief from her pocket.

She just needed a teaspoon, enough to extract the sample for the bio-key. Shoving the handkerchief toward him, she stepped up. "Let me help—"

He'd backed away, thrown out his arm, and of course, Stein had jumped in.

Declan bent over, letting the blood spill on the sidewalk. She put her hand to his back, practically shoved her handkerchief in his face. He grabbed it, her hand still holding on.

And maybe it was her movement, maybe she'd stepped too hard into him, maybe she'd hit him harder than she'd thought, but he stumbled.

Fell.

And he took her with him.

They tumbled into the bike lane, with the morning commuters pedaling hard.

Screams, and she looked up just in time to spot two bicyclists braking hard. She threw up her arms, turned away—

The bicycle hit her with the force of a truck, launching her into the air, the pavement coming back at her fast—too fast.

She put out her hand to brace her fall, felt the crack radiate up her arm.

Then she rolled onto the pavement. Squealing brakes. Screaming.

Everything went dark.

ELEVEN

H E JUST NEEDED A MOMENT OF FRESH AIR.
Conrad sat at the kitchen island, holding his cell phone, staring at Weston Winter's video image as he explained attorney-client privilege and the pro hac vice admission law that let West practice in Minnesota, should things go south. And yes, Conrad had anonymously called 911.

"You definitely need to make yourself available for the police to question you, but let me negotiate an immunity from your B & E before you jump in."

Jack sat at a stool, arms folded, wearing a King's Inn hat backward on his head, a sweatshirt covered in woodchips from this morning's refilling of the firewood to the fireplaces in the King's Inn houses. He'd been the one to suggest Conrad call his lawyer.

Penny also sat at the island, listening, drinking a cup of coffee, picking apart a muffin Conrad's mother had offered her when they'd arrived an hour ago.

Conrad had lost his appetite, his stomach still roiling.

"I'll be in touch," Weston said. "Jack was right to tell you to call me. Just sit tight and let me figure this out."

"Thanks, bro." Conrad hung up. Set his phone down. Looked at Jack, who had escaped to the coffee station on the far side of the kitchen.

"It wouldn't be the first dead-body discovery he's handled," he said as he poured himself a cup of coffee.

"I still think you need to call the police, Conrad."

Conrad spotted his mother backing into the kitchen, carrying a tray of dirty breakfast dishes used by the guests sitting in the dining room of the inn. She wore her blonde hair short, pulled back in a handkerchief, and a full-body apron with the words *The King's Inn* across the front.

She set the tray on the stainless-steel counter next to the dishwasher. "It's always the right time to do the right thing."

"Of course," Jack said. "But it's more complicated than that." He headed toward the door, back to his job as King's Inn's handyman. "Con's a public figure. He's got his image on the team to sort, as well as . . ." He glanced at Conrad. "Well, the last thing he wants is for the press to go hunting into his past."

"Oh, for Pete's sake, '*that past*'"—she finger quoted the words—"happened when he was seventeen years old. It's buried."

"Not deep enough," Conrad said. He glanced at Penny, who was reading her phone. She was probably okay.

And he needed air.

Jack had left, and now Conrad grabbed his coat from the hook by the door and stepped outside onto the apron porch that wrapped the old Victorian. Snow lay crisp and bright on the yard under an uncluttered blue sky, creamy-white snow stretching from the shoreline, marred only by the rectangular ice rink the family had carved out weeks ago for a late-night broomball game.

Guests probably used it also, as his mother kept a supply of used skates.

Conrad spotted Jack driving away on the four-wheeler they used to go between houses. Conrad pulled on a hat, his gloves, ducked his head against the sweep of wind, and stepped off the porch onto a worn path that led from the house to the garage, a newer building that housed the inn's summer furniture, lawn equipment, and snowplow.

And, more importantly, his grandfather's old daysailer, the one Conrad had been restoring for the better part of a decade.

The scent of woodchips and oil stirred as he walked inside. The garage held his father's woodshop, along with storage, and in the center of the room, the Catalina sixteen-footer, turned over on sawhorses, its hull up, the centerboard removed.

His fault. The last time he'd taken out the boat, he'd hit a rock, torn the centerboard in half. He and his father had pulled the boat from the water, and he'd decided to overhaul it, bow to stern.

The last time he'd worked on it eluded him.

The local news lifted from an old transistor, and he turned, spotting his father in the woodshop, holding a chisel and scraping a scrolled piano leg clamped in a wood vice.

He walked over. "Hey, Dad."

His dad jerked, looked up. "Hey, son. I didn't know you were here."

Conrad shoved his hands into his pockets. "Had a thing happen."

His father had stopped chiseling and now blew out the chips, stood up. They'd landed on his flannel work jacket, a few on his gray wool hat. Putting down the chisel, he walked over to a thermos and poured himself a cup of coffee. Gestured to the boat. "Anytime you want to finish sanding her, I'm ready to help."

"I got embroiled in Jack's new project."

"Me too." He took a sip.

"And frankly, I keep looking at all the mistakes I've made, trying to repair the boat." Conrad walked over, started running his hand over the hull. "I should have seen this rot earlier, but I just varnished over it. I'll have to rip out these boards and redo it."

His father lifted a shoulder. "So you redo it. More time for us to chat."

He let a smile free. "I hadn't thought about that."

"That's because you're only looking at your mistakes. From my point of view, the longer it takes for you to get her in the water, the more time I get to spend with my son. Which, from my point of view, isn't nearly enough time."

"Sorry."

"No need to apologize for your life, Conrad. I'm a fan. But I do enjoy it when you show up." He set his coffee down. "What thing happened?"

Aw. "Penelope and I are investigating a murder for her podcast, and . . . well . . ." He ran a hand behind his neck. "We sort of uncovered a dead body."

His father's mouth opened.

"I called Jack's lawyer friend, and he's sorting it out. But . . ." He shook his head. "I'm not sure how I got this far into trouble."

"With the murder investigation, or with Penelope Pepper?"

Conrad had been scrutinizing the sailboat and now glanced at his father. Raised an eyebrow.

"You've been showing up with her a lot recently. Your mother keeps track of your social media."

Oh. That. But, "Yes. We're . . . friends."

"Looks like more than that. She was wearing your jersey at the last game."

"You saw that, huh?"

"You didn't seem to mind." He winked.

Conrad nodded, found a smile. "I like her. She's . . . smart. Fun . . ."

"And exciting."

Oh. "I hadn't thought about that."

"Maybe not. Maybe you don't see it, but you like excitement. You're a guy who just jumps in first, thinks second."

"I try not to. I'm working on that."

"Oh, I know. Because then you spend years trying to untangle your past." Grover walked back to the piano leg. "You can't do anything about the past, son. You just have to learn from it and keep moving." He pointed to his project. "I repaired this years ago, but it was still weak, and it nearly broke on a guest. So now I need to go back and fix it again." He picked up a piece of sandpaper. "The thing is, when I first fixed it, I didn't have the skills I do now, so now I can go back and redo it, make it stronger. And now I'm repairing the entire bench, restaining, varnishing. It'll be like new, only sturdier." He looked up at Conrad. "I know you spend way too much time in your head, son. It might be genetic, because I've spent hours out here ruminating as I'm sanding. But what you're forgetting is that all things are used by God for good in your life, if you trust Him. He's in the process of making you stronger."

Conrad walked over, spotted the unfinished piano-bench parts. "I don't know. I keep making wrong turns, finding myself back where I was—"

"You talking about the panic attacks?"

He looked over at his father.

"Please. I'm your father."

Right. "Yes. They're still happening. And my worst fear is that it will hit me during a game. Which only makes it worse because the more you panic about a panic attack, the more likely it'll happen."

He looked away, unwilling to see that truth land on his father's face.

But his dad bent back over the piano leg. "I'm not going to pretend that you don't have a good reason for them. But the reason you feel so panicked now is that you still care what people think about you. Let's be honest—that's superficial. The only person whose opinion should matter is God's. So what does he say about you?"

Conrad picked up a piano leg, found a rough spot, and found a scrap of sandpaper. "I don't know."

"Yes, you do. He's already shown you. He loves you. And he doesn't love you less today than he did when you were first saved. You've already walked into God's love. Are already living in the abundance of it. So stop acting like you're going to lose it."

"In other words, stop panicking?"

His father looked up and met his eyes. "In a word, yes, although I know that's easy for me to say. I don't step out on the ice two or three times a week for a game, playing my heart out so that people can yell at me when I mess up."

Conrad shrugged.

"Good game on Sunday, by the way. When's your next game?"

"Wednesday. No physical practice today, but we're reviewing tape later. Then I need to head back out for tonight's practice with the Ice Hawks."

"The EmPowerPlay team."

"I'm helping out."

"Good for you. I wasn't sure you'd ever coach again after . . ." He made a face. "Well, good for you."

"Yeah, well, Jeremy Johnson is on the team, although I haven't seen him yet."

His father's smile dimmed. "Joe is in the hospital. Infection in his leg. Got a staph infection. Our church is praying."

Conrad stilled.

His father put down the sandpaper. Walked over and put his hands on Conrad's shoulders. "This is not your fault."

"It is, actually."

"The initial accident, sure—you had a role to play. But Joe has forgiven you, and so has God. I was there, Conrad. I remember you going in to apologize."

"I mouthed words, but I remember being pretty angry, mostly at myself."

"Defensive. I remember." His father considered him. "I know it doesn't feel right to forgive yourself, but you should . . . and then let it make you a better person."

"It just feels like I can't untangle myself from the guilt."

His father nodded. "Like Reuben."

"Reuben?"

"Joseph's oldest brother."

"Joseph from the Bible? As in the coat of many colors?"

"The very one. His oldest brother, Reuben, fought with his other brothers when they sold Joseph into slavery. And you know, it burned inside him for years, because twenty years later, when they went to Egypt to buy grain and Joseph tested their hearts by threatening to throw them into prison, Reuben offered himself as tribute. He still carried that guilt."

"And rightly so. They sold him into slavery."

"And that is what guilt does. Sells us into slavery. Only mercy, only forgiveness, sets us free."

Conrad was repentant. But maybe Joe Johnson didn't know that. Not really.

"Listen. You can't fix the past. Only God can do that. Consider Peter on the shore after he betrayed Jesus. He couldn't look at him. But Jesus forgave him, restored him. And this mercy impacted the entire church for the rest of time." Grover slapped Conrad's shoulder, turned away. "You don't need to unravel everything—you just need to put your reputation and your actions into God's hands and follow his voice. Learn, yes, but don't keep looking behind. Let mercy abound."

"Sometimes mercy just feels too big in the face of the fallout."

"That's exactly the point. Because to paraphrase my favorite Jack Nicholson line—'We can't handle the truth.' Now, can I get you to take this thermos in and get me more coffee?"

Conrad grinned. "Sure." He took the thermos. "Thanks, Dad."

"I expect a couple tickets at will call next time in I'm in town."
He picked up the sander.

Conrad headed outside, back up the trail. Frowned when he
spotted Penelope on the porch, coat on, pacing, talking on the
phone.

He looked at her, but she was turned slightly away, her jaw tight.
Huh.

He stepped inside and walked over to the coffeepot. His mother
had vanished. He filled his dad's thermos, then wrapped a leftover
bran muffin in a napkin and was about to head back outside when
Penny pushed open the door.

She wore darkness in her expression, a sort of panicked, horrified set to her jaw.

"What?" He set the thermos back on the counter.

"That was the arson investigator." She set the phone on the
counter. Pressed her hand over it. "They found a body in my garage."

It took a second. Then, "Your *burnt* garage?"

"That's the one. The body was in a bag in my old potato bin.
He wanted to ask me some questions to add to my statement."

"Who was the victim?"

She closed her eyes, almost pained, and then took a deep breath.
"They just identified him as Holden Walsh."

And he simply followed the impulse to walk over, wrap his arms
around her, and hold her tight.

●────────────●

Maybe she should just walk away.

The thought washed through her, turned Penelope to stone as
Conrad held her. Even her breaths had stopped, caught inside her.

"Did the investigator say anything about how they found him
or what the medical examiner said?" He let her go, leaned away,

so much emotion in his blue eyes it sort of melted through her, into her bones, put a dent in the terrible chill inside.

"No. He just said they found him in a bag in my bin. It's an old garage, and I used the bin for firewood, except after the remodel, I installed a gas fireplace, so I haven't used it for . . . well, since last year."

"So he could have been in there—"

"Since he left—or *didn't* leave—for Barbados. He was frozen through, so he might have been there for a while."

His mouth made a grim line.

She nodded, backed away, her arms around herself. "I don't know, but I was sort of thinking that Walsh might have killed Swindle . . ." She frowned, "But of course, why?"

"Maybe Swindle killed Sarah—you had thought that before . . ."

"I did, but I couldn't figure out a motive. I still don't have one— unless she knew that Swindle was involved in Edward's death." She pressed her hand against her stomach. Maybe she shouldn't have eaten that muffin, except how was she supposed to turn down one of Mama Em's baked goods? The woman possessed the skills of a French baker.

As if conjured up, Mama Em came into the kitchen, holding a half-eaten lemon-blueberry cake on a cake stand. She set it on the island. Looked at Conrad, then Penelope. "You okay?"

Conrad raised an eyebrow at Penny.

"Yes," Penny said.

"I have to run this out to Dad." Conrad left his gaze on her, a question in his eyes, long enough for her to nod. *Sweet.*

He picked up the thermos and a muffin wrapped in a napkin and headed outside.

Mama Em—the name that Harper had called Conrad's mom during the wedding—just felt right. The woman possessed enough mom in her to share with the entire county. No wonder she made such a good hostess.

Now it seemed she activated her inner mom as she walked over to Penelope. She pulled out a stool and patted it.

Penelope didn't have a bone to resist with.

"What has you so spooked?" She took a stool for herself, and her gaze went to the closed door. "My son hasn't done anything—"

"No. Of course not. He's . . . absolutely fantastic."

Her blue eyes warmed. "I had a feeling about you two at the wedding. And I've been seeing all the posts on social media."

Oh. Those. Yes. "We've been working on the Ice Hawks team together."

"I'm so glad he's coaching again. He carried his shame around too terribly long." She shook her head. "It wasn't even his idea to fool around with that Zamboni. It was out on the ice, and one of the other players got on it and started it up. He climbed up because the kid lost control. And then, of course, it all went terribly out of control." Her mouth made a grim line. "I think he sometimes feels like his life is still skidding along the ice."

And Penelope sure wasn't helping stop that feeling.

"What's that face?" She touched Penelope's hand. Warm, firm.

"I think I've gotten us into big trouble."

Her eyebrows rose.

"It's not . . . personal. But I've been investigating this case for my murder podcast, and I just lost my last lead."

"Oh, I'm sure you'll figure it out. I've been listening ever since the wedding. It's quite interesting. I love how you use Agatha Christie quotes."

"I was a huge AC fan growing up. My callers sometimes use her quotes too. There's this one caller who always signs off with 'If the fact will not fit the theory—let the theory go.'"

"That's a good quote. I was thinking of calling in, but I don't have anything useful to add." She gave Penelope a wry smile. "But I did agree with the caller you put up last week who said that it was probably someone close to Sarah. There was no forced entry, so she probably trusted him. Like her friend Kyle."

"He claimed all the way to the end that he was innocent." Penelope didn't want to add that he'd been found murdered too.

"Yes, well, I've read enough Agatha Christie novels to know it's the person you least expect."

"At this point, I don't expect anyone." Penelope folded her arms on the island and put her head down on them. "I just want to go back to the beginning and become a house flipper."

Conrad's mother laughed. "Why did you get into murder podcasting?"

"I don't know. I got sort of obsessed with true-crime novels as a kid, and then in college I thought about being a lawyer, but really, I liked telling stories. And of course, there was my own sense of justice, which probably started when I was a kid."

"When you were kidnapped by your nanny."

She looked up at Mama Em. "You know about that?"

Mama Em got up. "Coffee?"

"Always."

She headed to the coffee station. "I remember the story. I had my own kids at the time, and your mother's plea on television, for the kidnapper to give you back, really touched me. I prayed for you. And then when your nanny and her boyfriend were killed during the ransom handoff, I was so angry. We'd never know why they did it."

"For the money."

"Right. But to have the trust of a family, only to betray it . . . Wicked."

Penelope shrugged. "That's why my dad has multiple generations of the same family working for us. My bodyguard, Franco, is the son of my father's bodyguard, now retired. And our housekeeper stayed with us until she passed away. My sister was going to marry her son. But he was . . . killed." She didn't know why she kept the murder out of her story, but maybe she simply couldn't face how many bodies were dropping around her.

You, Penelope Pepper, are the connection.

No. She didn't even know Derek Swindle. Had never met him. And had only met Holden by phone, never in person, so there went that theory. Still, she didn't have to meet someone to be connected to their death . . .

"I know my mother was terribly hurt by Carmen's betrayal."

Mama Em put the mug of coffee in front of her. Pulled over a condiment tray. "Carmen?"

"My nanny." Penny doctored the coffee. "She started as a foreign exchange student and then ended up staying after my father sponsored her. She was with us for seven years before she . . . well, before she kidnapped me."

"Oh, that's awful."

"It might have been worse if I hadn't gotten away and then hidden until my parents got home, with the help of the housekeeper's boy, Edward. And then my father's bodyguard, Vincent, came to get me. I'll never forget seeing the light pour in as the dumbwaiter door cracked open, and then there was Mr. Vincent, holding his arms open for me. I'd never felt so safe. He carried me upstairs to my mom, and she just held me and cried. I'll never forget that. She was always so put together, so . . ." She sighed. "Anyway, I hated that I put them through that."

Silence, and Mama Em frowned at her. "*You* put them through that?"

She nodded. "I heard my parents fighting maybe a few days later. My mother sounded furious. She was yelling at my dad—I could hear them through the bedroom door. She said that he'd let it get too far, that I could have gotten killed."

She took a sip of coffee. *Perfect.* "I think it was because he refused to pay the ransom."

"He refused?"

230

"That's what Edward overheard from the nanny and her accomplice, Nicolai, one of the guys on the security team. But I never had the courage to ask my dad."

"Oh, honey."

"I don't know. Edward could have misheard. I did hear my dad tell my mom that if I hadn't run away and hid, they would have found me and it would have all been over earlier, so my guess is that maybe there are things I don't know." She took a deep breath. "It did make me aware of the danger of having money. And how I needed to be careful."

"That's a hard way to live your life. Always fearing someone is going to betray you."

Penelope looked away.

"And no amount of trying to understand the darkness that lurks in the human heart will make you feel safe."

She met Mama Em's gaze.

"I'll bet you were terrified."

She nodded.

"But you don't look terrified now. In fact, I remember you at the wedding, after Kyle hurt you, and I kept thinking, *She's one brave woman.*" Mama Em covered Penelope's hand. "And you are, Penelope. And smart, and determined to find justice. But the truth is that finding answers isn't going to give you peace. You think it will, but it won't erase what has been done to you. And it won't erase the crimes committed.

"The only thing that brings peace is knowing that, whatever happens, you are loved. You are carried. Worry—or even the relentless pursuit of justice—is just a form of control. You want to figure it all out, make sure none of this happens again. But really what you are saying is, 'God, I think your intent is to leave me unprotected and vulnerable, so I need to make sure that doesn't happen.'"

Penelope stared at her coffee. "My mother is a woman of faith.

And we went to the local Episcopal church all my life, but . . . yeah. I'm not sure where God was when I was kidnapped and locked in the basement cellar."

"Right there with you."

She looked up. And somehow heard her own voice. *"I ate some apples and then opened a jar of pickles. Two days in, the door unlocked. It was Edward."*

She had been warm, and fed, and spared.

"It's hard to see in the midst of the darkness, but when we need Him most, God doesn't abandon us. But we often don't look for Him. We keep our eyes on the darkness. God is the light that shines in the darkness, and not even evil can overcome it."

Steps on the porch. *Conrad.*

"Out of the depths I have cried to You, for with the Lord there is lovingkindness and abundant salvation. Paraphrase mine, from Psalm 130." Mama Em winked. "Don't let circumstances dictate the quality of your life."

Then she got up as Conrad came into the house.

It was like sunshine and heat pouring into the room, the way he walked, his gaze going right to Penelope's. And though his mother moved away to the sink, she could still hear Mama Em's words.

"That's a hard way to live your life. Always fearing someone is going to betray you."

Yes, it was.

But maybe not anymore.

"We need to get going," he said. "I have practice."

She slid off the stool. Walked over to Mama Em, who stood at the sink, her arms in the suds, and gave her a hug. "Thank you."

"Make sure you take a muffin on your way out."

Conrad held out her jacket, and she grabbed her gloves and hat.

"What was that about?" He hit his fob and unlocked his door.

She said nothing as she got into the truck. Then, "You can drop me at my house."

He actually laughed. "Sweetheart, until we figure out who put a dead man in your potato bin, I'm not letting you out of my sight."

His gaze landed on hers.

And she couldn't have walked away if she'd wanted to.

———•————————•———

He didn't know if Avery McMillan had done it on purpose or by accident, but either way, Steinbeck saw the entire thing in slow motion as he stood in the curtained bay inside the emergency room of the Hospital Clínic de Barcelona, watching doctors stitch up his bloodied boss.

Two seconds earlier and Stein would have been able to fully rescue Declan from traffic, keep the bicyclist from smashing into him.

As it was, he'd had a hold on Declan, managed to jerk him back, kept him from flying into the motorized traffic. The bicyclist had hit him, however, and managed to slice open Declan's shin, send him flying into a light pole, which he bounced off, landing on the pavement with a wicked bonk to his head.

Which was why Stein had insisted on the CT, just to make sure Stone's brains were intact.

Now they were stitching up his shin where the EMTs had taped on gauze pads, his blood saturating them as well as the ones packed on his damaged nose. He'd sport a couple raccoon eyes tomorrow, given the blood flow. In the tiled hallway, a few voices lifted, announcements made over the speakers, and the smells of antiseptic and bleach burned into Steinbeck's nose.

Memories. He shook them away, but he didn't know what was worse—the churn that always stirred in his gut over his own medical trauma so many years ago or . . . well, or his current epic fail.

He shouldn't have let the woman get that close. But she'd seemed . . . well, he'd just kept remembering the woman he'd danced with, and her smile might have hypnotized him a little, stirring to life the memory of Phoenix, and he'd been off his game.

And nearly gotten his boss killed.

Maybe he should resign.

"Calm down, Steinbeck. I'm fine."

He raised his head to look at Declan—his nose taped, his hands bandaged, a tech working on his leg. The gathered bloody gauze piled in a hazardous-material bin next to him.

"You're not fine."

"Please. I'm more worried about Avery. Have you checked on her?"

His mouth pinched. "Not since the EMTs put her in an ambulance."

Declan raised an eyebrow.

"Yes, sir," Stein said.

"Can you get me some water too?"

Stein stepped through the curtain and walked down the hall, past the other bays, some of them with their curtains drawn. A toddler with his mother in one bay, a teenage girl in another. He didn't see the blonde anywhere.

The nurses' station was empty, and he had to wait a long moment for a nurse to arrive—a woman, her dark hair pulled back, wearing a pair of teal scrubs, a stethoscope around her neck. She addressed him in Spanish and then changed to English. "Can I help you?"

"I'm looking for the woman brought in earlier—blonde, American, petite."

"And you are—"

"A friend. We were together." Close enough.

"Yeah, ah, she was sent to imaging and, I believe, orthopedics for casting."

"She broke something?"

"I'm not sure, sir."

He could still see her flying through the air, the hard slam into the pavement, right in front of oncoming traffic.

He'd nearly run to her, but Declan lay broken too—

A couple Vespas had stopped in front of her, one of the men getting off. And by the time the EMS had shown up, she'd been sitting up, holding her arm. Had glanced at him at least once with an expression he couldn't place. Almost desperation. Or maybe pain.

He nodded, ran his hands down his face. "Vending machine anywhere?"

"Down the hall." She pointed out of the ER area, into a hallway, and he headed out, into the austere waiting room with the orange formed seating, the windows that overlooked the stately courtyard. Of course the hospital had to be a historical building, with columns that cordoned off the monastic style, and inside, a grand staircase to the second floor, travertine tile flooring, a renaissance feel that suggested learning and grandeur alongside new technology.

He stopped at a vending machine tucked into a corner, dropped in a euro, and a bottled water fell to the gap. He scooped it up and headed back to the ER.

No more conference. He didn't know why, but the accident sat like a burr under his skin. Something felt off, not random . . .

He entered the ER, glanced at the nurses' station. The tech who'd been cleaning up his boss stood at the desk, talking with the nurse. Stein nodded at him—good, maybe now they could go home—and then turned toward Declan's bay at the end.

Slowed. *What—*

Avery stepped out of the curtained area, her satchel slung over her shoulder, holding a plastic bag. She wore a cast in a sling but seemed to be moving just fine.

But wait, wait—was that . . . bloody gauze? *What—*

"Avery!" He lifted his voice and she jerked, turned.

And just like that, memory slammed into him. Those green

eyes—had they been green all along?—and the scrape on her jaw, the set of her mouth. *"Are you with me?"*

The sense of it punched him in the sternum, and he froze.

Her eyes widened.

No—

She whirled around and took off.

What—

He dropped the bottle and sprinted after her. "Hey!"

She hit the doors, the ones to the street, and exited.

He caught them just as they closed, pushed out.

The wide plaza in front of the hospital teemed with university students.

Beyond, on the street, traffic whizzed by, and he spotted her entering the crosswalk, still at a run.

Sort of a run. Her sling pushed her off-balance. Except, even as he watched, she flung off the sling, left it on the sidewalk, and disappeared into the shadows.

Why was she running? For a second, he debated. Follow her—

Or stay with Declan.

He stopped, his fist clenched, glanced back at the hospital. What had she been doing in Stone's cubicle?

What if—

He spun and took off back to the ER, breathing hard as he pushed back through the doors into the secured area—

He alerted a couple security guards, but he nearly took out the curtain as he skidded into Declan's bay.

His boss sat on the gurney, working his running pants back on, his hospital gown discarded in a hamper. "You ready to go?" Declan's eyes widened. "You okay, Stein?"

Stein's breaths shoved out hard, and he put a hand to his mouth, glanced around the room.

Had she really stolen the hazardous waste from Declan's injury? "Was Avery here?"

"Yeah. She stopped in to see how I was doing."

"Did you see her take something?"

He shook his head. "No. I don't think—"

"The plastic bag with all the hazardous waste. Your blood—did she take that?"

Declan frowned. "I don't know. I thought the tech took that when he left."

Stein nodded, walked out of the room.

A bin sat across the hallway marked with the Unicode biohazard symbol.

Maybe he'd mis-seen.

Yes. It had to have been her bloody sweatshirt, or the handkerchief she'd used on Declan.

Still, the whole thing sat inside him, a fist.

He turned just as Declan pulled back the curtain. "They discharged me. Let's go."

"Yes, sir." Then he paused. "Is there any reason why someone would want your blood?"

Declan frowned. "My blood?"

"I don't know. For . . . DNA? Or some other reason?"

Declan blinked, then ran his hand across his mouth. "Yes. Yes, there is." He shook his head. "Wow. I didn't see that."

"See what?"

"Get me back to the hotel. Conference is over. I need to make some calls." He seemed almost shaken. "And then call my pilot. I need a flight out, to Montelena."

Stein nodded, pulled out his phone, his mouth tight as he dialed.

He didn't expect Declan to look over at him, frown. "You okay, Steinbeck? You look like you've seen a ghost."

He raised an eyebrow. *Maybe. Yes. That was it.*

Because in his heart, he knew—

Call Me Phoenix was very, very much alive.
And he was very, very much in trouble.

TWELVE

CONRAD DIDN'T KNOW WHY HIS TRUCK DROVE him to the North Star Arena, why he pulled in and sat outside, hanging on to the steering wheel, Penelope quiet beside him. Her brain had probably gotten stuck on Dead Guy in Her Potato Bin, and rightly so. But his seemed to keep rounding back to his father's words. . . .

"You don't need to unravel everything—you just need to put your reputation and your actions into God's hands and follow His voice. Learn, yes, but don't keep looking behind. Let mercy abound."

But he couldn't get past the sense that maybe he needed another go-round at an apology to truly break free of the past.

Of the hold Joe Johnson had on him.

So he took a breath, then reached for the door handle.

Penelope put a hand on his arm. "I know there's a reason, but why are we at the Ice Hawks' practice?"

"There's something I have to do," he said.

She just nodded and turned to get out, and he wanted to grab her back and kiss her. Something about her trusting him, not asking questions, felt like they might be a team.

And it hit him again, as she took his hand walking into the arena, that he could love this woman. Maybe he had already started to—the way she saw him, didn't make him feel like he had to be a superstar, kept his secrets, and even needed him—yes, he wanted Penelope Pepper wearing his jersey, in his life, in his arms.

He tightened his grip on her hand as they entered the chill of the arena, shouts and the slap of the puck pinging in the air.

"Why do they have practice in the afternoon?"

"Presidents' Day. No school." He glanced over at the stands and spotted a few familiar faces. Parents who'd shown up at the game last weekend and even at practice.

No Joe Johnson, but he'd only given a cursory glance.

He lifted a hand to Simon, who spotted him from the ice. Simon was running the kids through a puck-handling obstacle course, round and round the rink. Conrad and Penelope walked over to the boards, and he leaned down, crossing his arms, watching. Searching.

And . . . *there*.

Jeremy Johnson, thicker and sturdier in his breezers and pads, wove through the cones, not sloppy as he handled the puck, so the kid had some talent. *Okay then*. Conrad didn't know why seeing him out there released a fist in his chest, but—

"Hey, King! Yeah, King Con! That game last night was a joke, man. You call that playing? My grandma could handle the puck better!"

He stilled, looked over, and spotted, *aw*, Steve Bouchard in the stands. *Perfect*. And it seemed the guy had started his day drinking, holding a beer as he got up.

"We pulled it together in the end—"

"Pulled it together? Man, we need more than that! You're the center—you're supposed to be leading out there. The passing was sloppy, and it felt like you didn't even show up until the third period. These kids here are showing more hustle than I saw last night!"

He held up his hands. "Not here, okay?"

Steve jumped off the edge of the bleachers, heading toward him. The other parents seemed to tense, watching.

"Listen—" Conrad started.

"It's time to retire, old man. We got the Blade. We don't need you—"

"Hey." Penelope stepped in front of Conrad. "Back off! You don't talk to him like that. You have no idea how hard he works— both on and off the ice. This isn't the time or the place."

Perfect. Just what he needed—Penelope Pepper defending him. "Penny—let it go. He's just a jerk—"

"A jerk?" Steve stepped up to him. "I remember you, King Con—the hotshot from Duck Lake. Weren't you the guy who drove over Joe Johnson with a Zamboni? Crippled him?"

Conrad stilled. Especially when he realized that the practice on the ice had stopped, kids lining up against the boards.

He cut his voice low. "Let's just take it down a notch. This is a kids' event. If you want to discuss the game, maybe let's take it outside."

"Oh, you want to go outside?"

More than he wanted to admit. He held up a hand. "Not like that—"

"Yeah, buddy, let's go outside!"

Penelope took a step toward Bouchard. *Aw—*

Steve took one look at her, smiled, and Conrad saw something ugly take shape.

"Sure, honey. You want to go outside?" He tossed his beer away. It hit the bench, splashed. Penny held up a hand to the spray, but Conrad had stepped up behind her, snaked his arm around her waist, and jerked her back.

He took most of the liquid on his pants and shirt.

But he turned, set her away, met her eyes. "Stay."

Then he rounded on Steve. Lowered his voice, met his eyes. "You do not want to do this. Calm down."

Bouchard swung at him.

Conrad stepped back, dodged the hit, the momentum jerking Bouchard off-balance. The man went sprawling.

Silence in the arena.

Except for Penelope. "Stay down, jerk!"

Conrad turned, grabbed Penelope's hand. "Let's go."

"Steve!" Missy Bouchard had scrambled off the bleachers toward her husband. He pushed her away. His eyes lit, fire.

"That's assault!" He pointed at Conrad. Smiled. "Missy, call the cops."

Aw, seriously? "I didn't touch you—"

Steve popped up. "You pushed me."

"C'mon, Penelope, let's go." Conrad made to shove past Bouchard, but Bouchard stood in the way, got in his face.

And that was just enough. "Bouchard, back off." He put his arm out to push him aside, and wouldn't you know it, Missy had jumped beside her husband.

Conrad's gesture whacked her, not hard, on the arm. She stumbled back.

Screams as Missy hit the bleachers, fell. Landed on the pavement and then howled.

She held her wrist, writhing.

"Missy!" Conrad started for her, but Penelope pulled him back as Bouchard rounded to his wife.

"It was an accident," Penelope said, glancing at him.

"Call 911," shouted Steve.

And then everything just started to blur. Conrad's breath seized, a sweat broke out up his spine, and as Penelope came around to the front of him, backed him into a bleacher to sit down, his vision started to close.

She stood in front of him, her arms on his shoulders, as people started shouting, gathering around Missy, as Simon tried to corral the kids to no avail.

It all became clutter and noise as he held his head in his hands, just Penelope's voice cutting through. "Breathe, Con. Breathe."

He spotted EMTs as they came in, and with them, the police. Deputy Jenna Hayes came over, crouched in front of him, asked for a statement. But really, he couldn't speak watching the EMTs splint Missy's arm. Steve had leveled a litany of accusations at him, but he'd stopped listening, and then the man had turned to the cops, and who knew what he'd said.

Jenna led Conrad away, through the crowd, Penelope with him, and then said quietly, with a hint of regret, "I need to arrest you for assault, Conrad."

Oh.

"It'll be okay," Penelope said. "I'll call your lawyer—"

He looked at her. Shook his head. "You should go. Don't get tangled up in this." He reached into his pocket and handed her the keys to his truck. "Please, leave."

Her eyes widened, her mouth opening as she took them.

Then he hung his head as Jenna turned him, cuffed him, and read his rights.

He let her lead him out to her cruiser, still sweating, managing not to lose it as she pushed him into the back seat of the car.

He leaned his head back, listening to his heart beat, his jaw tight. But as Jenna pulled out, he looked out the window.

Penelope stood holding his keys, wearing an expression he couldn't place. Fierce, maybe even angry.

And behind her, a man, leaning hard on crutches, mid-forties, graying hair, brown eyes, his mouth a grim, tight line.

Joe Johnson.

So yeah, that had been a good idea.

243

"We'll get this sorted," Jenna said as she pulled out. "We just needed to get you out of there before a brawl started."

"It was an accident."

"They're taking statements," she said. "But you should let your girlfriend call your lawyer."

His girlfriend.

Yeah, she might wish it were fake, if she wanted to hold on to those social media followers.

"And she should get one for herself, given Steve Bouchard's accusations about her starting the fight."

"He's just looking for money." And that thought turned him cold.

Yes, he needed to distance himself from Penelope as fast as possible if he hoped to save her reputation.

"She's not my girlfriend," he said. "She's just working with EmPowerPlay. We both are."

Jenna met his gaze in the mirror, her eyebrows up.

He looked away. His stomach had settled by the time they reached the station, and he spent the next three hours giving his statement and talking to—for the second time today—Weston Winter, who told him to say nothing until he got there.

Which meant by the time he finished with his statement, any hope of a bail hearing had passed, and Jenna asked him what he'd like to have for dinner as he sat in overnight lockup. Apparently, they brought in takeout.

Instead, they let him call Jack, who showed up with a pot roast in a Tupperware container. They let Conrad eat it in the interrogation room with Jack, so he got an update on Missy. Not a broken wrist, but yes, Bouchard had found a lawyer.

And no, Jack hadn't seen Penelope. Maybe, for the first time, she'd listened to Conrad.

"I'm going to miss practice," Conrad said to Jack as he finished off dinner. "They'll suspend me."

Jack closed the Tupperware. "We'll get you out tomorrow, bro. It's going to be okay."

He didn't mention the memories that had suddenly crept back to haunt him. Only, this time he wasn't seventeen, arrested and on his way to juvie hall for interrogation, the horror of Joe Johnson's screams in his head.

"I don't think it's ever going to be okay," he said and motioned for Jenna to return him to his cell.

Where, probably, he belonged.

————————•————————

She'd made a mess of everything.

Penelope stood in front of the coffee maker, watching it drip, listening to Conrad's words yesterday thrum through her. *"You should go. Don't get tangled up in this."*

He couldn't have meant it the way it'd hit her.

Because she was already tangled up, right? If it hadn't been for her—

"You're up early." The words from her mother, who came into the room dressed in a pink velour day suit, her dark hair pulled back in a messy bun, diamond earrings and her makeup already applied despite the dawn's early-light hour.

Penelope sighed and stared back at the lake, where the snow reflected the sunset in a glowing fire, now sliding over the white toward shore. "Couldn't sleep."

Her mother kissed her cheek, then grabbed a mug from the cupboard. "Isn't Annette up yet?"

"I can make my own coffee, Mother."

Her mother patted her hand. "I know. You're so independent. It's nice having you around."

"I'm not really here, Mom. I just . . . well . . ."

Well, she hadn't known who else to call yesterday when she'd arrived at the sheriff's office and met the wall that was Deputy Sheriff Jenna Hayes. Apparently, Conrad didn't want to see her, words that had left her hollowed out and brittle.

He was panicking. She'd seen the expression he'd worn at the arena and in the cruiser.

And it was all her fault. If she hadn't baited the guy—

"I'm sure you will get it sorted out. Lucas is already writing up a press release about Kingston, distancing EmPowerPlay from the fiasco."

Penelope stared after her as her mother left her mug on the counter—maybe for Penelope to fill—and sat down at the kitchen nook, a padded bench that circled the bay window.

She picked up the remote to the flatscreen.

"Mother. It wasn't Conrad's fault—"

"Oh my, *Morning Brew* has picked up the story."

Penelope followed her mother's gaze. *No, oh*—

Of course she'd made the top headlines, a shot of her at the sheriff's office yesterday, getting picked up by Franco, flashing onto the screen.

Her mother turned up the volume on Ian Fletcher and Britta Turnquist.

Ian had leaned into the camera, wearing a white oxford, his sleeves rolled up, sporting a tan as if he'd been south, although Penelope knew a tanning-bed job when she saw it. "Today we're diving into a rather spicy topic from the world of sports. I'm sure many of you have seen the video that went viral yesterday—hockey star King Con confronted by a fan at a children's charity hockey practice."

And then the altercation played, including her jumping in to defend King Con, which, given his height and stature, felt very Minnie Mouse to his Incredible Hulk. Still, she winced when Missy went down—from this angle it clearly looked like he'd hit her.

"Oh my," her mother said, not helping.

"Yes, that's quite the scene, Ian," Britta said. Blonde, skinny, wearing a slim V-necked floral dress, an outfit that matched her personality. "We talked with the fan, Steve Bouchard, who said that he'd made a couple comments to King Con about the team's recent performance when King Con struck back. Things escalated when he accidentally spilled beer on King Con."

"That's not what happened," Penelope said.

"And then it got heated when Penelope Pepper stepped in, trying to defend King Con from the irate fan," Britta continued. "But here's where things get even more interesting—King Con later stated to officials that he and Penelope are not dating, contrary to what everyone assumed, seeing her jump to his defense."

Not dating?

She picked up the remote and popped up the volume.

"That's right, Britta. King Con's statement is that they are nothing. They know each other through EmPowerPlay, and she is not in a relationship with him, although recent social media has those two linked." Ian gave her what looked like a shake of his head. "Let's not forget, King Con is no stranger to being at the center of media speculation. A couple of years back, he was in the headlines for a rumored fallout with a teammate, allegedly involving another player's girlfriend."

"That was all misconstrued," Penelope said softly.

"It seems that wherever King Con goes, drama tends to follow, which really paints him as something of a wild card in the sports world. His talent on the ice is undeniable, but these off-ice escapades seem to keep him in the spotlight just as much," Britta said.

Ian. "It raises a big question about athletes and their personal lives. How much of this should affect our view of them as professionals? And where do we draw the line between their private affairs and their public personas?"

"Right?" Penelope turned to her mother. "Whose business is this anyway?"

"I think it's ours."

She looked up to see her father walk into the room dressed in suit pants, a shirt and tie, carrying his jacket. "Whatever the truth is about his relationships, King Con needs to manage these situations better. You can't have beer-splashing incidents becoming the norm. It hurts ticket sales. And now we have some damage control to do." He looked at her. "I think it's for the best if you stay away from Conrad Kingston, Pep."

She stared at him. "What?"

"They aren't together, Oscar," said her mother.

Wait—"Yes, we are." Weren't they?

"Not according to your social media," her mother said. "You posted it yourself—that Conrad and you were just working together to help EmPowerPlay."

Aw—Clarice!

"Good. Conrad is a loose cannon. I just wish I'd known about his former record before we drafted him." He shook his head. "What a fiasco." He walked over and kissed his wife. "Don't wait up. It'll be a long day."

He patted Penelope's arm. "Walk away. I'm sorry. I like Conrad Kingston, I do. I wanted to give him a chance. But clearly he's only going to hurt you."

She stared at him. "How? Conrad is . . . he's kind and protective and sweet and—"

"And just told the world that you're nothing to him." He raised an eyebrow. "You might want to realize that you're just not that important to him."

She stilled, and her father pecked her on the cheek, then picked up his suit jacket and walked out of the kitchen.

The television clicked off.

"Penelope?"

She looked over at her mother, who'd gotten up, frowning.

"Are you in love with this hockey player?"

Penelope swallowed. "I . . ."

"Oh, darling. You have to be so careful. Men like Conrad Kingston are after only what they can get from you."

"No. He's not—"

"Just like Edward and Tia. Oh, she barely escaped that tragedy."

Her mouth opened. "What? Mom, Edward was murdered—"

"Yes, that was terrible. But it would have been worse if Tia had married him only to discover that he didn't really love her."

She blinked at her mother. "What?"

"He was just using her to get close to your father."

"Mother. Edward *was* close to my father. He paid for his education—"

"Oh no, no, darling, that was just the agreement we made with his mother." And then her eyes widened. "Oh dear."

A beat. "What's 'oh dear'?"

Her mother sighed. "Well, I guess it's all over now. Inga was a treasure to the day she died. Without her, we might never have found you."

"What are you talking about, Mom? Found me—wait, is this about the kidnapping?"

"Of course. Inga and Edward were the only ones at home when you were taken. And it was she who found you."

"Edward found me."

Her mother shook her head. "Edward only found you because Inga overheard Carmen and Nicolai talking about where they'd stashed you. Inga took you and hid you in the dumbwaiter until we got back."

That wasn't how she remembered it. "Edward told me that Dad didn't want to pay the ransom. That he was negotiating, and he was afraid that Carmen and Nicolai would kill me."

"Oh no, darling. Of course we paid the ransom. We wired to the account Carmen gave us—but she wanted more. And that's when your father suspected there was a bigger plot, someone behind Carmen and Nicolai."

"Why?"

"Because we had insurance on you and Tia, and the ransom demand barely dipped into that. When the kidnappers realized we'd pay it, they asked for double more. Your father thought that maybe there was a bigger plot at play, and that's when he decided to stall. He feared that someone on his staff would leak the truth to the police, and the cops would lose their chance to capture Carmen and Nicolai and the mastermind behind the treachery. He asked Inga to keep hiding you. He told her he'd take care of Edward for life if she trusted him."

"He *kept* me in the dumbwaiter?"

"Oh my, darling, no, of course not. We didn't know where you were until we arrived home and Inga told us. She simply said she'd found you and you were safe. Of course, we sent Vincent to find you the moment we returned home. By then, the second ransom exchange had already happened, and this time, Carmen was killed, along with Nicolai."

"By the police?"

"No. They were dead when your father's bodyguard, Vincent, arrived with the ransom money. We never found out who did it, and we never retrieved the first ransom either. That's when your father decided to assign you personal security." She caught her daughter's face. "You just can't be too careful, honey. You have to know who to trust."

She did know who to trust. She thought she had, but . . .

"Please, leave." And *"King Con later stated to officials that he and Penelope are not dating."*

She sank onto a counter stool.

Then, *wait*—"Why didn't Dad trust Edward?"

"Oh, that. It's because Edward came to him with this crazy AI program he'd developed at MIT and wanted Quantex to buy it. He thought your father would risk his company just because of Tia." She sighed. "I'm just glad Tia found out before it was too late."

"Mom—Tia was weeks away from marrying Edward when he was murdered."

"No, I wasn't."

Penelope turned, a chill raking through her as Tia came into the room. She wore leggings and an oversized sweatshirt, her dark hair pulled back in a headband. "What?"

"First, this house is big, but it's old. Vents, people. My bedroom is right above this. And second, Mom is right. Edward and I broke up about a week before he died."

She came into the room, grabbed a mug, poured herself coffee. "It didn't mean I didn't love him. But . . . he was in love with someone else, and I couldn't deny it anymore."

"Sarah Livingston." Penelope didn't know why she said it. The name just slid out.

And Tia laughed. "Sarah? No. Hardly. They were friends, but Sarah had just started dating Edward's best friend, Franco."

"Franco? As in *my* Franco?"

Tia's brow went up.

"You know what I mean."

Tia shrugged. "Yes. Franco Bernatelli, Vincent's youngest son and Edward's childhood bestie."

"I was Edward's childhood bestie."

"You were Edward's true love."

The words hit her, rocked her back. "What?"

Tia sighed, glanced at her mother, back at Penelope. "I broke up with Edward because he was marrying me only because he couldn't have you."

"What do you mean? He didn't even ask!"

"You were four years younger than him, and . . . I don't know why he didn't ask. But after we were engaged, I watched you two at every family event, and . . . Edward never looked at me the way he looked at you. I finally confronted him and he admitted that he loved you. And me, of course. But I knew I couldn't be his second choice." She touched Penelope's arm. "I'm sorry I got in the way. He got back from MIT and there was something about him—more confidence, I guess. And you were away at college, and I asked him out, not even thinking. He said yes, and then things just started happening. He was really involved in his research, too, on his AI program. Said it would transform the way we drove cars. He even had applications for defense technology. I think he even got an RFP from a defense contractor after Dad turned him down for Quantex. He was so smart." Her eyes filled. "I did love him, Pen. But not like you did. I wish I'd realized how he felt about you sooner."

Penelope's eyes burned, filled. "Me too. But . . ." She pulled Tia into an embrace, held on.

"Oh boy, this man really did a number on my girls," said her mother, her arms around both of them.

"He was a good man, Mom," said Tia. "Not everyone is out to get us."

A soft shrug from Sophia as she eased her embrace. "I just can't bear the thought of you two getting hurt." She kissed Tia, then Penelope. Held their hands. "'One must seek the truth within—not without.'" Her mouth made a kind smile. "I suppose 'If the fact will not fit the theory—let the theory go.' To quote my daughter's favorite author." She winked.

Penelope stared at her mother and heard the echo of the caller who'd delivered that quote pinging inside. "Mom?"

"You'll figure this out, darling." She let her hands go and headed for her bedroom.

Penelope gaped.

"What was that about?" Tia asked.

"Does Mom listen to my podcast?"

"Of course she does. Seriously. We all do." Tia wiped her cheeks. "You deserve a happily ever after, Pep. With the right man."

Oh. "I . . . I think I've found the right man." The words spilled out, soft, testing. *Yes.*

Tia cocked her head. "Pen . . . I heard *Morning Brew.* And it's all over social media. I mean, you even came out and said that you two were over."

She had—*oh, that's right,* she'd texted Clarice. "Yeah, I know. But . . . don't believe everything you read on the internet."

Really. Because she knew Conrad, right?

"One must seek the truth within—not without."

Yes, she knew him. He was the real deal. No games. No fake dating. He'd been beside her when he didn't have to be.

The kind of boyfriend who stuck around, even when trouble circled her.

"By the way, in the end, Edward was right. Quantex did end up investing in Edward's program. He had sold it to a company called MetaGrid, who then dumped it after he died. Declan Stone picked it up but sold shares to Quantex to finance it."

"Yeah, that was the DOD company that Edward talked about. I remember him telling Franco and Sarah and me about it at dinner a few weeks before we broke up. Franco was weirdly mad that Dad didn't acquire Axiom for Quantex, because that had been Edward's plan. I had tried to talk him out of it, but he wanted Dad to have the first shot at it."

"Quantex made millions when they invested in Spectra, who finally acquired Axiom." Her sister slid onto a stool, sipped her coffee.

"How do you know that?"

"Seriously? Do you not read your quarterly stock reports?"

Oops.

"Yeah. In fact, Quantex was losing the AI race until they invested in Spectra. Edward's mother inherited all of Edward's stock, and she didn't have a clue what to do. I think Dad hooked her up with Stone, who bought the company."

"Why didn't Quantex simply buy it?" Penelope asked.

"It violated an antitrust act for them to have controlling shares in two AI companies that would create a monopoly on the market."

"Wow, Miss Economics Degree."

"It was in the report." Tia winked. "Stone's company owns the majority of Axiom shares."

"So, what happened to Inga's shares when she died?"

"I don't know. She has no living kin except Vincent, so—"

"Vincent. Dad's old bodyguard?" Penelope said.

"Oh, they had a longtime fling—did you not know this? Edward was sworn to secrecy, but with Vincent a single dad and Inga a single mother . . . Franco and Edward were practically brothers. Closer even than Franco and his own brother."

"Marcus, right? I only met him once."

"He lived with their mom, so he was never around. He's a couple years older than Franco. I met him once, in college. Franco and I used to see each other on campus sometimes. We actually took a class together. Anyway, his brother looks just like him, dark hair, blue eyes, built. I think Marcus went into law enforcement, or maybe security. I admit, I was a little surprised when Franco ended up back here. I always thought he'd be an investment banker or something."

"Why?"

"His degree was in finance. Or at least it was going to be. He dropped out of school his senior year. Showed up a couple years later working here."

"And just in time to follow me to college."

"At least he was cute." Tia slid off the chair. "Could have been worse. You could have had Geoffrey." She set her mug in the sink.

"For the record, I liked King Con. I thought you two were cute together."

We were cute together.

No, they were more than cute. They worked. Even when they'd been fake dating, it had worked.

No more games.

Conrad was the happily ever after she wanted.

She picked up the house phone and dialed their security office. Geoffrey answered.

"I need a car."

"I'm afraid your father has requested no more vehicles for you," Geoffrey said. "He says we are to drive you."

Of course.

"Fine. Then how about a ride?"

"Where to, ma'am?"

"Duck Lake. I'll be ready in ten minutes."

"I'll have Franco pick you up in front."

Good. Because she had some questions for him.

Ten minutes later, wearing leggings, an oversized sweater, a vest, and her hair pulled back, she climbed into the back of the warming Lexus, Franco at the wheel. He wore a wool jacket, gloves, and sunglasses, and was clean-shaven, her armed chauffeur. "Duck Lake?"

"The sheriff's office, to be clear."

"Ma'am—"

"We've been over this. Not ma'am."

"Miss Pepper."

"Just drive, Franco."

His pursed mouth said everything.

She sat back and pulled up her phone. Scrolled through her social media, reading the comments. So much love, so much hate. She'd gained followers, lost followers, and really, did it matter?

What *was* she trying to prove?

They'd left the city, rounding the lake toward Waconia, the sun having cleared the horizon to the east, the golden swatch of dawn fading into the blue sky. She should have gotten another cup of coffee for the road.

"I didn't realize you and Edward were friends." She didn't know why she started there. Franco glanced at her in the mirror.

"Yes, ma'—Miss Pepper. Of course. We grew up together."

"Why didn't I know this?"

"We didn't live in the house. And my father forbade any contact with you and your sister."

She frowned. And then, "You dated Sarah Livingston."

A muscle pulled in his jaw. "Yes. For a while. She broke up with me to date Holden Walsh."

"I'm sorry. You lost Edward and Sarah."

He nodded, and his hands tightened a little on the wheel.

"Any idea who might have killed Sarah?"

A beat. Then a sigh. "Not a clue."

"When was the last time you saw her?"

He lifted a shoulder. "Maybe a few weeks after Edward's death. She was pretty upset—said she thought he'd been murdered." He glanced in the mirror. "But you already know that."

She frowned. "Do you listen to my podcasts?"

He smiled. "Of course."

Oh. "Ever called in?"

"I'll never tell." He laughed then, low, deep.

And it nudged something inside her. *Wait. "You can run, but you can't hide."* One of her crazy podcast callers.

She swallowed, looked up, nearly met his eyes in the rearview mirror, glanced away, her heart hammering.

No.

That wasn't right—

Her phone buzzed, a text coming in. *Conrad?* She opened it. Janet Foster.

Janet Foster
_____
I found him.

Found . . . Wait—the man fleeing from Edward's apartment?

Then a picture came through, a grainy shot of a television screen, with fuzzy lines across the picture. Janet had clearly taken the shot of Penelope in front of the sheriff's office on her phone, then edited it, drawing a circle around a face in the background.

The face of Franco Bernatelli.

Oh . . .

"Aw," he said then with a sigh.

She looked up to see his gaze on her through the rearview mirror. "By the look on your face, I think this just keeps getting messier."

Then he shook his head.

And engaged the child locks.

THIRTEEN

H E NEEDED A HOT SHOWER, MAYBE A COLD plunge and a massage.

Thanks to criminal lawyer West Winter's appearance before the judge, all the charges had been dropped. And West had suggested that the entire thing might have been Steve Bouchard's fault.

The half dozen video clips of the altercation helped. And not a few fan sites that suggested Conrad had been baited into the fight.

Which *wasn't* a fight, as West had pointed out to the local judge in the cleared courtroom this morning. Hence the court clerk handing Conrad a manila envelope containing his wallet, belt, sunglasses, cell phone, and keys, courtesy of Penelope.

Who hadn't shown up yet.

Not that he expected her. After all, he had told her to leave. And with a woman with her history, that could feel like a betrayal.

No, if she listened to her manager and cared at all about social media, Penny would give him a public goodbye, sell his jersey on eBay, and start showing up at Timberwolves games.

Except he sort of thought she didn't care. Hoped, really.

Now he stood in the hallway outside the courtroom with Jack and West and his father—that had been a nice surprise this morning—listening to West's instructions.

He liked West in person as much as he'd liked him on Zoom. Smart. Had been Jack's roomie in law school. Too bad he lived in Iowa. Conrad would have had to find another attorney if this thing had gone to trial.

Thank You, Lord.

"There's a mob of press outside. You should probably be aware of the statement EmPowerPlay has issued." West held up his phone. "'EmPowerPlay is committed to promoting sportsmanship, integrity, and community values. We are aware of the incident involving Conrad Kingston and are deeply concerned by the actions reported. While we believe in the principle of innocent until proven guilty, we must also ensure that all of our coaches uphold our standards. At this time, we have suspended Conrad as a coach and do not condone any behavior that detracts from the respectful culture we strive to uphold.'"

"Nice support," Jack said. "Sheesh."

"At least it wasn't from the Blue Ox," West said. "Keep your statement simple, Conrad." West wore a black wool coat, black pants, glasses, and a Gatsby cap, his hair longer around the ears. "Just say that you love your fans and that you hope this misunderstanding will be cleared up in the near future. And that you wish everyone well. Then thank them, wave, and walk away."

Conrad sighed, glanced at his father, who wore a pinched expression, his eyes saying what Conrad felt—here they went again.

"Or you could say nothing," Jack said. "Just wave and walk away."

"The fans will want a statement," said West.

"They're going to trade me anyway. Especially if I don't make it to practice." Conrad had secured his watch and now glanced at it. "I have two hours."

"Time enough for breakfast at the house," his father said, clamping him on the shoulder. *Sheesh,* the man acted as if this might be akin to car trouble trapping him in town instead of the reliving of his worst nightmare.

At least this time no one had lost a leg.

He blew out a breath. "Okay, let's go."

West and Jack moved toward the door, but his father caught his arm. The man wore his canvas-and-flannel work coat, a wool hat. A working man, salt of the earth, the kind of man who earned respect.

"Don't let Satan use this to lie to you. You're not the reckless boy of the past, Conrad. You're a man who got caught up in something."

"I didn't think. I just followed my impulses, and someone got hurt, again."

His father nodded. "So you leave it with God. Humble yourself. The Lord is near to those who call on Him. He hears their cry and saves them. You don't need to fight this battle."

Conrad nodded, wanting the words to seep inside, nourish him, but a chill had found his bones, his cells.

He'd felt like he'd walked away from justice last time, really, had gone on to have a glorious career he didn't deserve. Maybe justice had finally caught up.

The chilly air burned his nose, caught his breath as he stepped outside into the sunshine. A blue-skied day, the sun burning over the treetops, and on the sidewalk below the steps of the court building stood more press than Duck Lake had probably ever seen.

Even after the terrible tornado that had nearly swept them off the map. But it wasn't every day that a storm like Conrad Kingston swept into town for a second time.

"Conrad, can you tell us what led to the altercation at the ice rink last night?"

He opened his mouth, but another reporter peppered him.

"Were you acting in self-defense, or was there provocation on your part?"

"Um—"

"How do you respond to EmPowerPlay's statement that they do not condone such behavior? Are you still affiliated with the team?"

"The Blue Ox? Of course I am."

"Do you believe this incident will impact your career in the long term? How do you plan to address your fans and sponsors?"

He stared out at the crowd, sweat trickling along his spine.

"Has there been any contact or reconciliation with the other party involved in the fight?"

He shook his head, the edges of his vision closing in. *Shoot*—

West held up his hand. "One at a time."

"What message do you have for young fans who look up to you and might be influenced by these events?"

He looked at the woman who'd thrown out the question. Mid-twenties, blonde hair—*wait*. He knew her. *Ava.* She met his eyes. "What is the nature of your relationship with Penelope Pepper, and how was she involved in this altercation?"

He leaned toward her. "She wasn't." More of a bark than a statement, and his stomach began to roil.

A hand touched his shoulder, and he glanced over at his father. He wore a tight expression. "You okay?"

No. But Conrad just turned back to the crowd. Opened his mouth.

Nothing emerged.

"Leave the man alone!"

The voice lifted from behind the crowd, more voices with it. "Yeah, leave him alone! Leave King Con alone!"

He searched and spotted—*what?* The Ice Hawks, or at least a good handful of them, pushing through the crowd to the front.

"Hey, Coach Con!" said one of the players—the winger he'd

taught how to shoot—and skinny Jeremy Johnson and even Tyler Bouchard, and coach Simon and then . . .

Joe Johnson. The man walked up on crutches, but wearing an Ice Hawks jersey and a wool hat, looking sturdy, his eyes clear.

And a smile.

He walked right up to Conrad and held out his hand.

What? Conrad reached out, his eyes wide at the gesture.

Joe tightened his grip, stepped up, and pulled Con to himself. "I see you, Conrad. I've always seen you. Let it go."

Conrad leaned back, met his gaze, and Joe smiled at him, kindness in his eyes. "Forgiveness doesn't have to be earned. It just has to be accepted." Then he squeezed Conrad's hand and let go.

Oh. Now Conrad really couldn't breathe.

Joe turned and held up his hands. "Leave our hometown hero alone. He has a game to get to."

The Ice Hawks sent their fists into the air with a chant of "King Con, King Con." And what. was. *happening*?

"My guess is that Steve Bouchard is not as popular as he thinks he is," Jack said, his hands shoved into his pockets.

Conrad swallowed, then raised his hands, and the kids quieted. He glanced at West.

"Keep your statement simple."

But the "simple" wasn't just a quick statement or a soundbite or a reel.

"I learned a long time ago that hockey, and life, is about teamwork. And about not just showing up but showing up with my best. I was not at my best yesterday, but I do know that I can't change the past. I just have to . . ." He looked at his dad, then back at the crowd. "I just have to keep moving forward. I can't change what happens to me—just what I do about it. Right, kids?"

More fist pumps.

"So, I am sorry for any hurt I caused the Bouchard family. And

I look forward to showing up with my best for our amazing Blue Ox fans. Thank you."

Cheers, and he couldn't help but scan the crowd for a certain brunette.

Then his father pulled him away, off the steps, toward the parking lot, where he took Conrad's keys and got into his truck. They backed out, the press still chasing Conrad.

"Your mom is making pancakes."

"Breakfast of champions."

"Yep." Grover looked at Conrad, winked. And somehow the drive home felt like redemption.

Conrad's mother met him with buttermilk pancakes, homemade maple syrup, fresh-squeezed orange juice, scrambled eggs with cream and gouda, and hickory-smoked bacon, and they ate in the big room because they'd been guest-free last night.

Mom gave him an update on Doyle and Austen, and Stein had left on Saturday with Declan Stone heading somewhere overseas, and then he pushed away from the table and carried his plate into the kitchen.

"I really loved getting to know Penelope better," his mother said, loading his plate into the dishwasher. "I just wish you two were really together, and not just . . . you know."

"Just . . . what?" He arched an eyebrow. Reached for his phone.

"That you two were just together for charity purposes?"

"Where did you read that?"

"Oh, on your Instagram account."

His account? He opened the app. Read his statement. *Aw . . . Felicity.*

"Don't believe everything you read on the internet." He kissed her cheek, then stepped away and dialed Penelope.

Outside, the sun shone on the cleared broomball rink, and he glanced at the thermometer. Above freezing, but just barely.

"Better watch the ice, Mom. There are snowmobile tracks on

the ice, but the snowpack can warm it up and turn it weak. And the wind has piled some ice flow on the shoreline, which says that the currents are rising to the surface."

Ringing.

"And the sun is getting hotter, so it could be melting the ice where we cleared it. C'mon, Penny, answer!"

Voicemail. He hung up.

Shoot.

No texts either, and it occurred to him then that maybe she didn't have his new phone number. Had he given it to her after she'd shown up at his house?

Jack barreled into the room. "Con, we have a problem."

Of course they did. "What?"

"I just got off with Harper—Penelope sent her a text. She forwarded it to me." He held out the phone.

> Penelope
> _____
>
> Franco killed Edward. Probably
> SL. He knows I know.

Conrad just stared at it. "SL? Sarah Livingston. And Edward."

"Who's Franco?"

"Oh, I know Franco. He's her supposed bodyguard, but he's hardly been around." He thumbed down past Harper's many unanswered responses. "She's in trouble."

Jack nodded.

Conrad swiped up his keys. "Call Harper and get me Oscar Pepper's cell number. We need a location on Penelope."

"If Franco did take her, he will have turned off any GPS," Jack said, reaching for his jacket.

Conrad bit back a word. "Right. Okay, so where then, tracker man?"

Jack ran a hand across his mouth. "He won't want her found. So that means he won't dump her body anywhere accessible."

"Please don't say *body*."

"Okay, so it's daylight. He'll have to take her somewhere he knows, somewhere remote, somewhere he can—"

"If you say *dump the body*, I'll hurt you."

"—deal with her." Jack had pressed dial on his phone. "Harp, babe. Listen, what have you found out about this Franco guy?" He put her on speaker.

"Nothing. He lives on-site with the Pepper family. His brother was found dead a month ago in a fire . . . a motel fire in Duck Lake—"

"The body we found."

"Wow. Okay, so that's a question for later, but if Franco was in on the previous kidnapping, he took her to the Loon Lake housing project last time—my guess is that he knows this area. But how—wait. His father has a house on Frederick Lake, on a small plot of land near Declan Stone's estate."

The world couldn't be that small.

"We can start there," Conrad said, heading to the door.

"I've been there," Jack said and pushed out behind him. "Harper, call Jenna Hayes, tell her that Penelope has gone missing again."

"I feel like the boy who cried wolf."

"That's why you have to do it—you'd never call Jenna unless it was real."

Conrad didn't hear the rest as he climbed into his truck. Jack took the passenger seat, glanced at him.

"You sure you want to do this? You'll miss the game."

He pulled out. "I'm going to miss everything if I don't find her."

"Right," Jack said, and buckled in.

———————•———————

Why hadn't she dialed 911? Penny sat in the back seat, the child locks on the doors, trapped, watching the winterscape of barren cornfields and remote farmhouses pass by.

Think.

Her face burned from where he'd grabbed her phone, a move she should have seen coming when he'd abruptly pulled over, turned in his seat, and lunged for the device.

She'd tried to get out then and run, but of course, he'd engaged the locks. And then he'd slapped her—which she most definitely *hadn't* seen coming. She'd sat dazed for a whole minute as he'd pulled back out on the highway, her phone sailing out his window.

Why hadn't she watched more car-hijacking videos? Then she might know how to disable him—but all she saw was herself grabbing the wheel, shooting them off the highway at seventy-five miles an hour, and plummeting through the windshield.

Think.

"I thought Edward was your friend. Why did you kill him?"

Maybe not the best way to calm Franco down, but hopefully she'd get him thinking. Regretting.

The man gripped the wheel with both gloved hands, his jaw tight, frustration radiating off him.

"It was an accident."

"Setting a fire doesn't sound like an accident to me—"

"It was an accident!" He hit the steering wheel. "He lied to me!"

Oh.

Franco took a breath. "It wasn't supposed to go down like that. I was just trying to get him to change his mind, go back to Quantex instead of taking the MetaGrid deal."

MetaGrid? "The company that wanted to buy his program?"

He nodded. "He told me he was just using the MetaGrid deal to entice Quantex to sell. I knew that when Quantex acquired Axiom, the stock price would soar, so . . ." His mouth tightened, and he shook his head. "I invested everything I had into Quantex. And then he betrayed me."

"He didn't betray you. Quantex couldn't acquire it—"

"He was going to cost me everything. And he didn't care. He didn't *have* to care—he was marrying Tia."

She looked out the window.

"And then they broke up, and he signed with MetaGrid and . . . my stocks were tanking and I was hemorrhaging money—" He turned off the highway onto a county road, the snowdrifts dark and grimy from the dirt that kicked up. "I just wanted to talk."

"With a 9mm."

He said nothing.

"So, why the fire?"

"That was . . . that my father's idea. Burn the place down. And maybe it would have worked, but Holden Walsh got suspicious."

"How?"

"Sarah betrayed me. She told her new boyfriend that she thought Edward was murdered."

And it hit Penelope then, all of it. "You killed Sarah. You were the unforced entry, the masked man."

He said nothing.

"Wait. How did you cover up the murder with the wrong forensic report?"

His mouth tightened.

"Your brother. He was in law enforcement."

"He quit a few years ago. Went to work at Turbo." His mouth pinched. "But yes, he knew the right people, and my father did the rest."

His father. "Vincent knew about this?"

He glanced in the mirror, and a tiny, eerie smile played on his lips.

What—

"How did you know about Holden's forensic report?" she asked quietly, trying to sort out the smile.

"Sarah told me. Said that she thought Edward had been killed and asked Holden to hire an investigator since he owned the building."

"And he discovered the bullet holes and knew the autopsy was faked."

"He would have caused trouble."

"You killed Holden too."

"He was leaving for Barbados. I couldn't let him get away."

"And you dumped him in my garage."

"Felt like a good place."

She shook her head. "And you set fire to my garage."

"That got tricky, since you were out of town—"

"Did you try to run me off the road?"

He made a face. "No. I would have gotten it done."

Her eyes widened. "Then who—"

He narrowed his eyes. Shook his head. "I told you it was getting messy."

She fought with her voice, kept it cool, the podcaster in her taking over. "It doesn't have to be messy. No one else has to die."

"It's gone too far. After Marcus was murdered, there was no turning back."

Marcus. "Your brother was *murdered*?"

"Sarah's friend Kyle killed him."

She stilled, the pieces forming, connecting. "Your brother was the one who kidnapped me a month ago and tried to kill me."

"You were digging too deep."

Her breath left her. "Then why didn't you kill me after I was found?"

"Everyone was watching. And for a while, you thought Kyle had killed Sarah. I didn't want to interfere."

"Until he was run off the road and shot—oh my. *You* did that too."

"That was for Marcus."

"Kyle was *innocent*."

"Hardly. He was working for Swindle. Who was trying to cover everything up after his partner, Holden, told him about the real forensic report. He knew Edward was murdered."

"I knew Swindle was tangled up in this."

"Swindle was on the board of Quantex. And he knew Declan Stone. He was the one who told Stone to buy Axiom."

"And my dad?"

"He felt bad for Edward's mother and voted to invest."

So he was innocent. A fist released in her chest. She should have trusted him. And then . . . *Wait.* "You killed Anton Beckett?"

"He contacted Swindle, told him that he'd gotten into Kyle's cloud, and asked about the video. Swindle called me, told me to grab the drive."

"And instead you killed him."

Silence.

"And burned down his house."

Again, nothing.

She might be ill. But—"Wait—who killed Swindle?"

He sighed.

"You did. Why?"

"Because he was an idiot—just like Edward. He was going to betray me." His voice lowered. "Fine." He sighed. "He freaked out—thought he'd be implicated in Beckett's murder because Beckett had called him. He went to Holden's place to get his computer, see if he could destroy the video."

"But you left the computer there."

"Deleted the entire hard drive." He shrugged. "Nothing to find."

She had gone cold. "You used Walsh's phone to text me. You were the one at Theodore Wirth Park."

He glanced at her, huffed. "You're more trouble than you're worth."

She looked away.

They'd turned off the county road, headed into a wooded area, a dirt road that led back to—Frederick Lake? "Your father owns a lake home?"

He glanced in the mirror. "You don't think you're the only one with money, right?"

Oh.

"He bought it years ago when I was still a child. Spent years renovating it."

So this was where it would end. "So, you're going to kill me, bury my body on the land?"

He glanced at her. "Aw, it can't be that easy. I think you probably need to do one last podcast for your listeners."

One last—"What, naming you as the killer?"

He laughed, and there it was again, from the recording, driving a frozen sliver through her. "Oh, I don't think so. I think we make this more fun." He pulled into a long drive, birch trees shooting through swaths of evergreen, the occasional barren poplar. Through the forest, light ahead suggested lakeshore. "I think you confess."

She stilled. "Me—why me?"

"I have Ring footage of you breaking into Holden's house. That was helpful. And of course, you had a reason to hate Edward— crime of passion and all."

"I didn't hate Edward—"

"Of course you did. You were in love with him."

"My sister was going to marry him!"

"No. She'd broken up with him. Edward wanted to marry you."

Her breath caught. Yes, Tia had said that, but—

Well, she hadn't believed her. Not really.

"He was in love with you from the minute he 'rescued' you when you were nine years old." He'd finger quoted the word *rescued*.

And that's when his eerie smile clicked. "I wasn't kidnapped."

"Well, technically there was a ransom paid, but not really. Yes, it started that way—with Carmen and Nicolai. But Inga discovered what they were up to and told my father. He got Edward to 'rescue' you and hide you in the dumbwaiter and then took over the negotiations. Your father had the money—and the insurance—to cover it. He made sure the transfer went down, killed Carmen and Nicolai, and then my dad and Inga pocketed the cash. Your dad was such a chump—he actually thought Edward had saved your life."

Her voice cut to a whisper. "Did Edward know?"

"Probably not. He thought he'd saved you. What an idiot." He slowed, the house appearing.

She gaped.

He glanced back. "What did you think we'd have—a cabin? It's not the Pepper palace, but my father restored every inch of the eight thousand square feet."

The colonial revival home sat back from the lake, sprawled along the shoreline, with a columned portico over the front door, and rose three stories, with dormer windows jutting from the roofline. Vines twined up the outside, like an old English estate, and a dry fountain centered the circular driveway.

"It was an old summer estate of some financier. Inga found it in a magazine, and my dad bought it for her. It has a ballroom on the second floor."

"Inga? Why did she keep working for my family, then?"

"Guilt, maybe. And if she quit, they'd ask questions . . ."

"And that would lead back to the money she'd stolen."

"Earned."

"By kidnapping me."

"You were fine. And Edward turned out to be a hero, so calm down."

Calm. down?

"Your father kidnapped me. Stole my sense of safety, made me believe that everyone was out to get me, to use me."

He put the car in Park. "It made you smarter, made you stop living in a fantasy. My dad did you a favor."

She had nothing for that.

He reached for the door handle, turned. "But you do know that if you hadn't gone poking around Edward's death, none of this would have happened. Sarah wouldn't have gone to Holden and started the mess." He met her eyes in the rearview mirror. "This is all on you."

"You, Penelope Pepper, are the connection."

She froze, even as he got out.

But not so much that she didn't realize he'd unlocked her door. And yes, maybe she was smarter—or at least braver. She opened it, barreled out the other side.

And ran for the house.

"Penelope!"

She ignored his shout, scrambled toward the front door.

Locked. She turned.

He slammed up behind her, trapped her against the door, his face close. "This is fun."

She kneed him, and he doubled over, shot out a word. Then she slammed the palm of her hand into his face, and his head jerked back.

He stumbled, and she pushed away.

Took off. This time along the length of the house, toward a sunroom-slash-greenhouse. If this house was anything like her father's, the sunroom door would be rusty, vulnerable.

"Penelope! You—"

She ignored his word, hit the sunroom door. Again, locked.

She backed up and kicked it, hard.

It shuddered open, and she shoved in.

Eight thousand square feet. Eight thousand square feet of nooks and crannies and closets and stairwells and maybe even an apple cellar.

More, she'd gotten off a text to Harper, her podcast investigator. Who'd had the brains to find her last time.
Time to hide.

FOURTEEN

WHAT IF SHE'S NOT THERE?" CONRAD SAT, his hand on the dash, bracing himself as Jack thundered up the dirt road, following the GPS that Harper had sent him.

"One thing at a time," Jack said. "If she's not there, we regroup, and by that time, the police catch up." He glanced over at Conrad. "We'll find her."

Conrad nodded, his jaw tight. He leaned back, his feet braced on the floorboards, his hand moving to the handle above the window. "At least you don't drive like a grandma."

Jack glanced at him. "Please. I taught you how to drive."

"Stein taught me how to drive."

"I remember one distinct driving session—"

"You yelled at me, and I panicked, drove out into an intersection and stopped. You were terrifying."

Jack grinned. "You were always a little tightly wound."

They'd turned onto a county road, the GPS indicating a driveway ahead. "I've been tightly wound since the day I went through the ice."

Jack turned quiet. "I didn't know that."

"Yeah. Just always waiting for the earth to crack under my feet. I live with a weird desperation inside, always fighting to get out—"

"Hence the panic attacks."

He nodded.

"And your focus on hockey."

"For a long time, yes. Although . . . I dunno. I started focusing on the fear of getting traded, and that messed up my game . . . and then I met Penelope. She sort of . . . gives me something to focus on. I forget about the roil inside when I'm with her."

He hadn't quite labeled it yet, but yes.

"So, Penelope Pepper, for all her craziness, outcrazies the crazy inside," Jack said. He looked over at Conrad. "I get that more than you know."

"Harper."

"She's always been the one."

"I didn't think there was a one for me until I met Penny."

Jack slowed, working his brakes on the slick road, then turned into the wooded drive. "We'll find her."

Conrad drew in a breath.

"You could pray."

He glanced at Jack.

"Just saying that if you need something to focus on, you could try God's love. His provision, His help."

"I'm not sure—"

"That God is going to show up for you?"

He shrugged, still trying to get Joe's words into his head.

"God's grace is bigger than your mistakes. At least, that's what I'm starting to figure out. And you've got to stop worrying so much. Thinking so hard. Trust those instincts God gave you."

A house came into view, and Conrad sat up. It sprawled across the frozen landscape, a miniature version of the Pepper estate.

"I know you're constantly trying to figure out how not to repeat your mistakes, how to make everything turn out okay. But you can't do that, Con. Even if you're in charge. So, who would you rather trust—you, or the God who loves you?"

"Both. There's a Lexus in the drive—the door is open."

"I see it." Jack pulled up, slamming on his brakes, skidding, and Conrad barreled out of the car, his gaze already finding the open door to a solarium.

He took off, driven by impulse more than strategy, and yes, he had to believe Jack was right about God. Because no, he didn't trust himself, not completely.

So he had only one choice left.

He slipped on the terra-cotta tile, nearly fell, grabbed a wrought-iron table, then took off into the house.

Jack came in behind him. "Con—be careful!"

Right.

He came into a breezeway, the floor bright-red brick, then into a butler's pantry attached to an expansive kitchen with a center island, French country off-white cabinetry, and a hanging copper hood over the center grill.

Despite the remodel, the place still hit him as . . . old.

He entered a dining room that looked out to the lake and spotted a boathouse down by the water. There was a zinc fireplace with a leaded mirror over the top, and the place smelled of oiled wood.

What if she was hiding? Jack had entered the living room, and Conrad found him there, standing on a white area rug, breathing hard. "We need to split up." Jack pointed toward the upstairs. "I'll check the bedrooms—"

"I know where she'd hide," Conrad said. He walked into the foyer that connected to the front door, a split staircase dividing the room. Not unlike the foyer at the King's Inn. He opened a door—*yep,* a bathroom.

The other led downstairs, just like he'd hoped.

Jack ran upstairs, his feet pounding on the treads.

Conrad headed down, found a billiards room, a theater, a wine-storage room, the smells of water, age.

Which meant—*yes*. It had to have cold storage. He scrambled back upstairs into the kitchen, found the door off the pantry that led down.

These stairs creaked, age having turned them brittle. The walls were cinderblock, and lower, stone. A poured-concrete floor, uneven, cobwebs clinging to the walls. Mustiness, the scent of dirt and stone, a cool dampness to the air, and the sweet aroma of apples.

Warped wooden shelves lined the walls, the darkness thickening the farther he went from the stairwell, but there at the end of the room, a door.

The rusty knob wiggled in his grip. *Please*—

He pulled it open. The door groaned, and he braced himself.

Just a room with a dirt floor, empty save for the wooden shelving and a potato bin.

No Penelope.

And probably this had been a stupid idea—why would she return to the one place that haunted her?

Think!

He turned and scrambled back upstairs, out of the butler's pantry. He'd find Jack and—

The blow hit him along his back, almost like a check into the boards, and he slammed against the counter. Fire exploded in his hip.

But he'd been hit before and knew how to round back. He caught the second blow—a fireplace poker—with his hand.

Why the man hadn't just shot him, he didn't know, but Franco jerked back. Blood on his mouth, so maybe Penelope had gotten a kick in.

And that galvanized Conrad.

He listened to his instincts and charged.

Catching the man around the waist, he propelled him back against the island, heard a whuff, then sent a fist into his gut.

Not before Franco cuffed him in the ribs, but he'd taken tougher punches before.

Franco grunted, hit him again, added a knee, but Conrad dodged it. He grabbed Franco around the neck, pushed him down into the crook of his body, tightening his hold.

"Bro! Ease up—you'll break his neck!"

He looked up to see Jack scrambling toward him.

Franco used the moment to elbow him in the thigh—near miss, but it shook him off-balance enough for the man to break free.

Jack jumped in, took him down, his knee to Franco's shoulder, wrenched his hand back.

Franco swore at him, kicked, and Conrad landed on his legs. "Where is she?"

"I don't know!" He writhed and Jack bore down on him. "She got away!"

Good girl. "You got this?"

"Secure his legs."

Conrad pulled off his belt, wrestled the man's legs together.

"Now a lamp cord."

What? But he scrambled off Franco. Franco fought, but Jack pushed his hand against the man's neck, held him to the floor. Conrad yanked a cord from a lamp in the living room, raced back.

Held him as Jack looped the cord around one wrist, pulled it back to meet the other. Then he sat on the man, who was still shouting, swearing. "This will hold until we get help. Find her."

"Penny!" Conrad stood up, ran to the living room. "Penny, come out—you're safe!"

Nothing but creaking in the old house, never mind Franco's shouts.

Then, in the distance, a motor sounded.

He ran to the dining room, and out at the boathouse saw—

A snowmobile. And on it, Penny, gunning out of the house, right toward—

"Penny! No!"

He took off through the kitchen. "She's going out onto the lake!"

He had to give her props for getting away, for thinking, but for a girl who'd grown up on a lake, she should know—

And even as he cleared the house, running out into the snowy yard, toward the lake, he saw it happen.

The snowmobile cracked through the ice, its back end breaking through not far from shore but enough that the current could grab her.

She fell and disappeared as the machine slipped into the water.

"Penny!" He ran to the edge of the lake and didn't stop. Just kept running, toward the hole thirty feet from shore, the hole that was widening as her head popped up and she grabbed at the ice.

Around them, the trees cracked in the wind, his breath and the crunch of snow breaking the air—

"Conrad!"

She'd spotted him.

"Hang on—hang *on*!"

But she slipped, vanished again, and he dove across the ice, his body landing, skidding through the snow—

Not far enough. She'd floated out into the middle.

He tore off his jacket, slapped it to her. She grabbed the arm— *good girl*—and he used it to reel her in. Then he caught her wrist. Grabbed her up, pulled her to the surface, the water brutal, stinging. He fisted her jacket with his other hand and yanked her to the edge.

She sputtered, shook her head, gasped. Whimpered. "Don't let me go—don't let me go—"

"I got you." He searched her face. A bruise on her cheek, fear in her eyes.

The ice cracked beneath him. She screamed.

"Just stay calm!"

"You're not calm!" Her eyes sparked.

Yeah, well, if he pulled her up, they'd both go in, the ice splintering beneath him even as he held her.

"I'm sorry," she said. "I should have stayed at the jail—"

"What? No—babe. I told you to go—"

"I didn't leave—not really. It was just—"

"Fake. I know." He smiled then, his hands gripping her jacket, holding her up. He'd lost feeling in his grip, and she'd started to slow her tread, probably turning hypothermic, dipping into the water.

"We need to get you out. Can you climb over me?"

"You'll go in."

Probably. "I'll be fine." He met her eyes, held there by the emotion in them. Fear, yes, but . . . trust. And maybe even hope.

And all the panic simply silenced, the terrible whirring inside stopped. And all he could think was . . . *"God's grace is bigger than your mistakes."*

Bigger than his impulses. Bigger than his fears. Bigger than his panic.

Bigger than his past.

And maybe, even though the world dropped out beneath him, God had him.

Okay, God, I got her. I need You to have me.

He started to shake, gritted his teeth. "Hang on, Penny. Help is coming."

And then, just like that—"Conrad, hold on!"

He glanced behind him and spotted Jack, and what looked like Harper and a couple deputies easing their way out onto the ice. Conrad worked his arms under Penelope, pulled her up to himself. "Listen, when I tell you, kick hard. I'm going to pull you up, and you hang on to me and don't let go."

Hands grabbed his feet, and he hooked them together, gave Jack something to pull. "Ready?"

Behind him, Harper had grabbed Jack's waistbelt. "Go, Con!"

Penelope kicked and Conrad pulled her up, and Jack yanked on his feet and the trio slid back, enough for Penelope to slide mostly free.

The ice beneath Conrad cracked, water slicking up. "Keep pulling, Jack!" But the ice kept breaking.

Penelope had found her knees, scrambling onto the ice, but started to sink. Conrad stopped thinking. He leaned up, grabbed her against himself, and rolled. Onto his back, then over, cradling her, and then again to his back, away from the hole.

Jack had fallen back, into the snow, scrambling hard away from the gaping hole.

Conrad let her go, sat up. "Move, move!" He grabbed the back of her jacket, propelling them away from the cracking ice.

Then he found his feet, scooped her up against himself, and they ran, fell, scrambled onto the shore.

He dropped onto his hands and knees, shaking, gulping in breaths as Penelope collapsed beside him, drawing up to the fetal position, shaking.

"Okay, we got you," said Harper, pouncing on Penelope with a blanket. "We need some help over here!"

"I'm fine—I'm fine!"

But Conrad looked at her. "You're not fine. You're bruised, and hypothermic—"

"Did you get him?" She pulled the blanket tight, her teeth chattering. "Franco—did you get him?"

"We got him," Jack said.

She smiled, and then turned to Conrad, so much emotion in her eyes it heated Conrad all the way through. "You came for me."

He gave a laugh, a huff. "Of course I did."

Her eyes shone. "I knew I could count on you."

Yes. Yes, she could. And then he followed his next crazy impulse, trusted his instincts, and kissed her.

And he didn't care who saw it, what pictures might land on social media. Didn't care that he'd lost his jacket, his clothes plastered to his body, Mr. June, in February.

Didn't care what might be ahead or behind. Just sank into the moment.

Finally he lifted his head. "I love you, Penelope Pepper. Just so we're clear. I love you."

Her mouth opened, still shivering a little, and then she smiled. "I thought we broke up."

"I can't keep up. But you shouldn't believe everything you read on the internet." Then he wrapped his arms around her, for, you know, body warmth, and kissed her again.

"And that about wraps it up for this final edition of 'The Case of Sarah Livingston,' the baffling and tragic case of Sarah Livingston. Thank you for tuning in today as we unraveled the final threads of a mystery that has taken us on quite the journey."

Penelope stood in the hallway outside the locker room area of the Blue Ox, one of her EarPods in, listening to the final take of her episode dropping tomorrow night.

Harper wore the other Bluetooth EarPod, leaning against the brick wall, her hand in Jack's. He scrolled through his phone, probably searching the latest missing-persons reports.

Through the double doors and down the hallway, a hum rose from the locker room, where reporters peppered the team about their win against the Florida Chill.

A win that'd had Conrad scoring one of the three goals.

Her picture, the one with Penelope wearing his jersey, had probably already hit social media, but she hadn't even looked.

Instead, she put her hand over her other ear, still listening to herself. "Over the last few episodes, we've dissected alibis, motives, and secrets. In the end, Franco's actions were driven by a tangled web of greed and panic. It's a classic motive, yet it never ceases to disturb how these base instincts can drive one to the unthinkable."

Harper gave her the thumbs-up, clearly happy with the monologue she'd helped write.

"In our quest for truth, we encountered numerous moments when panic could have swayed our judgment, when fear could have clouded our path. But here, in this space we've created together, we chose to push through. We chose to seek out the truth, believing firmly that it would prevail."

Sounds came from down the hallway, where a few players had emerged. She spotted Wyatt Marshall, the goalie, pushing through the double doors, his hair still wet, carrying a bag over his shoulder. His wife Coco and their son ran over from where they sat on a sofa near the door. He caught them up. *Sweet.*

"And this brings us to a vital lesson, one that transcends the confines of our podcast and applies to every aspect of our lives: We must never let panic dictate our actions. Fear is a powerful motivator, yes, but it's also a misleading guide. It propels us toward quick fixes, urgent cover-ups, and, as in Franco's case, disastrous decisions."

This was her favorite part. She met Harper's eyes.

"To quote a wise woman I know, 'It's always the right time to do the right thing.' This isn't just a saying—it's a principle. As we close this chapter and this case, I encourage you, my listeners, to be not just seekers of mystery but also seekers of truth in your own lives. Challenge the shadows of fear and greed. Embrace the light of honesty and integrity. And remember, the truth is not just about finding answers—it's about finding peace."

The outro music played. "And now, as we part ways, I leave you with a quote from the queen of mystery herself, Agatha Christie:

'The truth, however ugly in itself, is always curious and beautiful to seekers after it.' This is *Penny for Your Thoughts*. Remember, in a world full of puzzles, your thoughts might just be the missing piece. See you next time—toodles!"

She clicked pause on her phone and removed her EarPod.

"It's perfect," Harper said, handing her the one from her ear. "So, what's your next case?"

She put the EarPods back in their case. "I think maybe I'll take a break."

"What?" Jack said. "I think we can find you something riveting." He'd pocketed his phone, glancing through the double door.

Oh, she already had something riveting, and he was walking toward her, his blond hair wet and curly, long around his ears, his beard trimmed, those perfect red highlights turning him into a sort of Norse warrior.

His gaze on her landed in her bones and lit them, a spark in his blue eyes suggesting he'd seen her on the jumbotron rooting for him.

Her man.

Harper stepped up to her. "By the way, did he mention if he's getting traded?"

"I think after Dad found out how he saved my life, he might have found an advocate." She looked at Harper. "But for the record, where he goes, I go."

Harper raised an eyebrow.

"Don't give me that, Miss I'm Taking Measurements for My Stuff in the Jack-o'-Bus."

Harper laughed and King Con came out through the open doors, took two steps, dropped his duffel, and swept Penelope up in an embrace.

Her feet left the floor, her arms around his neck, her legs around his waist, her mouth pressed to his.

All in, for the world to see.

He tasted of some energy drink he'd consumed, and smelled of the woods, spice, the soap from his shower, and felt like a man who would reach into the darkness to pull her free.

Had done that, actually.

He leaned back. "This is serious PDA."

"Get used to it." She kissed him again but then let him put her down. He took her hand in his.

"Nice jersey."

"Told you that you weren't getting it back."

"I might have to try." He winked and her eyes widened, and then he grinned, squeezed her hand. "Just kidding. For now."

Oh.

He picked up his duffel.

"Great game, bro," Jack said. "Thanks for the tickets."

"Anytime."

"But—what was the deal with that last pass? You had a clear shot to goal."

"Blade had a better shot. The Chill goalie read me, and I was glove side. Blade had a better power shot—"

"Wow. Strategy."

"Impulse." He winked. "And strategy."

Behind them, Blade came walking outside. His duffel hung over his shoulder, and his arm draped around the shoulders of a woman who held his hand, fingers laced through his.

"Hey, Ava. Blade," Conrad said.

Blade held up a fist to Conrad. "Thanks, King. You were right." They bumped fists. He kept walking.

"What was that about?" Jack said, looping his arm around Harper.

"That was me telling him to loosen up and enjoy the game. To stop thinking so hard. It's freezing him up."

Jack raised an eyebrow.

"Whatever," Conrad said. "It's good advice."

Jack laughed. "Sammy's?"

Conrad looked at Penelope, heat in his eyes. "I have something else in mind." Her eyes widened, and he leaned close. "How about a cookie?"

"You know how to woo a girl."

He led her outside, under the star-strewn sky, where the wind stirred around them, the night full of mystery and even magic, then pulled her into his arms, away from the paparazzi and prying eyes. "No, Penny. You're still a mystery. But I'm just curious enough to try to solve it."

"Give it your best shot, King Con."

He laughed, his gaze in hers. "Brace yourself. Because I'm very good at this game."

Then he kissed her.

And yes, yes he was.

WHAT HAPPENS NEXT...

Lisbon, Portugal

"Did it work?" Emberly sat in her bedroom overlooking the harbor and the big bay bridge that resembled San Francisco's Golden Gate, icing her wrist.

That had hurt more than she'd anticipated.

Which, of course, she *hadn't* anticipated. Not really. But once she'd shaken away the fuzz of the accident, had her hairline fracture casted—that seemed over-the-top, really—she'd realized that she had one final chance to complete her mission.

Stein had nearly blown that too, with his too-soon appearance in the ER. He'd nearly caught her with the goods—the bloody gauze and other materials she'd packaged up and sent to Mystique.

"Yes, it worked." Her boss sat in her apartment on the other side of the video call, the snowy mountains looming in the window. Mystique wore her blonde hair back, her brown eyes concerned. "You could have gotten killed."

"And that's a consideration?"

"Always, Phoenix." Her mouth tightened. "There aren't a lot of Swans left. Watch your back."

"He made me." She still saw the recognition click into his eyes— and sure, she could hope it was from the wedding dance. But in truth, maybe something about her appearance had triggered a deeper memory.

She'd been so careful, but maybe her disguises weren't enough. Hard to disguise the spark between them, the way that twenty-four hours with him in a war zone had embedded inside her.

"He couldn't have. The trauma, the plastic surgery, changed your appearance."

"Not enough. And I had to take my contacts out after the accident—"

"Don't let it derail you."

Emberly had gotten up, walked over to the window where the white-and-black limestone streets glittered under a blue sky. Lisbon had seemed the right place to escape to, the flight only two hours. She hadn't seen her condo in months.

And it helped that John lived in Portugal. He could synthesize the blood into the biocode they needed to access Stone's cyberwallet in the mountains of Montelena.

"Did you get into the vault?"

A sigh. "Yes. We got into the hard storage of Declan Stone's account, but . . ." Her mouth pinched. "We were too late. He got there first, emptied it, took the program with him."

She sank onto the sofa. "No."

"Sorry." Mystique gave her a grim look. "I wouldn't ask if—"

"The world's safety didn't depend on it."

Mystique nodded. "There is no one who can run a solo heist like you can. And we need the program, Phoenix."

"I know." She set the ice pack on the glass table. "Okay, so what next?"

"Mariposa."

She closed her eyes. Opened them. "It's a fortress."

"We tracked him to the island. Yes, it's a fortress, but it's also the one logical place where he'd store his hard copy of his program, if he didn't think it was safe in cold storage in Montelena. We have the blueprints, and Luis will help you build the biocodes you need to get in. Come up with a plan."

She sighed, lifted her arm. "I'll need a week or two."

"Yes. Heal. Get strong. And then, pack sunscreen."

"Funny." She shook her head. "And what do I do about Stein?"

A beat, and Mystique's mouth made a grim line. "Pray he doesn't get in the way."

Aw.

She clicked off. Leaned her head back, closing her eyes, her arm pulsing with heat. And in her mind's eye, she saw herself staring at Stein in all his rugged, dirt-streaked glory, his blue eyes on hers, saying, "Fine, Phoenix. I'll trust you. But don't break my heart."

Maybe she should have gotten the same promise from him.

Yes, this might get very, very tricky.

There's Trouble in the North...

Meet Doyle, who finds peril in paradise in this rivals romance.

MINNESOTA KINGSTONS | BOOK THREE

DOYLE

USA TODAY BESTSELLING AUTHOR

SUSAN MAY WARREN

Book 3 in the Minnesota Kingston series by USA Today bestselling author Susan May Warren.

When love and danger collide, paradise plays by its own rules.

When Tiana Pepper lands on the lush island of Mariposa, she just wants to put her sad past behind her. Her goal is a new beginning as fundraiser and director of Hope House, a local orphanage.

Except she's not the director. She's co-director, and nobody told her she'd have to work with an impulsive, out-of-bounds, depend on his charm, annoying disaster rescuer, named Doyle Kingston.

She can run this show on her own, thanks.

Doyle Kingston, bearing the weight of his own grief, arrives at Hope House ready to leave behind a history of loss. He hopes to find forever homes for these orphans, and the last thing he expects is to have to work with a woman who thinks she's the boss of this island paradise.

And yet...they have problems.

Like becoming the target of a local gang.

And boss, Billionaire Declan Stone has invited his fancy friends to the island to see Hope House up close, in hopes they'll donate and get the orphanage on its feet. So...please, could they work together?

And wouldn't you know it but among the donors is a treasure hunter who believes a pirate left a stash under Hope House. Whatever.

Then an earthquake rocks the island, kids go missing and Tia and Doyle have no choice but trust each other if they hope to save the children and each other.

Doyle is a pulse-pounding romantic suspense featuring rivals turned rescuers, where opposites attract amidst peril in paradise, and where two hearts scarred by tragedy just might find a second chance at true love.

ONE

WEDNESDAY

FOUR MONTHS ON A CARIBBEAN ISLAND helped a man find clarity. Sunshine, sand and most of all, the children of Hope House orphanage had sort of loosened the grip that grief had on Doyle Kingston.

He might actually be ready for that fresh start.

At the very least, he felt in the best shape of his life.

"Over here, Jamal, I'm open!" He gestured for the ball from the eight year old as he ran down the rutted, weedy semi-dirt soccer field, the sun fighting through low hanging clouds, turning the field to shadow. The salt and brine hung in the air, waves crashing against the high cliffs where the former monastery-turned-Hope House orphanage sat, and it might be the perfect day to tell the boys the good news.

But not yet.

Jamal dodged a player from the other team—a nine year old named Lionel—and then glanced over at him. Jamal wore the yellow and white jersey of the Mariposa Wings, the number nine, from his favorite player—Ronaldo Viera, another striker.

Ronaldo and the entire team had donated the jerseys to Hope.
A move Doyle could only blame on Tia Pepper, his new...what,
co-director?

Annoying, wanna-be boss?

Doyle kept pace, running at centerfield. A glance in his pe-
riphery said that Aliyah had found a spot in midfield, her brown-
eyed gaze on him, ready to intercept. And at goal, fourteen year
old Kemar wore the gloves Doyle had received in a recent donor
package.

Again, Tia's doing. It had been more than a little awkward when
she showed up two weeks after him, saying she'd been hired by the
founder of Hope Home, Declan Stone, to "get the orphanage on
financial track."

He'd been hired—by Declan—to reorganize and help the kids
find a solid future. Whatever that meant. He was still trying to
do that for himself.

Jamal kicked the ball, and Doyle ran to intercept, caught it
and dodged Taj, one of the RAs in the boy's dorm, a big guy, wide
hands, a wider smile. He laughed, "Yow, Big D, you drink jet fuel
this mornin'?"

Something like that.

Doyle raced down the field, and spotted twelve year old Fiona
waving her arms, open. Pretty, her hair bound in tufts on her head,
she'd been easy to place, with her generous smile. He kicked the
ball to her.

Aw, it shot past her, out of bounds.

He stopped running, grabbed his knees for a breath.

Andre, another RA, ran to retrieve it, blowing his whistle. Lionel set up to throw it in, and his team lined up.

Under the heat of the morning, sweat poured down Doyle's
face, saturating the back of his shirt and he was tempted to pull it
off. Except, he'd already managed a wicked sunburn his first week

here. He didn't need a reminder of the way he stood out against the population of the island.

Outsider, from his skin to his mannerisms to his expectations. Like being on time for, well, *anything*.

So, yeah, he needed to loosen up, live and let live, breathe.

So far, the plan was working—start over, leave the grief behind, focus on something new.

Like finding permanent homes for these children in his care.

He stood up, moving to guard Lionel, the ten-year-old laughing as he pushed Doyle out of his way, stepped in front of him, then grabbed the ball and maneuvered it around him.

"Hey, that's illegal."

"Keep up, old man."

He took off after him, lit, and fought the kid for the ball. The entire team had improved since their last game, with nearby Sint Eustacia, and now Lionel shot the ball off to Aliyah.

Jamal intercepted and the game turned. Doyle again switched directions, heading toward the goal, and Jamal passed it off to another girl, Gabriella, who was a playmaker, lean and tall and fourteen. He hadn't found a home for her yet, but maybe she would age out of the home, go on to college.

She had the makings of a doctor, the way she helped out in the medical clinic.

Gabriella kicked it through the legs of an opponent, and raced toward the goal.

Doyle set up in front of the goal just in case—

She passed it over.

He ran to intercept—

Bam! The collision hit him so hard it spanked him into the air, and he flew, thudding into the weedy grass.

His head bounced off the ground, and the he lay, dazed. Blood erupted from his nose, down his face, his face on fire.

"Gotchya."

He held his nose—grimaced and looked up.

Kemar stood over him, holding the ball in his gloves, the sun against his dark head, no smile.

Right.

He sat up, and Kemar stepped away as Andre crouched beside Doyle. "You okay? Let's get you to the clinic."

"I'm fine," Doyle said, even as Gabriella ran up, holding a towel. He shoved it against his nose, then got to his feet.

The world spun.

Kemar stood away, smirking.

"Why'd you do that, Key?" Jamal had run up, now stood in front of his sixteen year old brother. "You didn't have to hit him." His voice shook.

Doyle held up a hand. "It's just a game, Jamal. We're all good."

Kemar laughed as he grabbed Jamal, his arm around his neck, "See bro? Don't worry about it."

Jamal pushed away from him, jogged up to Doyle. "You okay, Mr. D?"

He touched the boy's shoulder. "I'm good. Get back in there." But he didn't miss Kemar's shake of his head.

Or the clench in his gut.

Kemar would hate him if the Jamesons refused to adopt both boys.

Doyle sank onto a bench on the side as Andre blew the whistle. He'd run to get the out-of-bounds ball that had fallen into an old grotto, now overgrown at the edge of the field. Another project on Doyle's long fix-up list.

Kemar threw the ball back into play.

"Doyle. I've been looking all over for you. I thought you were going to meet me—"

He turned, still holding the towel, now soaked, to his face.

Tia, her long brown hair up, a few hairs falling out of the bun, wearing a green canvas shirt that only pulled the green from her hazel eyes—shoot, stop!—and a pair of black cargo pants and keens, strode over to him.

The look in those pretty eyes said oops, he'd landed in the doghouse.

Again.

She frowned at the towel, one perfect brown eyebrow dipping, and then shook her head. "You can't go like that."

"Like what?" He took the towel away, glanced at his shirt. Sweaty, blue, and, oy—covered in his own blood. Checking his nose—the bleeding had stopped, so maybe not broken—he stood up, trying to wipe the blood off. "Where are we going?"

"Seriously?" She sighed.

Oh, right. "The x-ray machine."

"Yes. It came in yesterday to the port in Esperanza." She braced her hands on her hips. "Never mind. I'll take Keon again."

He threw the towel over his shoulder. "No, I'm in. Just give me five to get changed."

"Ten, and you shower first. The harbor master is new, and..." She gave him the once-over. "We don't need you looking like you're a member of the S-7 Crew."

He gave a her a look. "Thanks. First thing I check in the mirror every morning—do I look like a gang member?"

She rolled her eyes. "Just change your shirt."

Of course. Sheesh. So clearly she hadn't gotten their first meeting out of her head.

Talking about needing a fresh start. He sighed as he started walking toward the monastery's back entrance, where an arched door in the wall hung open and led to the interior of the compound.

She followed him, glancing at the game, the kids. "Do they know yet?"

"No. I'm planning to save it. We still have a few days left."

"Scared about what Kemar is going to do?"

He glanced at her, his mouth tight, and didn't answer as he walked through the entrance into the cool embrace of the 18th century building. Freshly white-washed, the thick walls kept heat from invading, and a long shaded corridor aproned the complex. The middle courtyard repaved with the black limestone that turned slick and shiny over the years, held a granite fountain in the middle, with a statue of the Holy Mother holding her baby Jesus in the center. Beyond that, gates—now closed—opened to a dirt road and a view of the harbor town of Esperanza, the capital of tiny Mariposa, and home to some four-thousand inhabitants.

Red-roofed, white-washed homes, a few three-story, arched veranda hotels overlooking the pristine turquoise sea, and not a few fishing boats that cluttered the port, evidence of their main source of income—conch and snapper and mahi-mahi.

The smells from the kitchen—located in the remodeled wing—suggested Jerk chicken on tonight's menu, a blend of allspice, Scotch bonnet peppers and ginger over grilled chicken, and of course his stomach growled.

"You sure you don't want to stay—?"

"No. I just skipped lunch. I was working on the chapel." He glanced at the open wooden doors to the building, located across the courtyard. "Had to brace one of the beams—it felt loose."

"I poked my head in. The kids did a great job on the murals."

Was that praise?

"It's a great place to show their talents, as well as the focus of faith we have here." He reached the stairs. "I think the donors will be impressed."

"Impressed? Maybe amused."

For all her beauty, she had a way of poking a stone into his soul. He reached the stairs. Turned. "I know you think this is a waste of time, but having the donors on site just might get a few of these kids adopted. And that could change their lives."

She held up a hand, the wind catching her hair, whisking it

across her face. "It's not that I don't think it's a good idea, but let's not get your hopes up, Doyle—we need them to donate to the medical clinic, get some real equipment here. The only souvenir these donors want to take home is a conch shell."

Nice.

"I'll meet you at the garage in ten." She walked away.

He bit back a growl and headed up to his room, in the center area. The boys' dorms extended down one wing, the girls' along the other. He keyed in his code to his cell, and opened it to a small but tidy room, with an adjacent bath, a single bed, desk, standing wardrobe and a glorious view of the sea as it hit the basalt debris of Cumbre de Luz, the dormant volcano that lumbered along the north side of the island.

Even now, the smells from the surf, the lush rainforest vegetation that swept down from the volcano, filtered into his room, and as he stripped off his shirt, he breathed it in.

Fresh start meant he'd let Tia's cynical words roll off him.

He stepped into the shower, braced his hands on the tile walls and let the heat revive him. Who knew what Tia might be escaping in the states. He knew very little about her.

Except that she could drive him to his last nerve.

He stepped out, toweled off, pulled on a clean pair of jeans, boots, and a white oxford, rolling up the sleeves. He didn't bother to shave—most of the men on the island wore scruff, many of them fishermen. Others worked in the fledgling tourist industry, hosting divers who came to the island in search of the fabled gold treasures located in the thirteen wrecks caught in the coral reefs offshore.

He raked a hand through his short hair—good enough—and headed down to the garage, a building outside the monastery that Declan had added when he'd upgraded security. The garage also housed the small security offices, with the monitors that captured all the corners of the building, as well as the corridor and the main hall.

Thank you to the S-7 crew whose terror of the locals had only increased after the hurricane five years ago that left so many of these kids without parents.

Not anymore. He didn't care what Tia said.

He planned on finding homes for every one of these kids. It was the least he could do for the woman he loved.

God rest her soul.

Tia leaned against a lime-green, 1960 F-100 pickup, the straps a jumble in the middle. She glanced at her watch. "Twelve minutes."

He shook his head. "Let me drive, and we'll make it up."

She rolled her eyes, shook her head and walked around to the driver's side.

He took a breath. Exhaled.

Maybe it wasn't so much a fresh start as it was focusing on something new.

He forced a smile, and got in.

Like not strangling his co-director.

Note to Reader

Thanks for diving into Conrad's story! I hope you loved hanging out with the lively Minnesota Kingstons as much as I enjoyed writing them.

There's plenty more where that came from—four more books to be exact! So, stay tuned for loads of fun, a bit of mayhem, and some swoon-worthy romance.

If Conrad's journey touched you, would you mind dropping a review on the product page? It doesn't need to be long—a simple heads-up for future readers works wonders (just try to keep those spoilers to yourself!).

Big thanks to my fabulous team. Shoutout to my editor, Anne Horch—your magic touch really brings these stories to life. I couldn't do it without you.

Huge thanks to Rel Mollet—she's amazing, not only diving deep into content and giving fantastic feedback but also keeping everything on track behind the scenes. We successfully publish books because of her incredible organizational skills. Rel, I can't express my gratitude enough for everything you manage so well. You're truly indispensable!

Sending a warm embrace to my writing buddy, Rachel Hauck, and the ever-creative Sarah Erredge, who are always game for brainstorming sessions. You guys are the best.

A nod to my husband, Andrew, who has answers to everything,

it seems, from cars to breaking into cabins in the woods. ⊠ I'd be lost without you.

Cheers to Emilie Haney for the stunning covers that grab everyone's attention and Tari Faris for making the inside just as beautiful.

Thanks, Katie Donovan, for your eagle-eye proofreading, especially when we're racing against the clock.

I'm truly grateful for all of you; we're definitely a dream team!

To my awesome reader friends—thanks for bringing my books into your world. I hope you find a little joy and maybe some inspiration in these pages. I'd love to hear what you think, and what you're hoping to see next. Drop me a line anytime at susan@susanmaywarren.com.

If you're into sneak peeks, special freebies, and the latest news, sign up for my newsletter at susanmaywarren.com, or just scan the QR code I've provided.

Thanks for jumping on the journey with me! Doyle and his Caribbean adventure is up next!

Warmly,
Susie May

SCAN ME

Susan May Warren

More Books by Susan May Warren

Most recent to the beginning of the epic lineup, in reading order.

THE MINNESOTA KINGSTONS
Jack
Conrad
Doyle
Austen
Steinbeck

ALASKA AIR ONE RESCUE
One Last Shot
One Last Chance
One Last Promise
One Last Stand

THE MINNESOTA MARSHALLS
Fraser
Jonas
Ned
Iris
Creed

THE EPIC STORY OF RJ AND YORK
Out of the Night
I Will Find You
No Matter the Cost

SKY KING RANCH
Sunrise
Sunburst
Sundown

GLOBAL SEARCH AND RESCUE
The Way of the Brave
The Heart of a Hero
The Price of Valor

The Montana Marshalls
Knox
Tate
Ford
Wyatt
Ruby Jane

Montana Rescue
If Ever I Would Leave You (novella prequel)
Wild Montana Skies
Rescue Me
A Matter of Trust
Crossfire (novella)
Troubled Waters
Storm Front
Wait for Me

Montana Fire
Where There's Smoke (Summer of Fire)
Playing with Fire (Summer of Fire)
Burnin' For You (Summer of Fire)
Oh, The Weather Outside is Frightful (Christmas novella)
I'll be There (Montana Fire/Deep Haven crossover)
Light My Fire (Summer of the Burning Sky)
The Heat is On (Summer of the Burning Sky)
Some Like it Hot (Summer of the Burning Sky)
You Don't Have to Be a Star (Montana Fire spin-off)

The True Lies of Rembrandt Stone
Cast the First Stone
No Unturned Stone
Sticks and Stone
Set in Stone
Blood from a Stone
Heart of Stone

A complete list of Susan's novels can be found at
susanmaywarren.com/novels/bibliography/.

About the Author

Susan May Warren is the USA Today bestselling author of over 100 novels with nearly 2 million books sold, including the Global Search and Rescue and the Montana Rescue series. Winner of a RITA Award and multiple Christy and Carol Awards, as well as the HOLT Medallion and numerous Readers' Choice Awards, Susan makes her home in Minnesota.

Visit her at www.susanmaywarren.com

www.ingramcontent.com/pod-product-compliance
Lightning Source LLC
Chambersburg PA
CBHW022214190325
23791CB00006B/122